WEREWOLF INCORPORATED:

THE FAMILY PLOT

WEREWOLF INCORPORATED:

THE FAMILY PLOT

MICHAEL DON ANDERSON

CRIMSON WEREWOLF LIMITED • USA

WEREWOLF INCORPORATED: THE FAMILY PLOT is a work of
fiction.
Names, characters, places, and incidents are the products of the author's
imagination or are used fictitiously. Any resemblance to actual events, locales,
business establishments, or persons, living or dead, is entirely coincidental.

This book is an original publication of
CRIMSON WEREWOLF LIMITED.

Published in the United States by
CRIMSON WEREWOLF LIMITED.

ISBN 978-1-935698-64-7

Printed in the U.S.A.

www.crimsonwerewolf.com

WEREWOLF INCORPORATED:

THE FAMILY PLOT

By

MICHAEL DON ANDERSON

CHAPTER ONE

The bar was dark and smoky, a typical American drinking spot. There was a confederate flag on one wall because it was Alabama and the South was still holding onto age-long loyalties. My eyes adjusted quickly and I knew that this was gonna be a mess. The middle-aged bartender glared from an unshaved face, as if his customers owed him more than for a beer on tap.

I walked up to the bar and put both fists on the counter. I didn't bother to sit. I'd been through this routine before.

"What'll you have?" he asked out of habit. Then his gaze drifted down to the back of my left hand before he looked me in the eyes. "We don't serve your kind here."

I looked down at the tattoo as if I hadn't known it was there. When I looked up, there was a hint of gold in my otherwise deep-green eyes. He took a step back. We both knew what I was.

"It's against the law to discriminate." I lowered my voice so that it sounded even more menacing than normal.

A woman a couple of stools down also glanced at my hand. She swallowed hard and her alcohol-glazed eyes flared wide. "That thing real?"

I took a moment, wondering if I could get any entertainment out of playing a game with her. I settled for an honest question. "Who'd fake something like this?"

The tattoo of a crescent moon was filled in with red. And just inside the curvature was a small skull and cross-bones. The mandatory marking for anyone infected with lycanthropy. I figured it was better n' being in prison. Although, in a way, it was a life-sentence. I wasn't allowed to cover it up, either. So I put it out at the start. It played hell with my love life and I didn't make many friends, but at least I knew where I stood with people.

"You ain't gonna get a beer then." The woman shuffled off the stool, her mini-skirt riding up to reveal a surprisingly nice pair of thighs for a day-time drinker. She didn't even bother to tug the skirt into place as she backed away from the counter. She hit the door with her shoulder, startled as if something had attacked her and bolted out of the place.

The bartender had a shotgun in his hand. I was annoyed that I hadn't heard him reaching for it, distracted by the woman's tight dress and well-formed legs. Sloppy. If I wanted to see my fortieth birthday in ten years, I'd have to keep my mind on business.

"I said we don't serve your kind. The law in these parts is likely to agree with me." The bartender cocked the gun like he'd seen too many movies. Maybe that really worked on the average Joe. But I was a werewolf. What did I care about a shotgun? This place was too cheap to afford silver buckshot, so it would only sting a few minutes.

I stared at the man, ignoring the gun. Sometimes, I could stare at a gun with such intensity that it freaked out whoever was holding it. This time, I was going for a different approach. I hated taking jobs in the South, because here, the only thing worse than being a werewolf was being black or a Muslim. Or both.

"I'm meeting the sheriff here. So if you don't serve my kind, take it up with him as to why I left." I took my fists off the counter. "I get paid for just showing up."

"Whoa, whoa, whoa. Now, boy, no need to rush off," said a man from one of the dark corners of the place.

I turned to stare at him. Stetson. Law-enforcement uniform. I knew exactly what kind of rat-shit he was and he'd known just how the bartender would react to me. A small-town sheriff testing the new dog on his turf.

"That depends on whether or not you're buying me the first round," I replied.

"No way, Sheriff! Get that cocksucker out of here," demanded the bartender.

Oh, right. There was one thing they hated worse than a werewolf or a black man or even a Muslim in the South. Homosexuals.

"Your call, Mr. Sheriff," I said condescendingly.

The man was built like what the locals would call a brick shit-house. He had sandy-brown hair, pale-blue eyes and the beginnings of a beer-belly. But that wasn't too bad for a man who had to be in his mid-to-late-forties.

"You weren't invited here to drink," replied the sheriff unpleasantly. "I'd rightly not have you here at all. Except what we're dealing with is beyond our expertise." The way he said 'expertise' made me flash back to every country-hick movie I'd ever seen as a kid. My dad was career-military and I'd spent a lot of time in front of the TV while he'd been away. Like anything in life, you got out of it what you put in. I'd learned a lot from TV.

"Well, then. Good luck with that." I gave an open-mouthed smile to the bartender, letting my canines show a little bit more than they did naturally.

Not the best way to handle an initial 'meet n' greet' about a case, but I'd already gotten riled up just walking into this town. There were still signs that said 'no blacks allowed.' Legally posted and even preserved under the 'Historical Significance' bill enacted by President Bachmann. I'd almost left the country after she'd won the election two years ago, but there were worse places to be an American than in America.

The truth was, I loved my country. Call it a gift from dear old dad, but I'd do just about anything to protect her people. All of her people. Not just white folks like me. Correction, white folks who weren't like me. There weren't that many werewolves in the States and the powers that be wanted it to stay that way. I wanted to remain part of the 20% not in federal prisons. The ones who could control their killer instincts.

"You ain't getting on my good side," said the sheriff, but I didn't bother to turn around as I walked for the door.

My back itched and I sensed the bartender's shotgun pointed at me which really pissed me off. If the sheriff hadn't been there, I might have scared the barkeep with more than just a flash of teeth and wolf's eyes. I might have sliced my claws through the barrel of his gun and maybe even broken his arm. Nothing serious.

"Frank, put the gun down and get us two MGDs. That work for you, Greyson?" asked the sheriff and then I did turn around.

"Call me 'Mitch,'" I said, trying to sound friendly with an edge of threat.

"I ain't serving that thing in my place," repeated Frank. "And you ain't gonna make me. I'll call the mayor if I have to."

"Do that, Frank. And be sure to let me know what he says," replied the sheriff with a growl almost as dangerous as mine. "Of course, you might want to try him in the county morgue."

"What's he doing there?" asked the bartender, reaching for the phone.

"Being autopsied right about now, I reckon." The sheriff glared at Frank. The bartender visibly paled and I grinned that at least one of us had scared him. "Now, we get those beers or do I shut you down for serving alcohol to Muslims?"

"I don't serve no heathens!" shouted the man, frightened. "We don't even have no Muslims here."

I studied the few other inhabitants of the bar. All white Caucasian, wearing plaid work-shirts or outdated Polos. Jeans, no dress slacks, and several pairs of cowboy boots. Function, not fashion. A Muslim wouldn't be caught dead in the place. Wished I wasn't either, but a job was a job in these hard economic times. Not because I needed the money. I needed to stay busy or maybe I'd wind up in prison. 'Anger-management' the Feds called it. I called it 'most people sucked.'

"Mebbe. But what would people say if they thought you did?" asked the big man.

"You are a real bastard, Louis. I'm not voting for you next election," replied the bartender but he put his gun away under the counter and grabbed two bottles from the cooler. "And no tab, neither."

"Over here, Greyson," said the sheriff, not bothering with my first name.

I followed the sheriff and took a seat at one of the several identically scuffed, round wooden tables. At least there was no juke-box playing some country song about love gone wrong. Not that I didn't like country music when I was in the mood, but I was just not feeling the whole Southern-hospitality thing.

"You don't look like I pictured," said the sheriff.

I studied his square jaw and the breadth of his body and the way his guns flexed under a jacket that was just a little too tight. "We can't all be stereotypes." He didn't get the dig and he wouldn't stop staring, so I finally asked, "What did you expect?"

His gaze went from my blue-black silk Henley button-up and custom leather jacket, to the polished black work-boot visible under the table. Then he settled his stare on my fingernails, neat and filed, unable to hide his disgust. My partner handled my 'first-meeting' wardrobe. She had expensive taste. I wanted to look rugged. She wanted me to look professional. My office was based out of Los Angeles where image was everything, so she got her way. Here, the sheriff thought I looked soft. Not just my clothes.

"I dunno. Some weasely, low-life type. You know the kind. Live in cheap hotels and look over their shoulders, like they're gonna get busted for drug trafficking. Dirty clothes and dirty under the nails." His eyes raked me up and down frustrated. "The only thing that matches what I pictured is your dark hair."

"You expected me to look like a drug addict? Seriously? That doesn't sound like all of it," I pushed him.

"I dunno. Maybe I expected fangs or claws or glowing red-eyes." Closer to the truth. He fidgeted.

"Still not buying it." I took a swig of beer.

"You look too clean. That's all I'm saying." He was getting frustrated. That should have made me happy, but I was getting ticked off.

"If you don't think I can do the job, why the fuck did you bring me all the way to this hell-hole?" I'd accepted the retainer, which meant I'd promised to do the job unless he fired me. Would have made for some easy money, but I wasn't trying to push him that far. His attitude, however, didn't suggest he'd had any choice. "And don't blame it on my L.A. chic because my partner dresses me." That didn't sound as macho an explanation as I'd intended, but I left it alone.

"You don't like it here, do you?" asked the sheriff, avoiding the subject.

I studied him, leaning back and holding my beer. "No, frankly. I don't."

"Alabama, specifically? Or all of the South?" I shivered at the almost reverent way he said 'South.' I hadn't punched out a law-enforcement officer for weeks. Wanted to keep it that way, but this conversation made that doubtful.

"I love southern food. The world could come to an end and without southern cooking, it wouldn't matter," I replied honestly.

"That ain't no answer," complained the sheriff.

I was a werewolf. Of course I hated the South. And I hated the North and the East and sometimes, I even hated California. I had been imprisoned and tattooed and treated like a criminal when I had actually been a victim. There were laws banning me from working in certain professions and living in certain neighborhoods. Just for turning furry a few days each month. So, yeah, I pretty much hated everywhere.

But did I really, truly hate the South? Like I said, life would be meaningless without chicken-fried steak or biscuits-and-gravy and a whole mess of other foods that the mere thought of made my stomach grumble. The South had beautiful rolling hills, dense woods with running streams and it really was God's country as much as anywhere. What I didn't love was the way the ultraconservatives living in it wanted to see me dead. And the racism.

"Okay, so I like it here." I took another long swig of my icy-cold MGD. I savored the mild burn as it hit my throat. My biggest regret since becoming a werewolf was that it took more alcohol than I was willing to drink to get a serious buzz. Now I drank strictly for taste and that nostalgic burn.

"You just said you don't like it here."

"You enforce that 'no blacks' policy on the store next door?" I asked pointedly.

"Of course not. It's against federal law," he said.

I'd taken him off-guard with that question. He hadn't expected me to ask about things like racism. He had expected it to be about Christianity and Hell and the natural order of God. Things I had no interest in.

"Then I like it here as much as any place," I said pleasantly. "Any chance I can get an order of fried okra? My gran used to make the best okra west of Oklahoma but she passed a long time ago."

"What's your take on God, boy?" He ignored my request for food and watched my eyes for some sign of the monster inside.

There it was. The religious issue with werewolves. Was I a servant of the Devil? Did I hate the Baby Jesus and his Virgin Mother? If I had been Muslim, he'd have known for certain that I was against his God. Especially if he was too stupid to recognize that the Christian and Islamic gods were the same God. But as a werewolf, Christians wanted—no, they *needed* to know if I was a heathen as well as monster. I was a killer and a beast, but even a serial killer could find Jesus. Came up less in California and New York, but nearly everywhere else, someone made it an issue.

"That your only beef with me?" I asked him, getting bored already.

If I'd wanted a fight, I'd have told him that I liked God enough to tear His son's throat out and fuck his faggoty mouth. But only if I wanted to fight. The one thing that could provoke a Christian, even a lawman, was to besmirch the sanctity of Christ and his sexuality. I could say the same thing about Mary and I'd only get a rise out of about half as many people. Go figure.

"It would put my mind at ease to know where you stand." he said.

I obviously wasn't going to get anywhere until I answered. "What's *your* take on God."

"He's my Lord and Savior and Christ died for our sins. Do I go to church every Sunday? No. But I try to go once a month and I patrol the church yard on weekends to keep partiers out." He refused to break eye-contact. "Your turn."

"Fine. I was raised Protestant. Hellfire and brimstone, the whole nine yards. My father still believes and he blames me being a sinner for what I am now. My mother died in childbirth, so maybe he believes this happened to me because I killed her. Either way, his attitude affected me. And that gran I mentioned? She was as much a Christian saint as I believe in."

"You like to avoid answering things directly?" asked the sheriff. He took a sip of his beer, keeping his eyes on mine.

I gave him more truth than I expected to. "I take the Lord's name in vain and don't feel bad about it. I even say shit about Christ when I'm pissed off or want to piss someone else off. But, truthfully? I wonder why God would let this happen to me. Why he would let my girlfriend be torn to shreds by the monster that made me into this." I let him see the amber in my eyes, it startled him. "Do I pray to him anymore to help me out or answer my questions? No. Fuck him."

The eye-thing made him re-evaluate me. And I expected a punch in the jaw for the 'fuck God' sentiment, but he actually nodded to himself and relaxed. Shouldn't have been surprised. Most people didn't often react logically. Not how I expected them to, anyway.

"Well. As long as you believe, I guess that's better than what you're here to hunt." The sheriff snorted and he swigged his beer the way I had swigged mine. He wiped the foam away before he yelled over at the bartender. "Don't give me any shit, Frank. Two Saturday Night Specials."

"It's only Tuesday," complained the bartender but he trundled off into the back of the bar.

The sheriff used his beer bottle to push his Stetson out of his eyes and leaned back. "So, what exactly are you?"

"Pardon?" I wasn't sure which 'what' he was referring to.

"Your website says you're a hunter. But the FBI guy called you a private investigator."

"Investigator? Or consultant?" I asked, annoyed. I hated explaining this bit. Explaining why a werewolf bothered with a website and a long, standard contract. "If he said investigator, it was a sloppy use of language. I *am* licensed by the Feds to hunt the monsters. Vampires. Rogue fey. Even demons. I went through their weapons-training classes because I carry a lot of guns. Some of them otherwise illegal. I learned the laws about non-humans and hunting them to get the license. Took hand-to-hand martial arts training, a bit of this and that when I can find someone willing to teach a werewolf. But I don't have any police training if that's what you're getting at. I'm not Paul Drake or nothing. Most of my jobs have been as a consultant to local government agencies. I'm damned hard to kill. Like you calling me in. I rely on you boys for most of the detecting. I can do it, but it's a waste of time and your money."

"Then what good are you?" He was trying to talk himself out of working with me.

Not enough that I was Christian. I was still a monster in his eyes. That or like a lot of macho ass-holes, he thought he could do it on his own.

"Hell, Sheriff. I *hunt* the bastards! I track with a sense of smell no bloodhound could ever match. Fact is, bloodhounds and other tracking dogs won't follow a vampire's scent. Can't be trained to. And they'll run from anything demonic." He scowled at me and I shrugged. "Look. I took some community-college classes on criminal investigation, but I'm not that kind of investigator. I mean, sure. I figure stuff out because I have a good intuition. But it ain't formal training. My partner wants me to put a degree behind it, but I've been kind of busy catching, or more often, *killing* homicidal creatures the regular police can't manage. Didn't you read the specifics of the contract we emailed you?"

He ignored my question, prodding at his doubts about me instead. "How many vampires you fight before this?" It wasn't one of the facts on our website. The information recently posted to it mostly bragged about the demon I'd killed in Little Rock a month earlier. That had been one bloody Valentine's Day. But the standard-contract had pages about vampire details. For our own protection, not the client's.

"Shit. You didn't read the contract. That means this is gonna be a shitload harder."

One of the advantages I had was my nose. But if the local law-enforcement had muddled the crime-scene, tracking a vampire was going to be nearly impossible. The contract stated that in big letters because I'd learned a long time ago that people liked to blame the other guy. Maybe it was pre-emptive finger-pointing, but I'd saved myself a few problems by showing it to them in black and white when the matter came up.

"Answer the question." He wasn't letting me make this about him.

"Fought as in hand-to-hand? None." He cursed at that, but I ignored him. "And I hope it stays that way. Hunted and staked? Three independent nests. Eight if you count helping the FBI." I saw the growing doubt on his face. "There are things harder to kill than vampires, but finding them is what I can do better than humans. It's why you guys are supposed to stay away from the crime scenes. Which I'm betting you don't even know, because you didn't read the damned paperwork. Trust me, I can handle it."

"If you say so."

"Look, I hopped into my car and drove non-stop from some less-pressing business in Texas to get here. Breaking the speed-limit the whole way." Not as impressive as it sounded. I had police/traffic immunity in pursuit of vampires. Admittedly, I took advantage of that immunity when driving around L.A. sometimes. Even when it had nothing to do with vampires. "Rushed because you asked. Which means I don't know a lot about your circumstances. Except that the FBI wouldn't come. But I'm here to help you. Do you want that help or not?"

He just stared, studying me. Not impressed with what he saw. The feeling was mutual.

I realized that he was looking for evidence of extra hair or bones that changed shape for no reason. My fault. I'd done the eye-thing. "Go ahead. Ask, Sheriff."

He took another gulp of beer. "Is it true you can only change at the full moon?"

"Didn't you Google it?"

"Damned internet had too many conflicting pages. Kept getting that *Twilight* stuff."

His confession put me in a better mood. I stared down at the table, forcing my right index fingernail to thicken into a sharp, tough claw that I dug through the surface of the wood. The waxy line of varnish curled around the blackened nail and I tapped it loose to make sure he was watching. Subtle but I had made my point. "No. But I *have* to change when it's full. The rest of the time, I can change if I want. The more moon, the easier."

"You only super-strong when you change?" That helped me see what he wanted to know.

"Nope. Though I'm stronger the fuller the moon is. Tonight, we're a long way from the full moon. So I'm strong, but not nearly as strong as I will be. And I'm fast and I heal fast, all the stereotypes like that are true."

He grunted and sipped on the beer again. "Holy objects?"

"No effect on me because I'm *not* evil, Sheriff. Do I need to drink holy water to prove it?" I scowled at him. He thought about my comments before he nodded, satisfied.

"Sheriff Louis Williams. But no need to shake on it." Acceptance and a formal introduction, all rolled into one. "Just do your job like a good Christian, Mitch Greyson, and we'll survive this unfortunate working arrangement."

He surprised me with such a powerful turn-around. But it confirmed that he hadn't been given a choice in the matter. I thought about what I'd said and how it might seem to him that I was still a believer. I guess that made me a Christian. Even if I didn't really want to label myself. But I was a hunter, first. A killer second. And that's what I was there to do.

"How big is Resistance?" I glanced around the bar, nearly empty. Lunch-hour was over.

"We're up near to three-hundred. If you include the whole county. Why?"

Small. Fewer choices of victims and less chance we'd miss one. Something positive anyway. I shrugged. "It helps to know something about the area. Not enough people for a vampire to settle down for regular meals. Even a vampire has motives, Sheriff."

"Yeah. To kill law-abiding Christians. The mayor's dead, ain't he?" Williams pushed his beer bottle back, still trying to figure me out. It would do no good to explain to him that vampires didn't care about Christians any more than they cared about atheists. Bloodsuckers wanted to hunt and to live, just like humans. The problem was, humans had to die in order for that to happen.

"I need to see him. Make sure a vampire is what we're dealing with." I thought about the alternatives. Something that left bite marks and drained the blood? Certain demons and one or two of the fey had vamp-like fangs. Although technically, none of them drank blood the way a vampire did. And there was always the chance it was something new, never before seen.

"We better eat first. 'Cause after you see the body, you ain't gonna have an appetite," he said. Then he cocked his head and stared. "Or maybe you will."

I wanted to slap the grin off his face, but if he was happy mocking me, my life would be less Hell. Only time would tell if I'd regret not knocking him cold while I had the chance.

CHAPTER TWO

The Resistance County morgue was just a cold room in a cellar. Bundles of garlic hung on the walls and crosses covered any space not taken up by fliers or medical equipment.

"Watch *Dracula* much?" The coroner glanced up from the body to squint at me. He was tall, but managed to seem smaller than he was. He should have been named 'Archibald' or 'Horace.' Balding, jowly cheeks and pear-shaped. Not fat, just soft. Could have been forty or sixty, he was that unremarkable.

"Got silver bullets, too," he said. It was a silly threat. I'd have bet good money he couldn't fire a gun.

"You even know where the safety is on your pistol?" I asked.

"This is the South," said the sheriff, with a reverence that spoke of fanaticism. "Doc Madison can shoot the tits off of a fly."

"That big here?" I asked. Another insult that went over the sheriff's head.

"Anywho. We ain't had an incursion in sixty-three years," said the coroner. He picked up some 8x10 photos from a desk against the only wall with windows.

"Incursion?" Were we talking aliens instead of undead bloodsuckers? Not that I'd ever seen any creatures from outer space, but there were always rumors. Of course, I wasn't sure most people would draw a distinction between monsters from outer space and the fey creatures that came into our world from other dimensions.

"*Vampires*, Mr. Greyson," replied Doc Madison, snidely. He studied my bored features. "Would you rather be someplace else?"

"I'd always rather be someplace else," I replied. "But people have funny ways of putting things. I hear 'incursion' and I think military units. And that makes me think of special crafts and I naturally think of UFOs. At least, that's what the Wyoming state troopers originally thought had taken out their entire team up above Casper four years ago."

"I read about that. Turned out to be a drug cartel trying to get a foothold as I recall," said the sheriff, nodding.

"Try a religious cult who'd managed to uncork a very unpleasant djinn. A transdimensional creature actually stuck in a bottle. They had plans to worship him into the afterlife. Most of 'em are dead, so I guess only they know if they were right." I saw the anger on William's features. "The FBI and the djinn killed them, not me." He nodded, but I wasn't sure he believed me. I shrugged. "What the FBI releases to the press and what really happens are rarely the same thing."

"You were there?" A smidgeon of respect grew in Doc Madison's pale eyes.

"Yep. One of my first jobs. Cost me two good men, but I learned to carry assault rifles after that," I said grimly. "Now, can we get back to this vampire business?"

The sheriff studied me like I was a ballerina who'd turned out to be a quarterback but he motioned the other man to continue.

"As I was saying, we hadn't had a vampire incursion for sixty-three years. Got two black and white photos of the injuries back then and we're lucky to have them. Not the best quality, but I emailed the FBI for additional materials on vampires. And I sent photos of the mayor's body."

Sheriff Williams grunted in disgust.

"What?" I asked.

"We told 'em we had a vampire problem and they asked how many bodies we had. Doc told 'em 'one' and they said call again when it hit double-digits." The sheriff chewed angrily on a plastic straw. "*Busy* they said. Too friggin' busy for a vampire! I asked 'em what we do in the meanwhile and that's when they suggested you. Werewolf Incorporated."

"Nothing like a professional recommendation from the men in black." My tone made it clear that I wasn't real happy with the Feds, either. Just in case he'd missed my earlier comment about their typical press-releases and lack of disclosure.

I didn't tell him that the FBI had kept me locked up for nearly three months after the bite, no better than an animal. Then months more of psychological profiling and obligatory lock-up on full moons. I'd even been shadowed by seasoned lycanthropes until they'd been sure I wouldn't go rogue myself. Not happy with them at all. More like a necessary evil.

"We're hoping you'll keep the number down to one," said the coroner with a stern look of disapproval to the sheriff. "We lost the mayor, so the town is doing its best to maintain proper order."

"I'm the only order you got, Harv," said the sheriff. "Now tell the man what he needs to know so he can get his ass out on the road before dark."

"Alright. I was told that you needed to see the body and not pictures." Doc Madison pulled a sheet of plastic off the table in the center of the room and took a step back. "This is Mayor Ronald Cheswick."

Cheswick had been a plump man in his late fifties, with a large firm belly, which meant he had worked out to put muscles over his fat. Round face and jowly, he resembled the coroner except for a bulbous nose above a well-trimmed mustache and goatee. Several types of bruises covered the corpse's grey-white skin. Some had been made during the attack, but others were the kind that showed up after a violent death. Messy bite marks outlined by darker bruising surprised me. As if the vampire had been in a hurry or out of control.

I approached the mayor's body, taking slow, deep breaths as I filtered through the scents. There was no way I was going to lick the body, even if I could have gotten more information by tasting the dead-man. The garlic aroma was strong, but thankfully, it was one of those fragrances that didn't mess with my nose. It was like hearing music in the background while listening to a conversation.

I tilted my head to the side and inhaled again. There was something, very faint. "Did someone start to embalm him?"

"No. Why?" The coroner shuffled over as if he might be able to smell what I smelled, but his nose failed him. Humans couldn't have smelled anything over the overwhelming garlic.

"Just curious." I motioned him to keep away, mostly because of his own, personally distracting scents. I circled the body, looking at the jagged marks on the torn throat and fleshy hip, but I concentrated on the subtle aromas he gave off.

Traces of body wastes clung to his corpse. As a werewolf, it had taken me a long time to learn to ignore the smell of fecal matter on dead bodies. Even diluted by the other smells of death. I still hadn't mastered it on living people. No matter how well you wiped or what you used, there was always something left behind. It took its toll on my sex life, which lately hadn't been much. And God help me if a woman was sick. No matter how hot she might look, the smell of disease could have been bottled as 'impotence.'

"I have men watching the two public cemeteries. But we're still trying to get permission to check out the six registered family plots out in the countryside," said the sheriff.

"No need."

"What, you don't think they get buried and then break their way out when darkness falls?" The big man glowered at me for contradicting him.

"Urban legend. By the time a body goes in the ground, it's gonna be embalmed unless there's a religious waiver. The last ten years, that waiver only applies if you allow a blood-test to prove nothing's coming back from the dead."

"What does embalming have to do with it?" asked the coroner, more curious than dismissive.

Great. Their best medical expert didn't understand the first thing about vampirism. He probably knew just as little about people like me, which meant he'd probably tell the sheriff to avoid sharing food or to keep me from kissing the local ladies. Not that I expected to get laid while I was there, but you never knew.

"Embalming kills the virus that makes a corpse into a vampire," I explained. "So cemeteries are a waste of time. I assume that this area isn't known for mausoleums."

The sheriff shook his head, but his anger was directed at the coroner. "Why didn't you know that, Harv?"

"I should spend my time researching vampires?" asked the balding man. "Hard enough to treat all your social diseases."

"Very funny," replied the sheriff. "So what can you tell us about the body, Mr. Werewolf? What makes you worth so much money?"

I glared at the sheriff and he shrugged, a sort of deal with it response. I'd left my mood to fight in the bar, so I played nice for now.

"Any bodies missing from a local mortuary?" The smells of formaldehyde and other pre-burial chemicals were too prevalent not to be related to the killer. How much embalming would it take before a body couldn't rise from the dead? I'd never asked that question before, but it was suddenly relevant.

"Not that I know of. I can double-check. What kind of radius we talking?" asked the sheriff.

"Wait. I thought you said if they were embalmed, they couldn't be a vampire?" Doc Madison was smarter than he looked.

"The smell's there. So there's a connection. Just don't know what." The sheriff raised his brows because I hadn't answered his question. "Depends on how long this sucker's been running around. If this is his first kill, within thirty miles I'd guess."

"What makes you think it's a 'him'?"

"When a man sweats between the legs, it ain't the same smell as a woman," I said without my usual rough language. "Truthfully though, vampires don't normally sweat. I'm guessing in a serious rage the undead body will still produce traces of it. I can tell which smell belongs to the mayor. He sweated up a storm, but this is different."

"Your nose that good?"

"I'm part animal, remember?" My sarcasm was meant as a criticism but Williams nodded as if I was just reminding him of a simple fact.

"We probably should assume this is a first kill. No other law enforcement's reported anything like it," said the coroner.

Crap logic, but I wasn't going to argue. First kill would mean at least two vampires. The maker and the made. For one of them it wouldn't have been a first kill. I kept the distinction to myself.

"The thing is." The coroner stared at Williams uncomfortably. "I've compared the photos I have. Not just the two, but from the internet while I wait for what the Feds send me. There's something strange about his wounds."

"Like what?" I came around to look at his photos.

"Vampires don't normally take chunks of flesh out when they suck you dry." Harv pointed at the man's buttocks. He set down the photos and approached the corpse. Using both gloved hands, he pushed up on the body so that it rolled slightly onto its side. I could see that the mayor had lost a bit of cellulite-laden ass muscle. The bite was so messy that it left shredded skin all around the edges where the meat had been torn out.

"Nope. They sure don't," I agreed but both the sheriff and the coroner were watching me closely. "Oh, I see. No, this isn't a werewolf bite. I may not know what it is, but trust me. I know what kind of marks I leave behind." I smiled.

"You killed a lot of people, there, Mr. Greyson?" The sheriff's tone grew dangerous.

"Only when the government gives me a license to." I stayed calm and pretended that I didn't notice his hand going for his gun. "But I do like to hunt on occasion."

"Hunt?" asked the coroner with an audible gulp. He took a step away from me and his fear messed with the other smells in the room.

"Yeah. White-Tail Deer up in the Sierra Nevadas during the season. Only difference is, I don't use a gun." With my back to them, they couldn't see me grin. Nothing like playing with the locals to put me in a better mood. I pulled out my Glock G21 .45 caliber semiautomatic from my shoulder-holster and waved it sideways in front of me for emphasis. "For vampires, that's a different story."

"So, what now?" asked the sheriff, suddenly impatient.

"Now we go to the scene of the crime. Or at least where you found the body," I replied.

When we got outside and were walking to his car, I asked him the most important question about the case that I could think of. "Sheriff, why did you have us meet in that bar if you knew the owner hated my kind and wouldn't serve me?" I wanted him to admit he'd been provoking me. It would give me leverage down the road that I was pretty sure I'd need.

"Even though Resistance County isn't one of the dry counties, Mr. Greyson, the *Broken Record*'s the only bar in town."

Just great. I so did not like the South.

CHAPTER THREE

The crime scene was at the edge of town, in an alley that was a small dirt road between the government building and the Resistance County Old Folks Home. No, really. That's what they had named the place. The government building didn't have a name, but it housed the mayor's office, the courthouse and county recorder's office

"It was here? In the alley?" Garbage bins overflowed with debris, half of it rotting organic material. People had urinated in the alley. More than once the past few days. My nose screamed for relief. "Could have warned me."

"Right there at the back of the building. We figure he was working late. Got caught on the way out," said a young man in a deputy uniform.

He barely looked old enough to have graduated high school. Like he belonged on *Mayberry RF*D, only he was no Don Knotts. He should have been the quarterback of the local high school football team, screwing the homecoming queen. Too handsome and too polite to be in law enforcement. But that was just my opinion.

I was okay to look at, but it was my body that got me laid. When I got laid without paying for it. Put this kid in a cell and he'd be everyone's favorite dance-partner. He smelled clean and healthy, but the *Irish Spring* made him a problem. Another reason the sheriff should have read the contract. No colognes and no fragrances in the soap or shampoos.

"That the official guess right now?"

The sheriff gave the pretty-boy an unhappy look but nodded confirmation. "Unless you got something better."

"I guess I should do my thing then." I glanced at the deputy. "Any chance you could get your spiffy little uniform dirty and move that dumpster about fifty feet in that direction? And stay back, while you're at it. 'Manly, yes,' but it screws with my nose."

One little shove with my inhuman strength would have sent the dumpster rolling half-way down the alley. But I wasn't here to do grunt work. That's what deputies were for, wasn't it? Who says TV isn't educational?

"Of course." The deputy didn't take any offense. Yep, definitely *Mayberry*.

I looked at the sheriff. "You got the budget for a cybernetic deputy, Louis?"

"It's 'Sheriff,' to you. And Jason's a good kid. Don't fuck with him." The broad sheriff moved a little closer to me, putting muscle behind the threat. "I mean it, too."

"Don't worry. I'm not into little boys, no matter how pretty." I waved at the retirement home. "Did any of the old farts hear anything?"

"At 10:43pm? Most of them can't even stay awake for the early-bird special down at *Rhonda's Eatery*."

I knew some old people who couldn't seem to sleep at all. Four hours and they were raring to go. But the first rule of any kind of investigation was to never assume anything. Sure, believe the facts as they came up, but never fully vest yourself in any truth until it was conclusive.

"You didn't seal off the alleyway," I complained. "At least three vehicles have driven through here since the murder. One of them more than once. Bigger problem than Barney Fife's *Irish Spring*."

"Three? How can you know that?" asked the deputy as he brushed dust off of his uniform and sniffed himself.

"Cars are like women. They each have their own fragrance no matter what perfume they wear," I said. "They run at different temperatures. Have different exhaust systems. Even made of different metals or plastics."

"I heard tell that a werewolf's nose was like a chemistry lab." The young deputy was pleased to be learning all about me. I frowned, not sure I liked being liked more than I liked being loathed. If I grew attached to the kid, he'd probably wind up dead. That happened around me a lot.

"If you say so," I grumbled. "Makes things harder though, Sheriff Williams."

"Never occurred to me that we'd be using a scratch n' sniff approach to policing," he replied, deadpan.

I actually wanted to smile, because it was almost a sense of humor. But I didn't give him the satisfaction. "Well, now you do."

I crouched down on my heels and ran a finger along a patch of blood soaked into the soil. I closed my eyes and used only my nose, still getting a whiff of offal that didn't come from just the dead body which had been here. I could make out other smells as well, despite the blood, urine and *Irish Spring*.

"There's that trace of embalming chemicals," I said for the benefit of the sheriff and maybe because I thought better when I talked out loud. "Smell of old people from across the alleyway." Yes, old people had a unique set of smells. They used lotions and powders and denture creams that younger people didn't. And there was a gummy smell of growing old that was hard to mistake.

Then something a little different hit my nose. A perfume I'd once caught whiff of in a very dark, dank cave. Only it wasn't perfume. It was the smell of undeath.

"Vampire," I confirmed and stood up. "No question. But the cars through here ruined any chance of me tracking them by scent. I'm going to have to get my partner and start back at the morgue to see if I can get something else from the body. Vampires don't give off that much odor in the first place. Not like some fey."

"What do vampires smell like?" asked the deputy. The sheriff frowned at him and he took a step back. "Sorry, Sheriff."

"They smell like apples, Deputy Jason," I replied, just to annoy the sheriff.

"Bullshit!" exclaimed the deputy, like he was pleased as punch. "Seriously?"

"Apples just a bit more than overripe. But yeah, that's as close as I can come to describing it," I confirmed. Shit, I did like the kid. He had an appropriate sense of the absurd and personally, I didn't think there was enough of that in the world. It mattered to me if he died or not. Shit, shit, shit!

CHAPTER FOUR

Back at the poorly maintained motel with its cracked paint and overgrown hedges, I paused on the way to my room to examine the pool. The smell of excess chlorine didn't bother me as much as the urine. Our room was right across from the water and the smell came inside. There weren't many guests staying in the low-priced rooms but they still managed to soil the only source of exercise I was likely to get in this backwoods town. The alley and the pool, was there anywhere these people didn't piss?

"Hey handsome," said a small, but very feminine voice. I saw my current partner lounging nearby on the railing which surrounded the cool-decking.

"Littlewing. What the devil are you doing?" I asked her.

The sprite's real name wasn't 'Littlewing,' but humans couldn't make half the sounds of her native language. The first week of our partnership, after she heard me play the Jimi Hendrix song, she rechristened herself. Eight inches tall, she had golden, pupilless eyes, wings on her back and long, pointed ears. Otherwise, she could have almost passed for a voluptuous human with silky platinum hair in a fifties bob. Most of the fey were humanoid, but few of them as sexy.

At the moment, her bare-breasts were exposed to the sun. They gleamed with a golden sheen that wasn't just sweat or a reflection of the light. She wore a bikini bottom, but probably because I'd told her I'd fire her if she didn't. The topless thing I could live with. Maybe I was her boss, but that didn't mean she'd do everything I told her. You had to know when to fight your battles. Especially when you didn't really want to win them. She had a very nice rack.

"I'm 'sorbing the rays, Boss. Just like you told me." Her voice took on a sultry tone. "Don't pretend you don't like what you see. You ever get small enough, I know you want to tap this."

"I ever get that small, I'm gonna cut it off." I shook my head, although I didn't stop staring at her proportionately well-developed breasts. Her nipples were shaped like flower petals instead of circles. Despite her size, they didn't look youthful. They were sensual.

"How much of a charge you got built?" Her soft glow didn't tell me how much sunlight she'd stored in her sexy little body. For vampires I wanted her at one-hundred percent.

My gaze lingered on the fullness of her top-half and I wished she was a real woman. Not for the first time, either. Sprites had libidos that would have worn out the entire U.S. Armed Forces given a chance. At least, the females did. She wouldn't talk about the males of her species.

"Not as much as you asked for. That's why I'm taking the girls out for a walk," she replied, eyes closed.

She snuggled against her towel, a plush, monogrammed washcloth she'd stolen from one of the more expensive hotels earlier in the year. I watched as her breasts flopped about. Natural endowments, not implants. Being from Los Angeles, I encountered more fake than real. Not that I was complaining. I enjoyed breasts of all types.

"I knew it!" shouted a man. The short, red-headed motel-clerk rushed toward us, irate. "I just friggin' knew it!"

"What's your problem?"

"You have to find another motel. You can't stay here!" He stared at Littlewing's flesh and turned red to match his hair.

"Pardon?"

I'd been hired to work with local law-enforcement. Beating up employees in respectable businesses wouldn't make Williams any friendlier. That didn't mean that I couldn't imagine wiping that sour expression right off the clerk's face with one of my hands transformed into fingers with claws. The man had seen the tattoo and the sheriff had cleared my lycanthropy with the motel owner before I checked in. The bar had been a test. This was business.

"We don't allow no pets. You have to leave," demanded the clerk.

I stopped him cold. If I didn't, no telling what Littlewing would do for calling her a 'pet.' She had a worse temper than me. "She isn't a pet. She's a sprite!"

"I don't care if she's a Coca Cola, you can't have pets. You have to leave. I'll give you thirty minutes to find a new place to stay. And you don't get no refund, neither." He turned and trundled past me toward the vending machines.

"Great. That's just wonderful. Have I ever told you how much I love working with you?" I asked her angrily. She was oddly relaxed despite the incident. That should have been my first clue.

"You need to get laid," replied Littlewing with a giggle.

I sighed. "There's only one bar in this rat-piss town. You wanna bet there's only one motel, too?"

I scooped up the small woman and she shrieked indignantly as I carried her up to our room. Once we were inside, I flinched at the smell. My contract always specified certain criteria for cleaning a place, but when I was stuck staying in small towns and rural areas, I had to take what I could get. Here, the thing that got me was the mold. If it messed up my nose, I'd lose half my advantage over the Feds who might be pulled into this job sooner than later.

"Didn't I tell you not to leave the guns on the bed?" I let her go and she fluttered angrily into the air. Her fury lost some of its potency as I was distracted by the jiggling of her naked breasts.

"You pick me up again like I'm a Barbie-doll and I'll castrate you while you sleep!" she shouted. "And I don't care if it's as big as me, I'll eat the thing right in front of your agonized face!"

"The guns?" I repeated.

Littlewing had a thing for hardware and frequently took out all of our weapons and laid them out to admire, clean, or straddle them like vibrators. I had my own type of kink, so I left her alone. Except she had instructions to keep them put away when not in use. For moments like this.

She sighed and glanced at the guns. "I thought you'd be gone longer and I was gonna check the fire-mechanism on your backup Glock. Seemed a tad slow last week when we were on the range."

"Like a half-a-second or less!" I snarled, heading for the small table by the bed to search for a phone directory. I was a werewolf, but there were times when a gun came in handy. My weapon of choice was a Glock .45 caliber semi-automatic which held thirteen rounds and weighed a little over two pounds fully loaded. But I also kept a Rutger SR9 compact stuck in the back of my pants. The guns on the bed were extras. I even had an assault rifle which I'd picked up during the battle with the djinn. Without that, I'd have been killed that day. Werewolf or not.

"How many times is a half-second the difference between life and death?" she demanded as if I were being irresponsible.

"Put your top back on. I need to concentrate," I growled at her, but she was right.

She smiled to herself and began to pack the weapons in the case, with careful reverence. No, she didn't put the top back on, but I knew when to draw the line. Her bare chest was not one of those times.

"No freakin' phone book." I searched the only other drawers in the room. "Did you see any places as we drove through town?"

"You are such a caveman!" she laughed at me. "I did an internet search while you were packing for this job. I told you not to take it. This is the only public place."

"*Public* place? What's that supposed to mean?" She was trying to bait me.

"Well, there is a B&B just outside of town," she said slyly.

"Which is probably where you wanted to stay in the first place, wasn't it?" I shook my head.

"The job covers this dump, not the Misty Lake House." She fluttered over to me as I plopped onto the bed. "Though I did make a tentative reservation just in case."

"Oh? And when did you do that?" I asked.

"What day did you get the call to come here?"

"You know perfectly well! Yesterday!" I snarled at her

"Um, then, yeah, yesterday," she said and resumed packing the guns.

Her relaxed attitude about being called a 'pet' now made sense. "If I thought that you got us thrown out of here on purpose—!"

She acted like she couldn't hear me. Familiar with the routine, I gave up. It didn't matter if she'd done it on purpose or not. We'd lost the motel room and the B&B was apparently our only other option. "Fine. You call the sheriff and tell him we're changing rooms. Then we gotta meet the coroner, again. Daylight is fleeting."

"Yes, Boss," she said, grinning merrily as she zipped around the room, her naked chest glowing with success. "But if you're trying to quote *Rocky Horror*, it's 'Time is Fleeting.'"

"Shut up," I growled. I hated it when she did that. "And save your charge! I've got a bad feeling we're gonna need it!"

CHAPTER FIVE

When I saw the front of the B&B, I let my lupine rumble filled the interior of the black 1963 Ford Mustang. It had been my dad's idea of a family project during my high school years. I'd personally hand-polished and buffed every piece of metal, replacing a few wonky parts with hard-to-find authentic pieces while the old man supervised by glaring. He even made me airbrush five coats of paint on the primered body before finally grunting that it would do.

It had run like a charm and was pretty enough to fuck. But after all of that, dear old dad told me that I couldn't drive it till I was thirty. I thought he was joking at the time, but he'd only handed over the keys earlier this year on my birthday.

"Stop complaining. Werewolf Incorporated makes a decent fee for these jobs." Littlewing pressed her entire front against the interior of the windshield to see the B&B, but she had her top on. "It's not like you spend it on dates."

I parked near the door of the elegant, two-story colonial. It had white plaster columns and other period features. I could imagine a remake of *Gone with the Wind* being filmed here, except for the burglar alarm and iron security bars on the windows.

"It looks more like a prison," I said.

If Littlewing hadn't agreed, she would have made a snippy little comeback almost instantly. She turned to look at me. "The online brochure didn't show bars."

"Let's get this over with. But no letting any happy, yuppie-couple force us into dinner with them. We're here on a job and I don't want my privacy interrupted!" I reminded her.

"Sheesh! You'd think they named the local tavern after you!" she quipped. "That's what I'll call you from now on. 'Broken Record Greyson,' the werewolf who couldn't stop whining."

"It's called a 'bar,' not a 'tavern.' This isn't the U.K. and it isn't two hundred years ago," I corrected, just to get back at her.

"Oh, look! They have an herb garden. Yum!" Her sulk was instantly replaced with hunger. Sprites were omnivores, just like humans. Nothing more fun to watch than people's faces while Littlewing inhaled a twelve ounce porterhouse. Those wings burned a lot of carbs. "Can we eat before we go?"

"I already ate," I confessed and felt guilty. We didn't eat all our meals together, but we usually tried to time it so that we knew whether to wait or not. "Sorry. Forgot to tell you."

"Nice one, Mitch," she grumbled. "Guess I can wait till after the morgue."

When Littlewing first applied for the job as my partner, her size had been a problem. But I couldn't complain about her ability to fly or absorb sunlight and send it out in stinging pulses. It worked pretty well on vampires. The few opportunities she'd had to use it. Better still, she knew more about munitions than I'd learned my entire time as a monster hunter. But the best thing about her, besides her figure, was that she wasn't squeamish. Not at all.

"They have great fried okra at the *Broken Record*." I opened the car door and she buzzed past me. She headed for the stairs leading to the front door of the B&B. "Or not," I muttered, following her.

I grabbed the gun-bag and our one suitcase from the backseat. As I did, an older woman came out of the house, spry and smiling. She had white hair, not grey, cut in an old-fashioned bob that framed her withered face a little too youthfully. Littlewing noticed the similarity in their hair-styles and I grinned, unsympathetically. The woman wore a garden apron over an off-white dress and her exposed arms and face were softly tanned.

"Welcome to Misty Lake House," she called. "I don't see your wife. She sounded lovely on the phone."

The woman tried to look inside the tinted windows of the Mustang, but I stared up at the sky and shook my head before I forced myself to appear pleasant. Or as close as I came to a happy face these days.

"I think you mean my partner," I said. Littlewing hovered in front of the old lady's face.

"Oh, my stars!" exclaimed the woman. She staggered back, clutching her sagging bosom. "You're not human."

"I did ask you if you had a problem with werewolves," said Littlewing annoyed.

"But you didn't bother to tell her you were a sprite?" I raised one brow at her.

"I couldn't believe she'd be okay with you and care about me," grumbled Littlewing. "Seriously?"

"No, no. Not at all. I was just taken by surprise." The old woman tried to smile but her eyes were worried. "You did say it was official police business and I'm certainly aware of my civic responsibilities. Mind you, I can't cut the rate too much. Sheriff or not. I run this place alone and it's not cheap you know."

"I bet it's been harder since the invention of electricity," I muttered under my breath.

She turned and looked at me. "My hearing is actually very good since I've gotten the implant, young man!" She studied me for a moment. I really didn't want her to change her mind.

"I'm sorry. My welcome in town was a bit rough and I'm still licking my wounds."

I saw Littlewing make a face. I frowned to keep her from making a remark about me licking other parts of myself and mouthed, '*I'm not a dog.*'

"Investigating the mayor's death?" She motioned for us to follow her into the house. "Everyone's heard about it, of course. Tragic. And poor Mrs. Cheswick!"

I put out a hand and the sprite flew in ahead of me. Out of habit, I sniffed the yard before we went inside and couldn't have missed the herb garden. The most obvious scent was fresh garlic. I knew it had nothing to do with the vampire attack. These were nearly ripe bulbs, planted many weeks earlier. Still, I was skeptical of coincidence. I wondered if there had been other vampire 'incursions' that the coroner didn't know about.

"I hope you don't mind, but I'm a classically trained chef in the Italian school," said the woman as if she'd read my mind. "I love the smell of garlic in the garden, not just in my food. Some people think it's too much. I hope it doesn't trouble you."

"No, actually. I love the stuff."

Garlic was one of those scents which didn't mess with my sense of smell at all. It's why I hadn't complained to the coroner. Not that he would have known that. It wasn't common knowledge. The FBI controlled all research published about lycanthropes and other creatures for public safety. I didn't really care. The only part about lycanthrope biology I cared about was what would keep me alive.

The owner of the B&B led us upstairs just off the foyer. She walked past oil paintings of Union and Confederate soldiers in various scenes of war, past vases with freshly cut flowers and I could smell the garlic stems used as decoration with the flowers. I admired the lack of waste, wondering if we wouldn't all be better going back to an earlier time. Back when people did for themselves.

Then I shook my head at the downside. Women were no longer repressed by false morality and I could watch six hours of *Dexter* if I wanted. But it was nice to see pockets of environmental conscience.

Our room had a king-sized bed with a canopy of gossamer fabric. Littlewing preened with delight and darted around the room, inspecting every corner. Smaller vases held yellow roses, only mildly fragrant so I wouldn't choke. The garlic was pervasive here as well, but I liked the smell and anything was better than the stench at the motel. I was starting to get hungry again.

"The bathroom is just down the hall. Second door. The first door is a pantry closet, so you won't get them confused." The woman opened the drapes, pulling at them several times because she wasn't as agile as she'd seemed at first glance. "I put a basket of fresh fruit out. But if you're a werewolf, I suppose I should have taken some raw meat out of the fridge instead?"

I grinned. "I prefer my meat cooked. And yes, I do eat fruit."

She wasn't trying to be a pain. But the flip side of the South was that people were more social and spent more time being genuinely interested in their neighbors than in Los Angeles. Another reason to prefer California. "I'm sorry, Mrs.—?"

"Miss Ruth Conklin, Mr. Greyson. I never had the pleasure of marrying." A look of dismay flitted across her features but then she smiled again.

"Your brochure didn't show the, um, security features." Littlewing was staring at the window.

"Oh, dear. Is that a problem? I really didn't want to install the bars. They ruin the view. But, have you ever stared up at the night sky and got this feeling? Like a hand brushing at the middle of your back?"

"Yeah, I have." I glanced at Littlewing who shrugged. The fey didn't get those kinds of feelings.

"Maybe I'm just an old woman, but I value my life as much as any teenager." She scowled. "Not that the place isn't safe." She smiled then, embarrassed. "You aren't exactly a victim-type are you, Mr. Greyson?"

"No, Ma'am. Not since I was first bitten." I rubbed my face, hating this tender moment. An old lady understood me better than a tough sheriff? Crap. "I'm sorry, Miss Conklin, but we need to meet the coroner. What else do we need to do to check in?" I reached for my wallet but she waved her hand at me, dismissively.

"After I've spoken to the sheriff," she said. "And if you don't mind? I do prefer cash."

"We can do that," said Littlewing, making snow-angels on the plush comforter.

"Good. Well, then. Here's your key to the front door. The brass one is to the room. The bathroom is never locked except when being used, so there's no key for that." She walked as quickly as she could to the door, trying to get out of my way. I felt a flash of guilt, but I ignored it. "Will you be eating here this evening?" she asked before she reached the hall.

"I think tonight we'll play it by ear," I said graciously.

"Fine. Then I'll see you both at breakfast," she replied and disappeared down the stairs.

"Happy?" I asked the sprite, less annoyed than I'd expected. But I missed the convenient anonymity of a motel.

"Very," she said and giggled.

"Good. You can store the guns." I tossed the bag onto the bed. She screeched and flew out of the way before it smashed her. I chuckled but she went into professional mode. She began by stashing a few of the weapons around the room, then placing the rest neatly under the bed.

While she was doing that, I inspected all the exits. I tested the bars which had been welded onto the frame of the house and made sure I knew where everything was in the room. Down to the last smell. Not paranoid. Just standard procedures. Attention to details had saved my life more than once.

Five minutes later, we were armed and heading back into town. Maybe the coroner had new information. Or there was the chance that Littlewing could help with the body. Dark was a couple of hours away and I wanted to find the thing before it struck again. I'd never faced a vampire at night, but I was pretty sure that the results of a bloodsucker biting a werewolf weren't much different than it biting a regular human. I could die or be infected just as readily. Death before infection, but I didn't really want to find out.

CHAPTER SIX

At the coroner's, nothing had changed. Garlic and crosses still lined the walls. The body was still in the center of the room, covered in plastic. But it was new to Littlewing and she buzzed around the small cellar inspecting its outdated girlie calendar. She modeled some of the poses and I managed not to smile.

Doc Madison, the coroner, stood there staring. Staring at Littlewing and not telling me much.

"You get any help from the FBI files?" I asked, trying to get his attention.

"Is that a functional pistol?" Harv pointed at the gun in the holster at the sprite's curvaceous hip.

Most men noticed her boobs first and then the tiny gun. The gun usually got more attention afterwards. Something about an eight-inch Barbie-doll with a gun fascinated grown men. It was a custom made semi-automatic, crafted by a very skilled, very expensive gunsmith out of Texas. He occasionally developed new and unusual weapons for the tiny woman, but only charged me for what Littlewing decided suited her. What he did with the rest I hadn't a clue. That's where we'd been when Williams had first contacted us.

"Want me to shoot off one of your balls?" she shouted.

She didn't have to shout, because her voice was bigger than the rest of her. She could be heard quite clearly when she spoke, even across a room. But it helped if she belted it from the diaphragm. Some people said it made her sound angry. Me, I thought she was just being flirtatious.

"That won't be necessary," he said. He had to fight his hand dropping to his crotch protectively. "I'm afraid the FBI material just confirmed that the bites don't make sense."

"You mean the chunk of flesh?" I winked at Littlewing who beamed as she patted her gun lovingly. We liked to take turns at being more immature. It got pretty hairy when we both decided to act like jerks.

"No. The bites themselves." Doc Madison shuffled over to the mayor's body. "See, here? Typical vampire dentition is like human or animal dentition. You could hypothetically I.D. a vampire by the placement of the fangs and shape of the teeth." He looked up at me troubled. "But this thing has a double row of identical fangs."

"Not two vampires feasting from the same wound?" Littlewing hovered within inches of the injury. Her golden skin was a stark contrast to the grey dead flesh she inspected. I used my nose. She used her eyes and other senses unique to the fey.

"Not with identical dentition like we have here. And it's not the same vampire biting the same spot multiple times. One set is smaller than the other. You ever hear of a vampire with two rows of teeth?" The man glanced at the sprite and then her gun before he jerked his head away.

My feelings got kind of hurt, because I'd never met anyone more afraid of Littlewing than of me. And my gun was in plain sight, too. Well, one of three I carried. My Glock was in a shoulder holster, invisible when I zipped up my leather jacket. The ankle holster which held my compact Rutger SR9 was hidden by my relaxed fit jeans. And I always tucked a second one in the small of my back, down the pants, but affixed to my belt so that it was easier to draw when I reached back. The only problem was, if I took the jacket off, it was in plain sight. As a werewolf, I didn't usually feel the need to carry weapons that would pass a body search.

"Nope. Far as I know, there ain't no such animal." I looked at the body, lifting up one end of the plastic draped over his head and checked his throat. "But you said these were messy bites. That interfere with your dental comparison?"

There were two circular bites, one slightly smaller than the other. The indentations from the inner teeth were deeper. I flashed to *Aliens.* Those creatures had inner jaws that extended from between the main teeth. Most people assumed that vampire bites meant two punctures. But when a vamp sank its fangs into a victim, the ordinary teeth pressed hard against the flesh as well. It was like a nasty human bite except the eye-teeth punctured the skin. A full circle of teeth plus a couple of holes.

If I hadn't smelled the overripe-apple fragrance of a vampire, I would have suspected something else. Something fey.

"Some of the places, sure. But you can see here. And here. The bites are clean. No savaging. They just drained the mayor dry."

"Some new kind of vamp?" Littlewing gave me one of her 'what have I got her into now' looks as she waited for me to answer.

"I told you. Never assume anything. If it's something new, it'll die just like something old." I sniffed the body. Now that I'd inspected the location where the body had been found, I had something to compare. "You sure it's not fey?"

She looked up at me startled, then shook her head. It hadn't occurred to her. And I'd just reminded her not to assume anything!

"Why would a fairy work for a specially licensed hunter?" asked good old Harv and I flinched on his behalf.

He yelped even before Littlewing started reaming him a new one. She drew her gun and waved it in his direction. "I am not a god-damned, insect-brained fairy you oversized balding piece of meat!"

"Don't burn your sunlight," I warned her.

My eyes were still closed and my concentration on my nose, but I could feel the flashes of light. She grumbled a few choice swear words only I could hear but she didn't argue and holstered her gun. I was grateful and worked through the smells.

There was a trace of dust from the alleyway. And the slightly stronger scent of old people. Then that delicate bouquet of overripe apples, which said 'vampire.' Overriding those was the smell of the mayor's own body wastes, spilled when he died. The embalming chemicals that came through were the same signature from the alleyway. Nothing new at all. Except!

"Harv, did the mayor have a lady-friend come visit since I was here last?"

"No. No one's been allowed to see the body, not even Mrs. Cheswick," replied the coroner. He had moved to the far side of the room away from Littlewing where she hovered above the photos of the previous 'incursion' into Resistance County.

"Boss, sixty-three years is nothing for a vamp," said the sprite.

"So?"

"Well, this is an odd place for a second vamp attack in less than a hundred years. Maybe they're related." She looked up at Doc Madison. "Why is Resistance County so small compared to the rest of the Alabama counties?"

Harv puffed up with local pride. "Ah, well. Some people think it's because we didn't want to be a dry county. No alcohol allowed and such. That we broke off from Talladega County for that reason. But it was the influence of the local big wigs back in 1914. I'm something of a history buff and my great-great was one of those big wigs."

"Big wigs?" Littlewing wrinkled her nose.

"Not literally, 'Wing. Rich people. Powerful." I nodded at Doc Madison to continue. There was a chance his historical musings might tell us why a vampire had come to Resistance County.

"Well, my family fell to hard times during Black Monday in 1929, so we lost our political influence as a result. But not before we made this county a place to be safe from supernatural creatures!" He gave Littlewing an uncomfortable look.

"And just how did you do that?" she asked unpleasantly.

"By breaking off from the larger county in 1914. So that we could vote the way we wanted. It wasn't about booze. It was about the fey." He waved in the air, like he was pointing at someone not present. "When Woodrow Wilson was elected. 1913 it was. He passed all these amazing reforms, you see. *Federal Reserve Act, Federal Trades Commission.* Things we still respect in this country. But then he passed a law requiring a *Federal Fey-Preservation Commission.* They had a mandate to allow a county by county decision on the hunting or protection of fey." Littlewing made a face. She wasn't following what the man meant. "The Commission required a law on the books, under their authority, one way or another. Either we had to treat your kind like protected species. Or pests."

"Pests?" Littlewing could growl almost as well as me when she truly pissed off. I kept my mouth shut. I knew the legal history regarding the fey. It was part of the training the FBI required for my license to hunt monsters. What I wanted to hear was anything relevant to Resistance County and vampires.

"The way wolves were hunted to extinction in some counties." Doc Madison hesitated but something in Littlewing's gaze made him continue nervously. "Well, the people of Resistance rose up against Talladega and we voted ourselves a separate county. We didn't want the fey here and Talladega looked to be in favor of protecting them. I figure it was because the Talladega community was historically influenced by the local Creek Injuns. The Injuns respected a lot of the monsters that came into our world through those rips in the universe. Said they was part of nature sent by the Great Spirit and all that bullshit. This part of the county didn't cotton much to the Injuns any more than the strange critters, so it was an easy call."

"Hard to believe a president established a commission like that back then." I knew how much the average American hated the creatures that had come through the rips in the universe. Maybe the werewolf that made me hadn't come through one of those tears, but sometime, years earlier, the original lycanthropes had. The current levels of prejudice were based on decades of education and tolerance. In the early 1900s, I would have expected fear to rule the day.

Old Harv had an answer to my comment. "President Wilson created that damned commission because he was influenced by his strong Irish roots. The Irish almost worship the fey, even to this day. Of *course* an Irish-American president would feel the same. People gave Obama hell because of his African relatives, but Wilson was more connected to Ireland than Obama ever was to the jungle."

"You saying you can hunt my kind in this county?" demanded Littlewing. We both let the jungle comment slide.

"That's what we voted for back then." Doc Madison did his best to make it noncommittal.

Part of what Harv said didn't jibe with what I knew about current federal laws. "Some fey have earned citizenship. So Resistance County can't just do what they want. Littlewing was granted hers after coming to work for me. She has the same rights as any American. Even Bachmann can't take that away from her."

"That Obama *Fey Registration and Immigration Act* would have thrilled Wilson to death." Doc Madison rubbed his chest, sneering. "It doesn't protect *most* of the fey, though. We still go goblin hunting whenever a nest crops up. Almost became an annual event throughout the counties that didn't pass to protect the little monsters. No law against killing them here in Resistance."

Littlewing's anger faded. She hated goblins as much as humans did, but for different reasons. Goblins were natural predators and they fed on sprites. When they could catch them. She'd appreciate the fact that they were kept eradicated locally.

"Not entirely true." I couldn't let it drop. Littlewing's safety might be at issue if the locals were ignorant. "The *Fey Registration and Immigration Act* reclassified non-thinking fey from 'exterminate at will vermin' to 'animals.' PETA pushed hard on that and it was the reason the bill passed. Obama already wasn't popular after being unable to fix the mess George W. left him and the nation with." I sighed, hating politics. "It was his last serious bill and personally, I think it's what did him in."

"People around here aren't fond of Obama. But animals can be hunted, so what's the difference?"

"And by people you mean white people?" I saw his flash of guilt but dropped it. There was no point in trying to convince him that animals deserved protections from a humane point of view. I changed the subject. "I take it the town wasn't originally called 'Resistance'?" You never knew when local culture might provide some insight into people's motives and he still hadn't told me anything that might tie in with the vampire.

"No, sir. Used to be 'Talladega Springs.' Changed the name at the same time as we established the new county."

"Does any of this have anything to do with the vampire? Daylight isn't gonna last forever," I complained.

"Well, no. But she asked."

He was right. I glanced at Littlewing but her mind was elsewhere. "What is it 'Wing?"

"If it's the same vampire, where are all the victims in the years in between?" She was staring at the black and white photos, looking for anomalies that others might have missed. She'd lost interest in the history lesson faster than I had. That was a first.

"Vampires don't have very good self-control," I agreed.

I sniffed the body again, wondering about the mysterious female visitor that Doc Madison swore hadn't come by. I tried to lock the female scent into my memory. I'd know her again if I ran into her. "I don't care what you say, Doc, there was a woman here. Scrubbed down so that she left little scent. Someone who knew you had a werewolf on the case. How many people you tell about me?"

"The whole town knows after your confrontation with old Frank, the bartender," exclaimed the coroner. "Can't be the same vampire as sixty-three years ago. They killed that one."

"Staked or beheaded?" I asked.

"Um, does it matter?"

"Um, yeah!" I replied mocking him. "Staking immobilizes them. As long as the wood's in, they stay that way. But pull it out and it's party time come nightfall."

"How come that's not in the material the FBI sent?" asked Harv.

"They don't want overzealous crime-fighters to go around beheading innocent people." I looked at the missing chunk of flesh, wondering why a vampire would do that. A souvenir? Was I looking at a vampire trophy collector? It would be a lot more bodies and a lot bigger mess really fast in this town if that were the case. Most vampires took one victim a night just to live.

"But wouldn't staking kill innocent people, too?" asked Harv, confused.

"You'd be surprised. It's a lot harder to stake someone, than to chop off their head. With a stake, it's close and intimate. You have to really hammer that puppy in there. None of that *Buffy the Vampire Slayer* stab and grab that I can do. But a chainsaw to the throat and bzzzz, zapola! One permanently dead body. Human or vampire. I'm not saying that innocent people don't get staked, but it takes a different type of effort." I stared at Mayor Cheswick's corpse. "Speaking of staking, it needs to be done before dark."

"Oh." The man turned green at the thought of driving a piece of wood through the body.

That's why they hired people like me. Over time, when everyone expected you to be a killer, you sort of fell into it. And sometimes I wondered if the wolf instincts weren't slowly seeping into my humanity. Would I lose control one day? Become one of the monsters?

"Do I need to stake the mayor?" I watched Harv. If he couldn't follow through, bad things might happen. One in three chance the mayor might rise from the dead when the sun set.

"I can do it."

"You sure? Not *maybe*. One-hundred percent positive?" He swallowed, but nodded. I believed him. Hard to be a coroner if he couldn't cut up a corpse. Or in this case, hammer a stake through the heart of one.

"Boss, this first vampire was spotted outside of town at a place called Sliverton," said Littlewing, excited. "Maybe it wasn't hunting. Vampires require the same kind of protection from the sun now as they did back then. What do you think?"

"What is Sliverton, exactly?"

"That's supposed to be 'Silvertown,'" clarified the coroner. "It's a small mining establishment. Closed up about fifty-years ago. Boarded up to keep out the kids or treasure seekers."

The perfect place for a vampire to make a nest. "You think the owner would mind if I checked it out?"

"I doubt it." Harv nodded down at the mayor.

"You're kidding me."

"Mayor Cheswick was the current owner of Silvertown."

"Guess we don't need permission, then."

CHAPTER SEVEN

I was wrong, of course. We did need permission. The mayor wasn't the actual owner. His wife was. The sheriff also insisted that we sign a waiver indemnifying the town and its representatives from any harm to myself or my associate.

He was taking us over to the mayor's house to get Mrs. Cheswick's blessing. Littlewing crouched on my shoulder, clutching at my ear for balance at the man's rough driving.

"I want to be clear about one thing," said the sheriff.

"Don't fuck with Deputy Jason," I replied affirmatively, but I kept my face expressionless.

"Alright. If you want to play it that way. I want to be clear about *another* thing," amended the sheriff. He had insisted we go in his car so that he could keep an eye on me. He would wait while we investigated the mine. "Mrs. Cheswick is a respectable Southern lady and you will treat her with more respect than you've been showing around this town. She's just lost her husband and I don't want no half-animal upsetting her. I will—and I repeat this just to make sure you can hear as well as you can smell—I *will* shoot you in the leg if you upset her."

I'd been called a lot worse than 'half-animal' by a lot nicer people. I thought about it and shrugged. Littlewing grumbled as she fought to keep her balance. Then she yanked on my ear to remind me I needed to pay attention to my movements.

"How about you go in and get permission and we just wait in the car?" I wasn't serious.

"If you're going inside that mine-shaft, she wants to meet you. The place has been boarded up for years. Even before she inherited it from her uncle. If it collapses and kills you, she wants to know who, or in the case of you all, *what* she's risking."

I had questions about the investigation. He'd been tight-lipped and I couldn't tell if he was hiding stuff or just preoccupied. "What about the mortuaries?"

"Oh." He'd forgotten. "Only two in the county. I checked them both out while you were at the morgue with Doc Madison. Nothing."

"Nothing as in?" Tight-lipped and terse. It wasn't helping me figure out how to find the vampire.

"Nothing as in no one's dead who isn't supposed to be. Nothing missing and no extra dead bodies hidden on the grounds."

Why had the victim and crime scene smelled like embalming fluids? Williams slowed down and turned in between two enormous, iron gates. I forgot all about the incongruous bit of evidence at the majesty of it.

"Holy shit!" asked Littlewing as we drove onto a well-manicured estate. "Was the mayor fucking rich?"

Some people accused me of being a bad influence on the sprite because she cursed up a storm. But I'd learned my foul mouth from her. Just because she was small and had tits out to here, didn't mean she wasn't the nasty one in our relationship.

"His wife is," said the sheriff without elaboration.

"No story behind the money?" I stared at topiaries of stallions running alongside the driveway.

"None of your business."

"As long as it has nothing to do with why the vampire's here, I reckon I can't argue that." Of course, the problem was, the only way to be sure was to actually know the story.

He pulled his station-wagon in front of a large colonial. I had thought the Misty Lake House expensive for a B&B. This was the White House of Alabama. About 20,000 square feet, all of it two-story except for the east wing. The east wing was more window than wall, maybe a conservatory. The only splash of color came from a row of neatly trimmed yellow roses along the entire front of the house. Even the broad, marble stairs that led to the front double-doors were white. Expensive but boring. At least if you spilled a beer, marble floors were easy to clean.

"The dog gonna be a problem?" asked the sheriff as we started to get out of his car. I saw a huge Rottweiler on the porch.

"Now that's an impressive animal," I said with genuine appreciation. Even before I'd been bitten by a rogue lycanthrope and had acquired my less savory attributes as a werewolf, I'd loved dogs. I'd always had a way with them. Now, their reactions to me were entertaining.

The animal trotted gracefully toward us, eyeing us cautiously but without fear or aggression. Most dogs that peed on themselves or that attacked strangers got that way from abusive or neurotic owners. Whoever handled this dog was pretty well-centered emotionally.

"The mayor's?" Littlewing pressed against my neck and watched the dog's huge jaws anxiously.

"You really need to get over your fear of dogs," I chided the sprite.

"Yeah, well. You say that after your first encounter with a creature that can swallow you in one bite." She clawed at my cheek with a sharp fingernail, drawing a tiny streak of blood. "And I don't mean sexually."

The sheriff noticed and frowned. I would have thought that he'd smile, seeing us fight. Or her hurting me. But he looked curious. "Can she contract what you got?"

Ah, his real question was could *he* contract I what I had. Or could anyone else who came in contact with my blood. The easy answer was yes, he could. But it wasn't as likely as contracting something else. Take the risk of an AIDs infection from spilled blood and make it about only five-percent of that. So, lucky me. I was one of that rare five-fucking-percent.

A vampire bite was the real danger. You were better off dead. You might stay that way. If you survived the bite, the conversion rate was 100%.

"Sprites can't contract human diseases," said Littlewing, twitching her wings proudly.

"That's why they'd make great whores," I said as I knelt next to the dog. Instead of staying safely on my shoulder, she shrieked and flitted into the air. "If you dance around like that, of course he's going to bite you! You look like a toy on a string."

The Rottweiler took one sniff of me and froze. My scent, feral and lupine hit him with conflicting signals. I was a dangerous alpha. A newcomer onto his territory. But my smell reassured him at the same time. It was an instant biochemical rapport.

He didn't know how to respond for a heartbeat. He watched my face and saw something that people never seemed to, one of the good guys. He wagged his cropped-tail and pranced over to me happily. Total acceptance.

"Who's a good boy?" I rubbed his neck and back as he licked my face.

"I thought dogs freaked out over werewolves?" asked the sheriff, disgruntled. If a good Christian dog accepted me, his arguments against me were weakening. And the Rottweiler did more than accept me. He liked me. Didn't make Williams happy.

"That's horses." Littlewing tried to mask her nervousness by talking. "Dogs freak out over vampires. Can we go inside? We need to be out of the mine long before nightfall."

"When you are right, you are right," It was something my mother's father used to say when we'd go over to his house for rummy and sodas. Grandpa Lumley also said 'consider the source' whenever he disagreed with one of us. I hadn't understood how insulting he was being until I'd reached adulthood. But he was dead from drinking a long time before that.

I patted the dog on the head and stood up, following the muscular sheriff up the stairs. The doors opened before he reached them and he tipped his hat to a thirty-something black woman in a powder-blue maid's uniform. The uniform didn't do much for her figure, which was thick in that sexy and healthy way of a real woman. Solid hips, solid thighs, and strong arms from hard work. She was an ordinary woman who really worked for her living. The way my grandmother had worked for her living. The maid would never be considered beautiful in any conventional way, but she was very attractive. My kind of woman. I doubted I would be her kind of man.

"Afternoon, Madeline. Mrs. Cheswick is expecting us." Williams spoke politely and with more warmth than I would have expected.

"Of course, Sheriff. Please, come in." The woman glanced at me with curiosity but no fear.

"Is the dog allowed in?" I asked hopefully, mostly to mess with Littlewing. But I also liked the Rottweiler. Dogs were less deceptive and judgmental than most humans. And they didn't wind up dead during a case.

"Oh, no! Mr. Bixby has to stay outside," said Madeline, horrified. "Have you ever tried to polish waxed-marble with claw marks everywhere?"

"Not recently," I said. She grinned at my joke. "Glad you got that. A lot of people around here don't have a sense of humor." I stared meaningfully at the sheriff's back.

A very matronly voice interrupted the moment. "It's not exactly a time for levity. Is it, Mr. Greyson?"

I entered to see a stout but lovely woman in her fifties standing at the back of the foyer. Obviously this was Mrs. Cheswick. She was dressed like a stereotypical high-end lady, wearing a full-length gown with bits of lace and ruffles here and there. The dress was white, but her skin was almost as pale from a lack of sunlight.

"I'm sorry about your loss, Mrs. Cheswick. In rough times, humor is what soldiers use to get them through," I said respectfully. I didn't know the woman and it wasn't fair to be cruel just because I hadn't received a warm reception from most of the people I'd met so far. Maybe the cold lines around her eyes were from grief, not because she was a bitch. "I didn't mean anything by it."

"No. Of course not." It was rote. What refined ladies said when someone apologized for saying something unpleasant.

"Shall I take them into the library, Mrs. Cheswick?" Madeline shut the front door, more demure than she'd been with either the sheriff or me.

But I immediately wished that she hadn't shut the door. There was an expensive vase full of dogwood stems in the foyer and the disgusting, semen-like scent had bothered me long before I'd become a lycanthrope. Now it was nauseating.

"No, Madeline. They won't be staying long. Go about your business."

"Yes, Ma'am." The black woman glanced at me again with that frank curiosity before disappearing into the rest of the house.

"So, Mr. Greyson. I was told that you had an associate. A Native American, I presume?" Mrs. Cheswick frowned in disapproval.

Littlewing. The name had confused more than one person. I chuckled at her assumption, but the sheriff's scowl stopped me. He approached the woman and kissed her hand. She studied me quite openly, holding a handkerchief up to her nose as if something smelled bad. Maybe she thought she was being sly. She wasn't. I was starting not to like the woman.

"Littlewing isn't an Injun', Ma'am." Sheriff Williams looked around for my partner, embarrassed. "That's my fault. I should'a said. She's one of them there fey. A sprite." He glanced at me suspiciously. "Where'd she go?"

"Why are you asking me?" I shrugged. Littlewing was nowhere in sight.

"I will not have my home snooped about, Mr. Greyson. Please call your associate here immediately!" Mrs. Cheswick snapped at me.

"Why would that be? You being such a respectable Southern lady and all?" I watched her expression for any hint of guilt.

Something smashed into my jaw and spun me around onto the slick marble floor. Damn it! I'd been caught off-guard. There was something about this place that was making me sloppy.

I jumped up, grabbed the sheriff by his shirt and lifted him off the ground. Mrs. Cheswick screamed and I could hear a woman's footsteps running toward us. I threw Williams against one of the elegant writing desks. It happened to be the one with the vase of dogwood blossoms and his heavy body made a satisfying crash. The vase broke and the desk crumpled under his two-hundred and forty pounds of muscles. That was nothing compared to my strength.

As he stood, I decided that he looked better with the Stetson on, but he left it lying on the ground where it had fallen. I was breathing hard, but not because it had taken much exertion to throw him. I was just that pissed off.

"Gentlemen! I demand you stop at once!" Mrs. Cheswick raised her voice, although she didn't shout.

The sheriff didn't seem interested in what she said, because he lunged at me. This time I was prepared. I leapt into the air, using one hand to lightly pivot off of his head and I brought my feet down on the ground behind him. I gave him a serious shove, adding to his momentum. If I had landed on his back, I would have shattered his spine. Maybe done something worse. The contract specified I wasn't allowed to kill except in self-defense. That included the vampire. This was a job, and I planned on getting paid.

Williams hit the other side of the foyer with enough force that he crumpled to the ground, unconscious. Mrs. Cheswick backed out of the foyer and scurried deeper inside the house. Probably to call the sheriff's station asking for deputies to come save her. I felt points press into my lower lips and I ran my tongue ran along my upper teeth. Fangs in my mouth. I glanced down and saw that I'd changed my nails to claws and my skin had darkened with hair without meaning to. Anger could do that to a werewolf. No wonder Mrs. Cheswick had fled.

Madeline came rushing back into the room, but by then I was fully human again. She saw him lying there and threw her hands to her face. "Louis!" She knelt down beside the man and held his head on her lap. Then she kissed his face anxiously. "Baby! Don't you die on me."

I hadn't found very much I liked about the sheriff. The macho, werewolf-hating bigoted backwoods hick that he was. Only he wasn't a bigot. That explained why Madeline had been so familiar with him. And the sparkle in her eyes when we'd arrived. He was a white man dating a black woman in the South. I actually regretted knocking him out cold.

"I suppose he started it?" Madeline raised her gaze up to me. No accusation, no anger, just resignation.

"As a matter of fact, Ma'am, he did," I replied. Maybe she was the one with the balls. A black woman dating a white sheriff in the South had to be dangerous. The fact that she hadn't overreacted, that she knew *he* might have provoked *me*. Well, I didn't respect her. I liked her. And it wasn't just my attraction talking. How did the saying go? All the good ones were taken or gay? And she wasn't gay.

CHAPTER EIGHT

Mrs. Cheswick hadn't called for deputies. She'd gone to get a gun. I had to give her credit. She'd come back even after seeing me change some. Most people would have kept running. She couldn't hide her relief when she saw that I looked fully human again.

"Take Sheriff Williams to the small divan on the back porch." She took her queue not to shoot me from Madeline's calm demeanor.

When I threw the sheriff over my shoulder and complied with her demand, she put the gun down distastefully. I'd been wrong about the coroner not shooting, but Mrs. Cheswick hadn't taken the safety off. I was guessing that she'd never used a gun. No surprise.

"Mrs. Cheswick?" Madeline's expression said it all.

The mayor's wife, make that widow, scowled at the black woman before she locked eyes with me. "Very well, Madeline. You may attend the sheriff. It's the least I can do. I hired this—gentleman."

"Thank you, Mrs. Cheswick." Madeline went to get a cold, damp cloth and patted the unconscious sheriff around his face and neck.

Mrs. Cheswick stood there, waiting for me to look away first. Maybe people in Resistance didn't stand up to her. Maybe her money bought obedience. She had a lot to learn about the real world. With me, money didn't buy her anything but a dead vampire.

She broke first. Trembling with unspoken rage, she stormed into the house. Elegant and dignified, but she stormed.

Williams was protected from the sun by a broad extension of the roof while we waited for him to come to. Littlewing had been gone too long. There hadn't been any gunfire, but Mr. Bixby wasn't the only predator that could have snapped her up.

I hadn't reached the end of the expansive lawn to search for her before the sprite fluttered out of the woods. Not alone, either. A handful of colorful fairies followed a short distance behind. They were half her size. Around four inches tall, but a similar species.

"Picking up strays?"

"One of them came up to me when you went inside." She been buzzed by one of the inquisitive creatures and she'd naturally followed it off to the local hive. I should have known.

"I punched out the sheriff."

"What? I miss all the good shit." She flew past me, coaxing the smaller fliers.

I trotted after her back to the house. Williams was still unconscious, but Madeline stood next to him, gazing down. She heard us coming and smiled when she saw the fluttering fey.

"Madeline, this is Littlewing. My partner." I didn't acknowledge her friends. From what I could tell, they were more like mindless bugs than people.

"Hello, Littlewing. Would you like something to snack on?" Southern hospitality.

"I'm starving!" replied the sprite. She made one of her few coy non-flirtatious expressions. "Enough for them, too?"

Madeline smiled warmly and I realized it was genuine. She left for a few moments and returned with a tray of food and drinks. She set them down on a small glass table and touched my arm. She acknowledged me in a way that made me feel human, before sitting next to her boyfriend. Most women wouldn't get near me. Even the whores I paid only did enough to earn them their money.

Madeline was only being friendly, but I felt a surge of loneliness. It caught me off guard. I studied the house, then the sky to avoid looking at her. Anger replaced loneliness. We were wasting more precious daylight waiting on the sheriff, but this was still his dog and pony show. Make that wolf and jackass show. And it was my fault he was out cold.

"What the heck are those?" The sheriff blinked as he came to and sat up. I turned to look at him.

"Welcome back," I said, not at all apologetic.

He stared suspiciously at Littlewing. She stood in the center of a platter of coconut macaroons, tearing off bite-sized chunks for the swarm of fairies.

"Relax, Louis." Madeline smiled at him in mild disapproval. "They're just some harmless pollinators attracted to Mrs. Cheswick's flowers. But you! Starting a fight in the middle of a murder investigation. You promised!"

"He accused Mrs. Cheswick of hiding something," grumbled the sheriff.

"Did you, Mitch?" she asked me.

"Madeline! This familiarity has gone far enough. He is 'Mr. Greyson' to you!" Mrs. Cheswick came out onto the veranda as if she'd been watching and waiting for just such a moment. She took a seat opposite me and set down her tea, almost crushing one of the fairies.

"I'm surprised you let anything fey in your garden, Mrs. Cheswick," I said.

I resumed staring at her to make her uncomfortable. I'd be more interested in talking to Madeline and finding out about the black woman's relationship with the sheriff than listen to this old biddy. Anything I wanted to know about Madeline's personal opinion of the mayor would probably require his help anyway. She seemed exceptionally honest and loyal, so she'd keep the household confidences better than most.

"I don't care for unnatural things, Mr. Greyson." No beating around the bush with that insult. But I let it slide. "However, Miss Jackson assures me that they are responsible for the lack of pests in my garden and they typically do not come around the house," she said dryly.

Madeline Jackson. Good to know, in case I wanted to ask questions in town about her relationship with the sheriff. "Now, really. Let's get this mine business out of the way so that I may resume my busy schedule." Code for get the nasty werewolf out of my house.

"Fine. Do I need to sign another waiver or anything?" I asked her. She had been the one to insist on meeting me. "I want to find the vampire that killed your husband. But if you want me to stop—"

"No. As a law-enforcement associate, assisting in the investigation of a crime, my lawyer assures me I have no liability should you get injured," she replied. "I only wanted to know what kind of *man* was looking into my husband's death." She watched Littlewing a little too intently as she made that last comment. I knew what kind of man she thought I was. A perverted letch who hired voluptuous eight-inch tall sprites.

She seemed torn between loathing Littlewing and intrigued by her interaction with the local fey. Either way, it was an excuse not to look at me. The real monster in the group.

"We wasted all this time for that?" I gave the sheriff a look of disgust. "Really?"

Mrs. Cheswick looked guilty and I perked up, leaning toward her. It unnerved her more. Maybe I let a little flash of fang show again, too. She reached for her glass but her fingers trembled and she pulled the hand back. Whoever said that Southern ladies don't sweat was full of shit. She reeked of it.

"I have no reason to suspect anything, of course. But I do have a concern." She looked at the sheriff for reassurance.

"Go, on, Ma'am," said the big man. I didn't need the warning in his eyes.

"Well. Ronald was planning on selling the mine, you see. A big company, the Silver Earth Consortium was interested in it and they sent a man."

"Yes?" My gut said trouble was coming.

"I'm getting to it, young man!" she said indignantly. At least she still referred to me as a man. After a moment staring at the fairies which danced in the air, oblivious to us, she continued. "Well, he left without giving us any indication of what his assessment was. Now this could be nothing, except—I'm concerned that perhaps the mine may have collapsed on him. It was closed for being poorly set-up in the first place. Until innovations in the Silver Earth Consortium's newest technology, it just wasn't practically to start it up again."

"Why didn't you notify me?" demanded the sheriff, like a kid whining to his mother.

"Well, until you said the mine might be involved with my husband's death, it never occurred to me. My first thought, of course, from too many mystery novels, was that Ronald had been killed for the deed. But as I am the only heir to his interest in the mine, I realized that was foolish."

"Who gets it if you die?" Littlewing asked. Despite her fascination with the distantly related fairies, she had part of her mind on the job.

"We didn't have any children. So we've left our estate to the good people of Resistance County, in trust." She sat very straight and kept her shoulders back as if the question had offended her.

"That's a lot of suspects." I stuck a finger out to one of the fairies but it zipped away from me apprehensively.

"I don't see how it ties in with a vampire kill," complained the sheriff.

I had expected Mrs. Cheswick to know that it had been a vampire that had killed her husband. After all, she'd paid for me to come to this shit-hole in the first place. And truthfully, why else send for a werewolf? But personally, I wouldn't have told a soul if I'd been the sheriff. Get more surprise out of them that way. But I was there to find the thing and kill it. This wasn't my town.

"Is there any threat to the town? I mean, does it need your money to survive? If a vampire was planning on hiding out here a long time, it might want the town to last. Provide fresh blood," I suggested.

"No. We're fiscally responsible. My husband saw to it." She put her hands on her lap, indignant. "Revenue from two local natural gas wells provides for the entire county's budget. The rest of the income is used for reserves and improvements."

"Wouldn't a vampire want to make the town collapse? Get rid of people sniffing around that way?" asked Littlewing, sadly out of macaroons. She came to land on my shoulder. "Not that there're that many people in the first place."

"I really doubt it was related to inheriting our estate," countered the woman.

"Mrs. Cheswick has a reputation for being quite the philanthropist," warned the sheriff.

I looked at the woman and her stiff, superior dignity. Sometimes people gave money away to seem better than regular people. It didn't matter. That she was willing to give her money away suggested that it wasn't about inheritance. But there were other motives. Especially if this was related to the vampire's activities sixty-three years earlier.

"Anyone want to keep the mine from being sold?" I asked, curious.

"Not to my knowledge." She sighed. "Look, I really just want someone to make sure that the mine didn't collapse on that investigator. And for that matter, Mr. Greyson, if the mine becomes a working prospect again, that's even more income for the town. So I think you're barking up the wrong tree."

I stared at her but she had the decency not to smile. She didn't even seem to realize she'd made a dog-comment to a werewolf. I was itching to be out doing something and the sun was getting lower with each minute.

"I agree with you, Mrs. Cheswick. We'll keep an eye out for the man. How long has he been missing?" I stood and Littlewing did a little dance to keep from falling off. I could feel her glare at me.

"Three days." Cheswick stood also. It was a dismissal.

"Thank you for your time, Mrs. Cheswick." The sheriff rubbed his head but bowed at the neck like she was royalty. In a place this small, with her kind of money, she was. "Madeline can show us out."

"Yes, fine. Please let me know if you discover anything. I keep expecting the Silver Earth Consortium to call anytime. If they ask about their man, I'd rather not sound foolish." She walked off into the house.

"Let's go around. The air's less stuffy out here," I said when the maid started to lead us inside.

"Alright," she said with a chuckle. She glanced at the sheriff but he seemed to be keeping some distance from us. "You don't rightly respect a lot of folk, do you?"

"Not if I can help it," I said honestly. "It really ticks me off when I meet people like you and I don't have a choice in the matter."

"Why, Mr. Greyson! Flattery?" she asked, but there was nothing coy or flirtatious in her tone. Only amusement. "If Louis hits you again, this time I won't assume he started it."

He ignored us, so I grinned at her as we walked back to the station-wagon. I studied the sky, estimating that we had about two hours of light left. Littlewing zipped around, trying to shoo away the fairies. They wanted to follow us inside. That's what you got for feeding strays.

"Oh, Louis, your hat!" Madeline raced inside.

"Let's go, Littlewing. I don't want to deal with a mine at night when we're hunting vampires." She buzzed into the car and I slammed the door.

The sheriff refused to get in the car, waiting on Madeline and his hat. I couldn't argue. All that time wasted and I'd learned nothing except that another victim might be out there. Things were not looking up for Werewolf Incorporated.

CHAPTER NINE

Sheriff Williams didn't speak as we left the town limits. We entered a mix of farmland and uneven woodland, and the road rolled with the terrain. Few structures, lots of trees. Perfect terrain for a vampire or a werewolf to live in relative safety. If they weren't sloppy. Take a stray cow here and there. Maybe a child went missing in the woods once in a while. The locals wouldn't think anything about it. But this vampire had killed a high profile victim in the middle of town. Why draw all that attention?

I considered the illogical profile I had of the vampire so far. There were two types of bloodsuckers. The first were animalistic killers that were more dead than alive, whose brains served only to house an instinct to hunt, drink and hide. The second were nearly perfectly human undead, who killed to survive, but their minds were intact. They were the more dangerous of the two. They killed for more than hunger, just like the living. For love. Hatred. Revenge.

But neither type would choose a target in the middle of a town when easier and sneakier prey could be had elsewhere. Not for food. I kept coming back to the fact that the mayor's death was not just an accident. He'd been killed for a reason. Not for blood. But what was that reason?

We passed one of the two natural gas rigs Mrs. Cheswick had mentioned and the sheriff nodded. "We're not far, now."

A master of understatement, the sheriff almost immediately made a hard left onto a side-road. It jerked me out of my analysis of the mayor's death. I was unable to concentrate on anything other than William's reckless driving. He made a sudden right which I thought was going to send us over a cliff, but instead it was a steep dirt road, strewn with gravel, that led down into a quarry. He only slowed enough not to slide over the lip of the road.

I'd pictured the mine set in a picturesque hillside, lush and rustic both. Like something from a Dungeons and Dragons campaign. But this was all broken rock and dust and strewn bits of equipment which obviously dated back to before the closure of the mine in the mid-1900s.

"What are you thinking?" asked the sheriff as he pulled up close to the entrance boarded up with heavy planks.

"Mostly how ugly it is." And creepy. Something about the place set the hair on my arms on edge. But I couldn't have said what. Just one more piece of Resistance County unpleasantness.

I inspected the wall of the quarry above the mine, looking for small openings or tunnels. Vampires couldn't transform into bats any more than they could transform into wolves. But a small vampire could worm its way through a narrower opening than a human could. They didn't need to breathe and they could claw through any tight spots. And by small, I meant young.

Children could be made into vampires just like adults. I never forgot that fact because the meanest and most evil vampire I'd ever met was a nine-year-old girl. Of course, her surviving sister had said she'd been like that before she'd been made, but you get my point. Staking the brat had actually been a pleasure.

Unfortunately, Utah was one of the few states that banned beheading of vampires. It was a religious issue of some kind and the federal government had backed down for a change. But God help me, if she ever got de-staked and escaped. She'd sworn a litany of horrible deaths upon me.

If anyone had asked me, it was better not to interrogate vampires after capture. The Feds said they did it for closure for the families. To make sure there weren't any more bloodsuckers on the loose. I'd never known a vampire to tell the truth about anything except how much they wanted to kill their captors. If there were more vampires, they wouldn't say. But I was one of the monsters. No one listened to me.

"There's no car," said Littlewing. We were looking for a corporate suit, not only a vampire.

"Might have parked up at the top and walked down. To keep the dust off of his ride," I replied. "How many times do I have to remind you? Never assume."

"It was an observation you lunkhead," she said offhandedly, not really angry. We bantered to keep our wits sharp. It also helped the bad guys to assume that we weren't a tight team. Some of it was real, but neither one of us carried a grudge for a little name-calling.

"What do you know about the Silver Earth Consortium, Sheriff?"

"Never heard of it before today." Truth mixed with anger. Mrs. Cheswick should have told him in his opinion. He believed that they were close friends. She didn't. I felt a pang of pity for him. Madeline's fault that I cared about him one way or the other.

"You coming into the mine?" I asked the sheriff.

"No, Sir. I do not get paid enough to risk my life foolishly." He got out and sat on the hood of his vehicle with practiced nonchalance. "But if it gets dark and I hear you screaming like a girl, I'll come running."

"Speaking of paid enough, where's the money for our fee coming from?" We'd been wired a deposit of ten-thousand dollars and the balance of forty-thousand was payable just for showing up. It wasn't dependent upon the death or capture of the bloodsucker and it kept my employers from not paying in case they didn't like my attitude. But I wouldn't get very many referrals if I didn't do the job. Some people thought that it was a lot of money just to hunt a vampire. I always told them, fine, you go do it. The only taker to my challenge was now six feet under, in a cemetery in Hershey, Pennsylvania. Not my fault.

"Mrs. Cheswick authorized a withdrawal from the town reserves," he said. "Don't read nothin' into that. She ran this town as much as the mayor did. Just not official like."

"I didn't say a thing." I sniffed the air. "Sheriff, do me another favor. What I said wasn't just for Deputy Jason. When we work together, don't use cologne or *Irish Spring*. Try something scent-free. It's good for you, too."

He sniffed himself and shrugged. Just like his deputy had done. I hadn't noticed the cologne when we'd first met, but maybe it had worn off and he'd automatically reapplied it. Or maybe he had known that he'd be running into Madeline and the man had spruced up a bit for his piece of tail. And she was a nice piece of tail. I liked women with big brains, so long as they had other parts just as well-endowed. I hadn't needed my nose at the Cheswick mansion, but the mineshaft was a different situation. I did him the courtesy of assuming he hadn't spritzed himself just to fuck with my ability to get the job done.

"I'll just go over there."

I walked along the gravel, sniffing the air and studying the ground while I waited for my nose to clear. There weren't any tire tracks, which suggested that I'd been right. A big company wanted to buy the mine. Obviously the suit had an expensive car. He'd probably rather walk down than risk a gravel chip to the paint. Or risk getting stuck in one of the steep ruts.

I didn't smell any gasoline or oil or that metallic odor from a hot engine. Either he hadn't made it here or he'd left his car someplace else. It was possible that he left more personal fragrances in the mine itself where the breeze and elements wouldn't dilute it.

"Littlewing? You mind doing a short reconnaissance? Not more than ten feet inside."

She nodded. "You got it, Boss." Unholstering her gun, she zipped into the mine through one of the gaps in the lumber over the entrance.

I studied the boards. One of the lower pieces showed fresh scuff marks. It moved when I tested it. It slid up and down, but it wasn't really fastened to anything. There was a faint whiff of cologne lingering on the wood, mingled with male sweat. Not the sheriff's cologne either. Much more high end. A rich man had spent some time prying it loose recently.

The sprite reappeared, her gun in her hand. She shook her head. "Tunnel goes pretty deep, but nothing dangerous around the entrance. No evidence of fey or left-over explosives."

Another reason Littlewing was my partner. She had a sprite's natural ability to deal with explosives. Sprites mostly liked to blow things up. But that same knack also allowed them to find hidden devices, defuse bombs and even chemically neutralize old T.N.T. I'd once seen her lick the sweat off a stick of dynamite like it was an aphrodisiac. Maybe for her it was.

Littlewing couldn't do a whole lot of magic besides absorb and discharge light. But she could take care of things that went boom, and that was one of the things I counted on her doing when the need arose. Not to mention, *she* always checked for her own kind. Some of the fey were just as dangerous as vampires.

"We're going in now, Sheriff!" I called to him. "Someone's been in here. May still be."

The faded expensive scent of the man was about three days old, just like Mrs. Cheswick said. The more expensive it was, the more chemically nasty it was to my nose. I couldn't name the brand or type, but there were thousands of scents on the market. Most of them only made me sneeze. This made my nose curl up even in human form. And he had perspired a lot. It supported my guess that he'd hoofed it from up top.

"I know I'm saving my sunlight for the vamp, but we gonna go in dark?" asked Littlewing. I pulled out a glow-stick. She scowled at me. "Really? We looking for a vampire or a rave?"

"I don't want you distracted by a real fire." I stepped through the loose board into the dark mine. "There might be pockets of trapped gas or explosives further in. No sense in taking a chance."

"Oh," she said, sheepishly.

I didn't hold that error of judgment against her. We'd never really done any tunnel work before. Not in a mine anyway. Vampires selected places underground, but something about their former memories made them pick mausoleums or basements. Or even the gaps in the foundations of homes. A mineshaft was a new one on me. Only some of what people saw in the movies was based on fact.

The tunnel was narrower than I was expecting. It had irregular pockets chiseled out of the walls at various intervals where they'd tested for ore. I took the lead, getting used to the patches of dried guano mixed with fresh, so that my nose could focus on the important smells.

Littlewing kept her gun ready, which meant the place unnerved her. Not because of the bats that inhabited the dry, musty shaft. They would ignore her. But sprites weren't cave-dwellers. I figured she was hiding claustrophobia from me. Another advantage of my turning furry once a month. My former fear of enclosed spaces had become pleasure.

"Smell anything?" she asked.

"Nothing." Meaning no vampires. The suit's odor was still strong and the trapped air, musty. No scent of fear, which meant he had done this sort of thing often. Why would a high-end suit double as mine-inspector? "Not yet anyway."

We walked until the tunnel branched. "Check out the left, I'll do the right. No more than twenty feet this time," I instructed. She darted down her tunnel and I sniffed my way down the other one.

Not a vampire, but something. Faint. That didn't mean the smell wasn't fresh. The sun was still out, barely. The vampire would likely still be unconscious. A really strong vampire, far enough underground, could move during the daytime. I'd learned that from the FBI the first time I'd worked with them. If the feds were wrong, well, I'd err on the side of caution. I didn't call for Littlewing. Instead, I gripped my gun and held it close to my gut to keep it from being knocked out of my hand. Just in case.

The glow stick was bright enough for my lycanthropic vision to make out a recent collapse in the tunnel. Rather than closing a passageway, it had revealed an adjoining tunnel. I put my face to the opening and sniffed deeply. Yep, this was the way. Overripe apple met nasty, expensive cologne and sweat. I was beginning to get the picture.

I sensed Littlewing coming down the passage toward me before I saw her. I motioned at the new opening. She grew grim and prepared to confront a bloodsucker as I headed into the narrow passage. The smell of the man was stronger here and it wasn't all cologne and sweat anymore. He'd pissed himself. Something had scared him more than a dark tunnel. Something *in* the dark tunnel. He'd discovered our vampire.

"Apples," I whispered. Littlewing nodded. She couldn't smell as well as I could, but that wasn't her best organ anyway. "He died here."

I moved with preternatural stealth as the tunnel curved, although the light would give us away if there was a day-watcher. Day-watchers were humans that protected the vampire while they slept. Vampires rarely had them. But rarely wasn't the same as never. A family member or a paid thug had been known to attack vampire-hunters in the middle of the day, when their undead master's lair had been discovered. Of course, the cave-in and sixty-three years argued against a human being involved.

The smell of blood was strong, but not recent. Stronger, however, was the sickly sweet fragrance of undead. Strong because the tunnel had been sealed up until recently. Either that, or we'd discovered a really large nest. I was really hoping on the former.

"Empty," said Littlewing and she zipped past me. I saw what she saw. A dead-end with a piece of sharpened wood on the ground and the dark-stain of human blood and urine soaked into the rocky floor.

"Damn it." I knelt next to the blood. "Our guy is dead."

"The suit?" she asked and I stuck my gun back into its holster.

"He pulled the stake out." The stupidity annoyed me. "Always, *always* cut off the sucker's head after staking. Except in fucking Utah."

Unlike the FBI, I didn't have an obligation to interrogate the vampire once I caught them. If the Feds wanted to do that, that was their prerogative, no matter how stupid. After Utah and what the state put me through testifying to satisfy their religious concerns, I'd never work there again.

I took a minute to study the scene. "Okay, so it was just one vampire. The one from sixty-three years ago. Just like you guessed." Not an exact science, but one stake sort of confirmed it. More than one vampire, any of them not staked would have dug their way out. More than one stake, well, they wouldn't have taken the wood with them.

"We gonna check out the rest of the tunnels?" Littlewing sounded impatient. Yep, claustrophobia.

"Yeah. But I'm pretty sure we ain't gonna find anything. If a vampire was trapped in here for years, they'd probably want to get as far away as possible."

We spent the next hour searching and as usual, I was right.

CHAPTER TEN

We found the missing man's car at the opposite side of the quarry, in a wooded patch overlooking the mine. It was a sweet, burgundy Mercedes Benz SL550 class roadster with all the extras. Big money for sure. So far, all the pieces continued to suggest that the vampire hadn't chosen the mayor by chance. The mine was the only obvious connection, but the cave-in troubled me. No explosives or tools, just a natural collapse opening the tunnel. My gut still said something was fishy about the timing of the suit and the opening.

I asked myself again, why had had he inspected the mine personally? Had he been a vampire junkie? A small number of people, usually rich ones because they had the resources to thwart legal barriers, had been caught chasing vampires. Not hunting. *Chasing.* They spent unholy amounts of cash to get peeks at or a chance to encounter a real-undead bloodsucker. Sometimes not just an encounter. Some of them hoped for everlasting life. They wanted to get bitten.

It might make sense why this guy from the Silver Earth Consortium had gotten dirty instead of hiring an engineer. Local people knew a vampire had been seen here sixty-three years earlier. If he'd thrown enough money around, the suit would have uncovered that fact. Was his interest in buying the mine nothing more than the hope for a slender chance at everlasting life?

The alternative was that he was just a thrill-seeker. Some rich and powerful men had hunted everything. The idea of untapped big game left only vampires or the fey. He might have come here to hunt the vampire and kill it. Lucky me, I got paid for doing it.

Either hypothesis made some sense. But neither accounted for the cave-in. How had that happened?

"Where would the body have been dumped?" asked the sheriff while I was busy looking at the sky. "Or did it become another vampire?"

"You do realize it's gonna be dark anytime?" I replied.

"What? You can't handle one lousy vampire who's been locked up without blood for years?"

"He's had blood," snapped Littlewing. "He drank the suit and the mayor." She didn't say it loud enough for Williams to hear, but she added, "Dumbass." Her idea of diplomacy.

"I wasn't worried about me so much." I studied the terrain. If I was a vampire, newly awakened, which direction looked appealing? Closer to town? Or away from the people who staked him in the first place? "Problem is, Sheriff. If this vampire knows the area, was made here for example, he'd go someplace based on that knowledge. A newbie, someone who didn't know the area. I'd go that way. Toward the gas rig. That shed looked like it would keep the sun out." I glanced at the sky, estimating just how much light we had left. "It's the only manmade structure that sticks out. And it looks safe. Vampires tend to like the idea of hiding in buildings."

"But if we know it already went into town. Why check out here?" Not the dumbest question he'd asked me so far.

"Because there's a chance it will come back to the first safe place it finds after escaping. And we need to find the suit's body if we can.

That helps exclude it as a second vampire." I watched him and was pleased that he didn't fight me on it.

"There might be other victims. Workers or night watchmen at the gas rigs," added Littlewing. "Let's check it out."

"Fine, my little queen of fairy. But *you* get to fly!" I told her with a mean smile.

"Why for fuck's sake?" she demanded, fists on her hips. I loved the way her chest jiggled when she was angry. Unfortunately, there was nothing that tiny body could do for what ached me.

"Because we're looking for the suit's body, remember? I'm guessing the vamp drained him so dry that he had nothing left to come back to life. But we aren't taking any chances. His corpse could be anywhere between here and the gas rig. If that's where the vampire headed first."

"Oh, fine," she huffed and buzzed off. "See you at the shed."

"Stay safe!" I shouted at her. There was the crunch of boots against gravel and someone stepped up close behind me. I spun without warning and growled but it wasn't Williams.

Deputy Jason jumped backwards and I had to grab him by the shirt to keep him from stumbling off the quarry edge. "Holy crap, Mitch! No need to give me a heart-attack."

I hadn't heard the second patrol car pull up. I'd been lost in the smell of expensive leather seats, artificial musk to make the car manly inside, the scent of money clinging to the doors. Not literally, but there was a smell to expensive things that reminded me of money. I rarely concentrated that hard, but a werewolf wasn't much different from a human when it came to certain interests. I wanted to see if the vampire had spent any time around the car after he'd killed the driver, but smelled nothing. And then I'd been arguing with Littlewing, giving the deputy a chance to sneak up on me. If he'd been upwind, I would have noticed him a lot sooner.

"Mr. Greyson," corrected the sheriff and I wondered if he was trying to out-wolf me with his exaggerated gruff mannerisms.

"Sorry, Deputy. Not real comfortable with people sneaking up at my back. Defense mechanism an' all," I said by way of apology, but I frowned at the sheriff. The sun was almost gone and he was just standing there. "You made me leave my car at the station. Shall we?"

Williams looked at the junior officer. "Check the thing for fingerprints and fibers, not just the registration." He waved a packet of papers from the glove-box, protected from contamination by a plastic baggie he'd snatched from one of his men. Then he looked at the darkening sky. "You got silver bullets?"

"Sheriff, that ain't gonna work on vampires," complained the pretty deputy. I would have grinned if I hadn't been horrified by Williams's disregard for the young man's safety.

"You aren't gonna leave him out here after dark are you?" I didn't hide my disdain from the sheriff. "And Deputy Jason's right. Silver is for werewolves and demons."

"Never know." Williams pointedly did not look at me. "Don't take any dumbass chances, alright?"

"That's why I got the garlic oil!" Jason pulled back his collar to show that his skin was slick and greasy.

"I thought you'd eaten Italian." I scowled. "Boy! Garlic will not keep a vampire from biting you!"

"It won't?" he asked blank-faced.

"Sheriff, if we make it through the night without finding that bloodsucker, I want to address your entire force about the dos and don'ts of vampires. You got me?" I didn't wait for a reply. "You can't kill 'em with bullets, but you can slow 'em down. Shoot for the brain. Messes up their ability to think until they heal. The heart, if you don't have a better target, cause it will hurt the fuck out of them. But they heal. Forget shooting them anywhere else unless you just wanna give up living."

"Garlic really won't bother them?" Jason didn't want to believe all of his pop-culture knowledge was crap.

"It interferes with their ability to assimilate blood, but it doesn't hurt them. You might give him indigestion while he's drinking that pretty neck of yours dry. And you better hope he drinks you dry. Otherwise, I'll be coming after you next." I marched off toward the sheriff's wagon, really pissed off. The kid was gonna get killed just because the department paid more attention to movies than the FBI dossier they'd been issued or the details of my contract. I had expected Deputy Jason to be more attentive to its contents considering his excitement about meeting a real live werewolf. Apparently I was wrong.

I got into the car, slammed the door and waited. A moment later, the sheriff joined me and we bumped along the rocky, irregular terrain of the quarry toward the road. I kept my eyes open, but I wasn't going to roll the window down and give the sheriff the pleasure of watching me sniff the air like a dog. The wind would have carried away any trace of the vampire anyway.

"We heading straight for the gas rig?" he asked when I didn't say anything.

"Any reason not to?" I sniped back.

"Only if you need time to take your head out of your ass."

"Excuse me?" I turned and stared at him.

"I warned you not to fuck with my deputy."

"No thanks. I don't want your sloppy seconds," I muttered back.

He slammed on the brakes. If he expected to throw me forward because I wasn't wearing my seatbelt, he was being stupid. I slapped a hand onto the dash and hardly moved at all. His vinyl, however, had my hand-print embossed in it.

"I'm getting sick of you, Greyson." The muzzle of his gun pressed against my cheek, hard.

"That was a stupid mistake, *Louis*." I moved so fast he only had time to make a gurgling noise as my hand was tightly around his throat. My other hand pressed his gun wrist against the back of the seat. I squeezed them enough to make it painfully clear I wasn't joking. "You never, ever pull a gun on me unless you want to die. And if you think me warning your deputy about his mistakes is out of line, you sanctimonious *prick*, at least I don't want him to get killed for being stupid like you! If I can scare the shit out of him so he'll take it seriously? And not rely on something dumb like garlic, then I've done a better job keeping him alive than you have."

I could see the hatred in the sheriff's eyes. But he listened. I could see him thinking in that big-jawed head of his. He was strong and he'd probably never been manhandled like this, but I was always gonna be stronger than any ordinary human. If he wanted to challenge me like equals, he'd have to get his ass bitten by either one of my kind or one of the things we hunted. I doubted that was on the list of things he'd consider to fight me fair and square.

"I'm gonna let you live and let you go. But you only get one warning like this," I spoke low and deep at his ear. I could smell the wax and the cologne and even something he used in his hair. It was common and cheap, which made me think about Madeline. I felt sorry for the woman. If I'd lived around these parts, I might have asked her out. And not only to piss off the sheriff. "Are we clear?"

He nodded at the expectant look on my face and I released him. He clutched at his throat, hacking and I watched him carefully as he put his gun away. His eyes were still full of hatred, but there a special kind of anger in them that made me smile, spitefully. I may be an asshole, but I really had done it to protect his people. That made him angrier than anything else I could have pointed out.

"Besides, Sheriff. I think the quarry is the last place we'll find the vampire again. He would hate this place enough to stay clear."

"Then why are we checking out the rig?" he rasped, as if I hadn't already explained.

"We're not looking for the vampire, so much as evidence of his passing. He killed the mayor in town and I suspect he's staying closer to his food source. Near Resistance. But there might be some clue, some bit of evidence about who he is. Or why he went after Cheswick. If this has anything to do with the mayor personally—he owned the mine after all—then I suggest you have people watch the mayor's wife."

"You think she's in danger?" He grew suddenly anxious. The 'she' he had in mind was not Mrs. Cheswick.

"If it's personal, yeah. So far, the only dead people we have are related to this mine. Though." I rubbed my chin as we sat in the growing dark with the car running. "Though if the suit pulled the stake out, which is the only scenario that plays out, then the vampire killed the suit, took the body and got away from its former prison as soon as dark fell. The mayor is too young to have been involved in the staking of the vampire, what, sixty-three years ago? You told me that Mrs. Cheswick inherited the mine. Maybe her father or uncle was involved, and this is a family thing."

"So, the vampire figured out that the mayor, not his wife, was a descendent and took revenge?" asked the sheriff. "I thought these things were less human and more like hungry animals?"

"Those are the ones that get the most publicity because they get themselves noticed." I counted to three in my head. It was either that or drive my fist through his dash at his ignorance. "This is a thinker. Nearly as human as you or I. At least with regard to loving and hating and planning its actions. As for the revenge angle? I didn't say it was the best motive, but I'm not going to ignore the connection with the mine." We were in this together and lives might depend on it. I told him a little known fact about vampires. "This isn't public knowledge, so keep it to yourself. When a vampire drinks the blood of an individual, their strongest, most recent memories are shared. The suit would have had the purchase and Mrs. Cheswick on his mind. It would have been almost a guarantee that the vampire would know that the mayor was selling the land to that corporation."

"And where the mayor worked and lived." Williams was thoroughly concerned about his girlfriend, which was what I'd wanted. "Jesus Christ, Greyson! You might have told me." He grabbed his radio and called into the station. "Get a group of the boys over to the Cheswick Estate. Tell her that she might be a target and apologize. But don't let her drive them away. You got me?"

"How long?" asked the female dispatcher.

"All night."

"Like as in till morning?" Littlewing might have asked me the same question, but she would have been joking. The dispatcher was serious.

"That's right. And armed to the hilt."

"They need to get ahold of some silver cartridges?" She sounded anxious.

He glanced at me. "No. We don't need silver shot. Tell 'em to radio me immediately if anything suspicious goes on. Over and out." He replaced the handset and gripped the wheel tightly. "What else can I do?"

"If we don't find him tonight, I should check out those mortuaries personally. Not because you didn't do an okay job. But people lie and maybe I can find something they didn't share." I scratched my ear. "I think we need to go back in time though. I've seen the coroner's file on the original vampire killings. But I need anything supplemental you have from the police investigation at the time. Assuming there's a separate police file?"

"There is. I read it from top to bottom the moment we found the mayor dead. One night the killing stopped and there's nothing to indicate why." Great, another dead end. The people here were worse than useless. Almost made me miss working with the FBI. Only almost.

"Let's get to the gas rig. If Littlewing beats us there, I'll never hear the end of it."

CHAPTER ELEVEN

The sun was down by the time we reached the big metal structure of the natural gas rig. The pump projected into the sky like a poor-man's Eiffel Tower. Tire tracks and foot-prints had worn away any grass that tried to grow up around the rig, and it bore the remnant evidence of a busy production that seemed abandoned at the moment. All the eighteen-wheelers used to haul the extracted gas were missing, and the on-site trailer was quiet.

Despite the cap used to seal the rig against leakage, I could smell the gas. It clung to everything. The rig also smelled of grease and sweat and nasty things that my werewolf nose didn't like. I fought a momentary distraction. The smell of axle-grease always reminded me of a favorite uncle in Texas who'd been a mechanic. His gas station had an old-fashioned bottled-coke dispenser and as a kid, my brother, sister and I had tried their local ritual of putting peanuts in the Coke to flavor the drink.

The only real fun we'd ever had as a family was on those trips. My hard-ass military father would actually relax around his younger brother and he'd let us kids play. That all changed when my older brother, Cole, drove our uncle's four-wheeler off an outcrop into a ravine and died. I had been seven, my sister Tabby eight. Cole was ten.

The old man hadn't blamed me for my brother's death, but he did blame me for surviving. After that, my sister and I never saw my uncle or Texas again as a family. Cole had never been his favorite, but you wouldn't have known that after my brother died.

"Sheriff, this is dispatch." It was that same female voice and I heard the fear instantly.

"Go ahead, dispatch," replied the burly man. "What's wrong, Erin?"

"Sheriff, we had another attack." She hesitated on the word 'attack' as if she didn't know what to call it.

"The mayor's place?" asked the sheriff urgently.

"No. County records."

"Fuck," said the sheriff. I was surprised to hear him cuss. "Was Sally working?"

"Gabby," replied dispatch her breathing ragged. "He was doing the rounds mopping. You gotta get over here, Louis. His blood's everywhere and we've got it trapped."

Williams was pissed. "You went?"

"Had to see, didn't I?" She sounded brittle and afraid.

"I'm on my way!" He slammed the radio back into its cradle. "Call your little friend. We need to get into town."

I shouted for Littlewing. Despite the natural gas, my nose said that there was nothing dead stashed nearby. A corpse would have stood out. Nothing worse than the smell of death gone a few days.

The sprite reappeared, her body a faint glow against the dark sky. "We gotta go. Fresh sighting in town."

Littlewing followed me with a grim expression. "If the vampire passed through here, it didn't stop."

"Small favors," I muttered as we got in the car.

Even Littlewing said nothing as the sheriff drove like a bat out of hell. But she clung fiercely to my seatbelt. If I hadn't known better, I'd have sworn that the sheriff wanted to kill us with his recklessness.

We went up on two wheels once and I cracked the door arm-rest by gripping it too tight. It would be another reminder of me after this was done, but it wasn't coming out of my pay.

He didn't slow down until he hit town. A crowd of anxious townspeople had gathered outside the government building, held back by armed men who weren't in uniform. Not deputies. They weren't Feds either.

"Who are they?" I asked. They had shotguns, revolvers and a few hunting rifles. Nothing ordinary folk couldn't legally own.

"Local militia. Left over from the good ol' days," grumbled the sheriff. "We only have three deputies in this town. More if we pull the whole county, but we only do that if a shovel's up our ass."

"That happen a lot?" asked Littlewing, breaking her silence. She'd been irritable since we'd left the gas rig but I wasn't going to ask why in front of Williams.

"What? Pulling deputies?" He skidded to a stop at the edge of the crowd.

"Sticking things up your ass while pulling on the deputies?" I glanced at her tiny face, surprised at the venom. No smile, not a joke. Something had pissed her off big time!

"I don't take insults from grown men. I ain't gonna take 'em from a Barbie-doll bug, neither." The sheriff opened his door angrily. He hit it with his shoulder as it unlatched, impatient to get out and it flew open.

"Good thing he's got a bigger priority, 'Wing." We got out of the station wagon, but I watched Littlewing curiously.

"Is that what they're calling it these days?" she mumbled, folding her arms before she flitted into the air and hovered near my face. She saw me watching her. "What?"

"What's wrong with you?"

The sprite started to say something but there was a scream from inside the courthouse. Her tender moment of confession never happened and we chased after the sheriff. Williams barged in through the front door a few yards ahead of us and I startled the militia by racing past them with superhuman speed.

"Find a window." Littlewing could fly as fast as I ran. She buzzed up into the sky without a reply.

We'd worked well together from the moment she'd joined me. This silent sulk was a new one on me. No matter. I could count on her to do her job. She'd track me from above while I went in the front after the sheriff.

The smell hit me. Fresh blood and gore. It was the smell of a dead body voiding all of its fluids at once. There were also spices from a recent meal mingled with the offal. Cilantro. Pepper. Chilies. Good tasty scents mixed in with death.

The courthouse was dark, but flashes of light came from down a hall. Even with my werewolf reflexes, I slipped on a wet patch and skidded into a wall. Even without lifting my hand to my nose I knew what it was. Blood, thick and cooling. *Gabby.*

"Sheriff?" shouted Deputy Jason. His voice was shrill and a gun went off, more than once.

"Jason?" replied Williams. The sheriff's shadow came into the hallway from another doorway followed by the man himself. I was still sitting on my ass.

"You gonna get up?" He flashed his light into my face. I growled, but it was a human sound.

"Slipped on the blood." Reflexes and strength didn't do much good if you couldn't get any traction. "The room to the right."

He held the light in my face for another second.

"You checking to see if my eyes glow in the dark?" I asked.

Williams turned his back on me and tried the door knob of the room I'd indicated. His gun was drawn and he pointed the flashlight at the ceiling as he turned the handle. Throwing the door open, he took his weapon in both hands. There was no mistaking him for a seasoned professional. His elbows were bent to keep flexibility in his grip in case someone tried to smash the gun away from him.

I pulled a stake out of my jacket. It was one of three six-inch bits of mahogany which I used when my hunting gear was in the car. It was more effective against a vampire, but the human in me still liked the weight of a gun in my hand. And the bang bang bang sound it made. So I used my free hand to reach for the Glock in my shoulder holster. Weapon in each fist, I followed the sheriff into the room.

This was the kill room. I saw a hand dangling limply over a counter, blood trickling down like some perverse faucet drip. I followed the line of the hand to the arm but it ended with a knob of bone, white and glistening. It had been torn out of the shoulder socket.

"It's not in here," I whispered to Williams, unnecessarily. We could both see the imprints of footsteps through the blood. They led to the far door. An office of some sorts, or supply closet. Whatever it was, the vampire was there. We heard another gunshot behind the door and rushed toward the sound.

"Take that you mother-fucking zombie piece of mother-fucking shit!" It was a woman shouting. I recognized the voice we'd heard on the radio. Erin, the dispatcher.

There was more gunfire as Williams and I smashed through the door together. Erin wasn't the one shooting. Deputy Jason was to the left of us, emptying his gun into the body of a man trapped under a filing cabinet the width of a Volkswagen. No, not a man. A thing, in filthy clothes which had been torn beyond recognition was pinned by its arm. It moved like a wild beast fighting to get free. The thing had pale skin and dark hair framing its savage face.

Jason's gun click, click, clicked. All his rounds spent. The female officer, Erin, had an axe in her hand. Pulled from the emergency-fire insert most buildings had. She sliced down on the throat of the vampire in a two-handed overhead motion. She looked like a monster herself, smeared with blood. It was splattered on her uniform top and her face.

But it wasn't hers. She'd come in contact with Gabby's blood. Slipped in it like me.

"Stop!" I cried out, but my command seemed to galvanize her and she swung harder.

I held my gun so hard I heard the synthetic grip crack and I cursed under my breath. The cost for replacing it was gonna eat some of my profit from the job. Littlewing was going to chew me a new one if I wasn't more careful.

I squinted against the explosion of flames. It set the dispatcher on fire as the explosion consumed every atom of the vampire's body and clothes. Her scream was one of the worse sounds I'd heard in a long time. Shit. I hated fire. Although I could heal from it. Didn't make it any less painful for the female officer. In this case, I was upset about something else. Any evidence to connect the monster with the killings had just burned up with the bloodsucker.

Deputy Jason just stood there in shock as Erin screamed, her polyester uniform melting to her skin. It smelled awful and I could only watch. But Sheriff Williams acted. He grabbed a jacket from the back of a toppled chair and threw it around the woman. Then he knocked her to the ground.

I could hear the public service announcement from my childhood. Drape. Drop. And roll. The way to stop a person from burning to death. No one ever warned you about the smell of cooking human flesh. Or how similar it was to pork.

"Mitch!" Littlewing rapped me on the ear. "Stop daydreaming! Upstairs is cleared."

I moved quickly, avoiding the smoldering woman and Williams as I searched the room. There were no other bodies. Alive, dead or undead. "Downstairs, too," I muttered, unhappily. "You see that fire? Gonna be a bitch to check her skin for bite marks."

"Cut its throat," Littlewing acknowledged. "At least we know it's dead this time."

"Yeah, it's dead," I agreed but I wasn't happy. "But we didn't do it."

"Who the fuck cares." Her mood hadn't improved. "We still get paid."

CHAPTER TWELVE

I washed the blood off my clothes and then we followed the sheriff to the morgue to wrap up loose ends. The coroner held out his hand and stared at me. Not for a handshake. I handed over the file I'd grabbed out of my car, folding my arms across my chest. Littlewing perched on my shoulder, sitting with an arm across her knees, holding onto my jacket's lapel with the other hand. Not nearly as intimidating as before.

"How is Erin?" Doc Madison looked to the sheriff for his answer.

"Burned pretty badly. She'll be in the hospital for a few weeks I imagine." William's voice was hard. "Jason's messed up, too. Try to touch him and he screams."

"Did he get bit?" Harv pulled open a drawer and put the file away.

"No. Neither of them. Thanks to Erin." The sheriff was growing impatient.

"Never expected her to take out a vampire." The coroner stared at me accusingly.

I knew what he was thinking. It was my fault she got hurt. As if I was the one who told her to go inside and try to catch a vampire. Right. I kept the sarcasm to myself.

"Guess that's that," said the sheriff. He had decided to personally escort me around town until I left for good. Figured he'd get rid of me faster that way. Nope. Wrong approach. I'd find reasons to dig my heels in just to fuck with him.

I pointed out the obvious. "We don't know if there were any earlier victims. Vamps usually take one a night." The case didn't feel finished to me, but it wasn't my call. "There were two nights between the suit and the mayor."

"No other attacks. It's done. You're done." Not subtle. Get out of town. We don't want your kind here, now that we don't need you.

"I am planning on having a drink before we settle in for the rest of the night," I warned him. "And we do get our expenses paid through check-out tomorrow."

"That's all this is about, to you. Isn't it? A job!" The sheriff glared but Littlewing could teach him a thing or two about intimidating looks. "I've had two good men killed. And a deputy who stares at a wall without even knowing who he is. Worse, my dispatch officer has burns all over her body. And this is just about money to you?"

I offered him my own hard stare. But I had advantage. I made my fangs prominent and let my eyes turn from dark-green to that amber-death seen in the eyes of predators. "I don't like people dying. It's why I don't make friends with them. You accept a paycheck for doing *your* job, Sheriff?"

"That's *not* the reason I do it."

"So if there was no paycheck, you'd still risk your life to protect these people?" I asked. Doc Madison studied the sheriff again, waiting for his response.

"Gotta eat," he said with a gruff nod. He hated agreeing with me. "These are my people. So I care. But you? You're a stranger." Normally this was where Littlewing would go ballistic at being ignored, but something was eating at her. She sat on my shoulder silently.

"I think what the sheriff really wants to know if there's anyone you care about more than the money." The coroner glanced at the pieces of Gabriel Hernandez, the janitor. Gabby had been carefully arranged on another metal gurney, awaiting formal autopsy. When the victims were torn to pieces like that, they didn't come back. It was one body I wouldn't have to stake or behead.

"Yeah. Myself." I stormed out of the morgue. The sheriff didn't follow me.

"Can we just leave tonight? Get out of this fucking town?" Littlewing stood up on my shoulder and used her wings to keep balance. A little booze might lighten her mood. I knew it would help mine.

"I think we both need to celebrate some easy cash," I said as I wandered toward the *Broken Record.*

The town was quiet after the early evening's tragedy. There were only a few people out on the streets. But one thing that happened when you became a bona fide predator. You knew when someone was watching you. And someone was watching me real hard.

I didn't break my stride or even turn my head as I scanned the street ahead. As a lycanthrope, I could see great in the dark. And give me any kind of light, I didn't miss a thing. But the person watching me wasn't hiding. She stood under the glow of a lamp across the street, in front of a closed pharmacy. Not waiting for a friend then.

The woman stared at me. I returned the favor. My gaze traveled up her body, starting at the corseted, ankle-high, black leather boots. Then it moved to her pale, perfect calves. I paused to enjoy her incredibly sexy thighs, lean and strong. They could break a man's back in the middle of an orgasm. Her hips were curvy in a painted-on red dress, and her waist was cinched by a wide, black belt with an antique gold buckle. Higher up, I admired her two silky, round breasts. They weren't Dolly Parton heavy. More Angelina Jolie as 'Laura Croft' in *Tomb Raider,* perfect. The nubs of her nipples were evident beneath the sheer red fabric of the dress.

After a moment, my gaze rose to the sexy hollow of her clavicle and the pale skin of her throat. The muscles there filled me with a desire to press my mouth hard against them, to lick the smooth length of her throat, one hand entwined in the hair at the back of her head. I noticed then that her lips glistened under the lamplight. A red as deep as blood. She was young, but not innocent. She had the bright-blue eyes of a woman who knew what she wanted. And she was looking at me.

"Of course, if you don't want to go drinking," I said to Littlewing, not taking my eyes off the auburn-haired woman as we walked to the bar.

"You're about as subtle as a dick up my ass," said the sprite. Normally she didn't get jealous if I saw a beautiful woman. As much as she liked sex when she could get it, which wasn't often given her size, she liked to watch, too. As long as she didn't critique my performance, I didn't mind.

"What's eating you?" I studied Littlewing's unhappy expression before glancing back at the woman. She was still there, leaning against the metal of the lamp with the allure of a lady but the promise of a prostitute. The tight, short skirt said it all.

"Nothing. We gonna drink or what?" She buzzed off my shoulder and headed for the bar which was now in sight. "With or without that piece of nineteen-year-old tail."

As she flew, flashes of sunlight slipped along her skin in tempo with her anger. It didn't matter. Littlewing wouldn't need the energy she'd absorbed now that the vampire was dead. I'd have chased her, but she could take care of herself. Besides, I'd earned a nice sum of cash and needed to relax.

Except. I paused, grinding my teeth in frustration. Not much a small town like Resistance had to offer a werewolf. The law said I had to tell my partners about my lycanthropy before I had sex. That and I had to take precautions. No claws and no fangs to tear a woman's flesh. That was easy enough. But where the hell was I supposed to find *Preter Peter* condoms in this tiny burg? I hadn't planned on getting laid, so I wasn't packing. I couldn't remember the last time I'd had spontaneous, casual sex.

"God damn it all to hell," I gazed at the sexy woman. If I started talking to her, I wasn't going to want to stop to scour the town for the only brand of legally authorized condoms for lycanthropes. There weren't many of us in the world, but the government had voted to allow us to live our lives the same way people with HIV lived their lives. Not in a prison cell or celibate, but very, very careful of other people.

I sighed and shrugged as I offered her a sad smile. She tilted her head as I began to walk off, frowning. She hadn't expected me to turn her down. I held up my tattoo, showing her the back of my hand and tapping at the circle with a finger. Her eyes flashed with confusion and I let my eyes turn amber. My ears grew a little longer, changing shape at the pointy tip and there was just a trace of the wolf about my nose. That was enough to startle her and she fled.

She hadn't known what I was and it had mattered. It always mattered. Even for the few working girls I'd approached. I wasn't looking for love. I had trashed that idea the night a werewolf had first turned my human life upside down. But no sex? Why live?

There were always people with werewolf fetishes in the big city. Although most of them were too freaky, even to satisfy my desperate needs. Mary in Detroit and Rhonda in Los Angeles were willing, but expensive, pieces of tail. Not the best in the trade, but at least they didn't make me feel like a mercy fuck.

With another sigh, I marched toward the bar to look for Littlewing and maybe—just maybe—to look for another fight with the bartender. As long as he started the fight, I could finish it. Or maybe Littlewing would finally open up and tell me what the hell was bugging her.

Inside, Frank was waiting for me. Littlewing was at the counter, with two of the local young studs next to her. They wore jeans, tennis shoes and clean t-shirts a size too small. She was bent over a shot-glass, lapping tequila and they watched her. Like they were gonna find a way to get sexual satisfaction with a woman only eight-inches tall. Not if I could help it.

They saw me and I still had amber eyes which made them jump, literally before they shuffled off to a booth along one wall. I hadn't said a thing, so Littlewing couldn't complain. If she did, I'd have that fight I was itching for.

"Sheriff said I have to serve you. Your leaving and all, tomorrow. I reckon I better," said Frank without any smile or kindness in his eyes. "But you can take this bottle and your little flying Barbie and go sit in that corner back there. It's dark. You can drink to your heart's content and you won't scare my regulars."

I pulled out a hundred and slapped it on the counter next to Littlewing. She bounced off the glass into the air, instantly irate. "Watch it, you oversized piece of cock!"

"That's it!" I grabbed Littlewing, the bottle which the man had set on the counter and her shot of booze, and carried them toward the booth. She was screaming and scratching at my hand but I held her tightly. She was a tough little creature. The fey were nothing if not resilient.

"Sit down and tell me what the fuck's up your snatch!" I plopped down on the vinyl bench-seat, dumping her onto the table. That got her attention. Two words I never used both referred for the same bit of female anatomy.

"You don't like that word." She blew the hair out of her face and stared at me like I was the one acting weird.

"What happened?" I sat there, the bottle neck in one hand and the other tapping the table next to her drink. It also happened to be next to her feet.

"You won't like it," she warned me.

"Yeah? So what else is new?"

She sighed, glanced around the bar and then propped her back up against the bottle. The nearest people were three tables away. We had privacy even though they stared. "You know those fairies in the old broad's backyard? The insect-like ones?"

"Did you try to fuck one and it wasn't interested?"

"Oh, for Christ's sake! Like I would have any use for a pencil dick!" No laugh or smile or clever comment. It was that serious.

"Sorry." I asked with what little patience I could muster. "What about them?"

I tolerated Littlewing's foul mouth and her erotic obsession with explosives and guns because she was the best partner I'd ever had. She was good at what she did and made me a better man. We made an efficient team. I respected her. But I'd never seen her so upset.

"That isn't their nature," she said, watching my expression. "Keep up, Mitch. They aren't like that in the wild."

"Like what?" She wasn't make much sense.

"Fer fuck's sake, Mitch! Dumb animals!"

"Don't take your anger out on me," I warned her. "How do you know they're not like that?"

The various fey creatures in our world had come through holes in the universe. Holes opened up at various times by the powerful physical forces of war. The atomic bombs which the U.S. had tested locally and then dropped on Japan in the 1940s had admitted a slew of creatures that we were still trying to find and kill. The smaller bombs since then had caused less trouble, fewer holes between dimensions. But it still happened.

Didn't have to be a nuclear bomb, either. Sometimes nature did it. Scientists were still trying to figure out what had let in the first vampires or caused the first strains of lycanthropy. Sometimes it was a simple as a lightning storm. If the energy hit the right spot in just the right way, that could tear holes between dimensions. The only thing humans had figured out so far was that there was no way to keep the holes between worlds from opening. But maybe we could learn to track them. Keep the monsters from getting very far.

The trouble with having so many non-indigent fey was that too little was known about them. The Federal Government didn't allow public research in the interests of national security. Same reason they didn't share what they did learn. Something about protecting the people from themselves. Hell, I worked with the Feds from time to time and they were even tight-lipped with me. Someday I'd get curious enough to snoop. When I was willing to risk getting locked up for good. Like that was gonna happen.

But we did know that the creatures didn't all come from the same alternate universes. Littlewing's world wasn't the same one in which the vampires had originated. Or rather, *a* vampire. As far as the world's governments could tell, only one bloodsucker had slipped into our universe. As a result, they believed that that particular dimensional rip had stayed shut ever since. DNA testing on the vampires who hadn't turned to ash all traced back to a single donor. That didn't mean there weren't others, but the evidence was against it. These days we had less to go on despite better technology. The FBI, Mossad, the KGB or whatever equivalents existed around the world had destroyed any they got their hands on. Probably for the best.

"I saw one by the gas rig. A normal one." Her anger was palpable. "He was so afraid. He warned me to flee."

"Flee? Flee what?" I asked, intrigued. "It talked? The ones at the Cheswick's didn't."

"Someone lobotomized the ones in the mayor's yard." She gritted her teeth and slammed her tiny fist against the wood of the table. "They took out part of their brains and made them into mindless bugs, Mitch!"

"Son of a bitch," I muttered, leaning back. It was like that moment when Charlton Heston first discovered his fellow astronaut had been lobotomized by the apes. Only this wasn't a movie.

"And we can't do anything about it!" She slammed the table again, while her body shot out bits of daylight that illuminated the bottle of *Cuervo*. Pretty but harmless.

"Not much difference between hunting goblins and lobotomizing some animalistic fairies, is there? After all, most of the wild fey are dangerous." I wanted to touch her, but in this mood, she'd get violent.

"Damned straight we are! But they aren't animalistic! Not naturally." She put her hand on the miniature gun at her hip, pulling it from its holster and scratching her cheek with the muzzle. "I told you you weren't going to like it."

"I mean, sure. It sucks. But normally you'd vent about it and then let it be," I said. She wasn't an advocate of the fey any more than I was a poster-boy for lycanthropes. "Why the big deal?"

"You saw *One Flew Over the Cuckoo's Nest*. You telling me that some things don't strike closer to home than others?" When Jack Nicholson had been lobotomized, I'd wanted to rip the heads off the entire hospital staff. And that had just been a movie. Didn't feel the same rage when I saw footage of kids being gunned down in the streets. And I couldn't say why. I understood her meaning perfectly.

"Okay. So it pisses you off. I respect that." I tapped the bottle. "I'll even drink to it. It's not like we can do anything about it."

"Yeah, well. That's the part you ain't gonna like. I'm going to the mayor's house tonight to snoop around." Littlewing folded her arms defiantly.

"We don't get the rest of our money wired till tomorrow," I warned her.

"I know. And it's the old broad who's fronting the dough, right?"

"Yeah."

"Told you you weren't gonna like it," she repeated. She was drunk. Golden light was seeping out of the corners of her eyes and the energy from her hands made the alcohol glow with a swirling, diffused warmth.

"Normally you can hold more liquor than I can," I said suspiciously. "Did you take something besides alcohol?"

"Nopes." She slurred that one word.

I picked up her drink, pulling it gently from her arms. Holding close to my face, I sniffed. Filtering past the bitter tang of the tequila, I got a whiff of something mediciny. I glanced first over to the two young men who'd been at the bar with her. They weren't paying attention to us. A strawberry blonde girl with big tits had them distracted in the corner. Not them, then.

My eyes searched the rest of the bar until I spotted Frank. The bartender jerked his guilty gaze away from us and reached for something under the counter.

"God damn it all to hell!" I snarled, mostly to myself. "Can't a man just get a drink in a Podunk town like this without people trying to kill him?"

I scooped up Littlewing and leapt to the side as a spray of buckshot tore holes into the vinyl upholstery. Customers screamed and scrambled away from our corner in surprise, none of them close enough to be in danger. The bottle on the table shattered, spraying us with glass. A shard tore through one of the sprite's wings and that pissed me off. I could heal faster than a human, but she was basically mortal.

"You crossed a line, Frank!" I tossed the sprite behind the booth-seat for her safety, and leapt to my feet.

I didn't want to take a round of buckshot to my chest, because it would still hurt like a bitch. But I was betting that he wasn't faster than me. And it would distract him from shooting Littlewing. One of those times I didn't even think to draw my gun as the beast took over.

I drew on the power of the moonlight, hidden as I was from it, like a fine mist in the air. My muscles shifted slightly into the heavier, stronger meat of my wolfman form. My jacket was loose enough that it took the extra mass, custom-made for it. But the seams of my shirt sleeves stretched and ripped, ruined. I didn't summon the wolfman hair on my body. It wouldn't make me any stronger or protect me from bullets. But my fingers grew claws and my fangs stuck out over my lower lip as I snarled the way no human could. Finally I had my fight!

I was half-way to the bartender before his eyes flared with fear and he squeezed the trigger again. I leapt but I wasn't faster than a speeding bullet. Or a spray of tiny metal pellets. I'd wasted precious seconds transforming.

The buckshot stung and I roared like a lion at the zoo. People screamed, more afraid of the big bad werewolf than a shotgun going off in their only watering hole. I heard them through the rush of adrenaline, but I kept moving toward the man who futilely pressed the trigger over and over. Like Deputy Jason after he'd emptied his revolver into the vampire.

My blood was splattered on my clothes and the floor. I didn't care if the old bastard got infected, I was gonna rip him a new one. Then the room lurched and I saw the strange grin on Frank's face. It was an odd contrast to the fear in his eyes. I smelled the stench of ozone from the muzzle and then—the unmistakable smell of hot silver.

"You fucker!" I said as my knees buckled. Silver was poison to the blood of a lycanthrope. It sapped the strength as the body fought itself. And it hurt like hell.

I hit the bottom of the counter with one shoulder and the side of my head, hearing the crunch of wood as spots flashed before my eyes. People ran for the door. I saw feet leaping past me. I was too weak to stand. Or to pull myself up the wood to reach Frank over the countertop. But I was pissed. I shoved my hand through the base of the bar and grasped at something on the other side. I felt the satisfying pressure of my claws breaking skin and Frank the bartender screamed as his bones shattered.

It was the lullaby which sang me into the darkness, but I made sure that I didn't let go.

CHAPTER THIRTEEN

Blinding florescent lights blazed above me and the world vibrated as I came to. I wasn't dead, which should have been a relief. But I had a flash of disappointment. Some part of me had been hoping my lonely miserable life would finally be over. I growled, telling myself I was happy to be alive. I hadn't given into to despair when I'd first turned. I wouldn't now.

I smelled that antiseptic hallmark of a hospital and focused my eyes. I saw scrubs on the woman walking alongside the gurney that they used to move me through the hallway. The assault on my nose triggered a growl of disgust. It stirred memories of the past.

For a moment I was back on the operating table. Before the lycanthropy had taken hold. I remembered shouting voices and that copper-stench everywhere. Unpleasant FBI agents had stared down at me with heavy assault rifles aimed at my head. There were older memories that made me hospitals, too. My grandmother's death being the worse. That image shook me out of the past.

I growled again, this time piteously. The helpless sound shocked me into silence. Over the smell of blood, piss and disease, the wash of alcohol implied more than sanitation. It offered hope. The smell lied. It tried to hide the approach of slow, unstoppable death. I couldn't speak for fear of sounding like a wailing child in my despair. My grandmother's face kept flashing in the back of my mind, even though I fought it like it was a vampire on my ass.

The rectangular lights of the hospital passed overhead. I tried to lift a hand to cover my eyes, but I couldn't move. It wasn't just the silver in my system or my fear of the past. I was strapped down.

"What the fuck are you doing to me?" I asked and the word 'fuck' made me flinch.

It wasn't the hospital that made me regret the word. It was my grandmother. Her lifelong disapproval was alive in my brain because I'd been reminded of her death. It was Littlewing's word and God-fearing little boys didn't use it. My grandmother's plump, gently-lined face always scowled at hearing it. But it had come from my father's mouth back then, not mine. Years of his military service.

You'll not teach the boy to swear, by God! She'd warned Adam Greyson, as much a soldier of life, as he was of war.

More than twenty-years had passed. Grandmother Adelaide was dead. And Mitchell Greyson was a full grown man with a foul mouth of his own. Being in the South reminded me of my conservative upbringing and being in the hospital made me ache for the only loving arms I'd ever known as a child.

"I'm Dr. Gwen Walker. We're trying to get the buckshot out of your system, Mr. Greyson." The angry voice tore me out of the past. I turned my head and saw an older woman with a doctor's ID. She was gloved up to her elbows and there was blood all over the latex. My blood. I couldn't see her mouth or hair because they were covered in standard operating garb. "Stop fighting the damned restraints!"

If I hadn't been weakened by the silver, I could have torn through the leather and plastic shackles. I could have broken them even if they'd been cast of any metal less than 2" thick. But at the moment, my sweat-drenched body was more helpless than a kitten. A kitten, at least, could have still dug its needle fine claws into a person and inflict pain. I could only lie there, wanting to kill the bartender for putting me in the hospital.

"Where's my partner?" I struggled again, but it was useless.

If Littlewing had been unharmed, she wouldn't have left my side. No matter what threats the doctor laid at her wings. Her absence worried me as much as the silver in my system.

"She's here. Worry about yourself." No compassion for her patient. Only anger.

"Why are *you* pissed?" I asked in a hoarse whisper as unconsciousness threatened me again.

"Frank Lynch." The doctor had to bite back her emotion.

"Did I hurt the bastard?" I smiled, woozy from a morphine drip. My metabolism would burn it off quickly, even with silver in me. But in high enough doses it could give me a buzz most things couldn't.

"Yes." She sounded not only angry, but vulnerable.

Great, Frank was someone she cared about. And this woman was going to cut into me to remove the silver the bastard had put inside my well-muscled flesh. If she got to it all in time. Before so much poison was in my blood that the buckshot wouldn't matter.

"He shot me." I put my own anger into the words. My consciousness swelled toward the pain of awareness for a moment. "For just being here." I saw something else in her eyes. "Don't worry. My claws in his ankle won't spread what I got."

Was that true? If I'd had my own blood on my fingers when I'd crushed his bones—. No, I couldn't have. I'd die before passing it along. Even to an asshole like Frank Lynch.

Dr. Walker started to say something, her expression fierce, but she bit back her reply. She spoke to the nurse instead. "Increase the morphine. The monster can handle it."

"Am I gonna wake up dead because of you?"

"More," barked the doctor. I felt it start to work quickly, at a lethal dose for a human. She turned back to me and leaned forward, just a little. Despite what she knew as a doctor, she was still afraid of being infected by the big bad werewolf. "You'll just have to wait and see."

Shit, I thought to myself. I was too lost to the drug to speak. Blackness overwhelmed my mind's eye, but it brought no sense of relief. I might not wake up.

All I wanted to do at that moment was to live so that I could punch the bitch in the mouth. But not because she'd threatened me. I just hated doctors that much.

CHAPTER FOURTEEN

I was in the woods. There was water running nearby. I could hear it. A wind blew, warm and green. It made the campfire flicker. Shapes played in the flames. Someone I should recognize. The figure was elusive, frightening in what should have been an idyllic redwood setting. Giant conifers all around, the stream somewhere out of sight. I recognized it. Dinky Creek, California, near Shaver Lake. My favorite spot. Before that night.

There was movement behind me and I turned. Slowly, the way a normal person turned. The moon was full above the tree-line but I couldn't feel it in my blood. No stirring of the beast in me. No ability to be more than a man. *The dream.*

I hadn't had it in years, but I recognized it. I knew what was coming next and my stomach knotted.

"Mitch!" Jenny's voice, warm and loving. I looked. I always looked.

She knelt at the opening to the tent, the flap thrown back. Her tight, white tank-top was torn open, along with her right breast and half her stomach. I could see her entrails and blood seeped into the cotton of her clothes. I always stared at the torn nipple, a flap of loose skin. My gut tightened even more with remembered pain, not anger. That constant anger had come later.

She smiled, long black hair framing her features. But the claws had gone through her face, too. Teeth like a corpse, grinning without lips. One eye staring, the other hanging out. Just enough to be horrifying.

"Jenn." My voice was a whisper, playing a scene I had no control over.

He came out of the shadows. Shadows that hadn't been there an instant before. Dusk to full dark in a heartbeat. The monster appeared, silent and deadly. Just like before.

Jenny had her back to him, no longer torn up. Events happening backwards. Meant to impact with the greatest guilt that they could. My sadistic/masochistic subconscious punishing me.

Black, wolf eyes, full of human intelligence watched me. A wolf-man muzzle full of white, glistening teeth that dripped with gooey saliva. That was my imagination, not a real memory. Because when I changed, my spit was spit. This was about something else. Another guilt. A different fear.

The naked man-wolf grinned at me, knowing I was helpless. Impotent in the dream. Each step, its obscenely oversized genitalia dangled from a wet patch of curly hair between two rippling thighs. He was anxious, ready. A rapist, not just a murderer in the dream. But it hadn't happened like that. Not in real life.

He'd torn her to pieces before he could satisfy that urge. The doctors had confirmed it. So why did I repeatedly imagine he had?

The monster stood tall, arching back to face the moon, his nakedness full of sexual prowess. His mouth opened for a sound that never came. Always the same. Only Jenny and I spoke in the dream.

He finished his silent howl and faced me. His body hair, coarse and black stood up off his shoulders. It made him look bigger. Feral.

"It's fur, Mitch. He's an animal." Jenny's voice said things she had never said. Would never have said as the werewolf was about to slice her to bits.

I didn't hate having this conversation. It was a chance to hear her again. To pretend she was alive. Maybe my subconscious wasn't as cruel as I thought. Except, by pretending she was alive, watching her die again hurt all that much more.

"There's no difference between hair and fur." A New York mammologist had told me that during my post-bite rehabilitation. I hadn't known it when Jenny was still alive. Our final conversation and my mind chose to argue with her. "People use 'fur' for soft animal hair or undercoats, Jenn."

I tried to say 'I love you.' I wanted to say 'I'm sorry.' All I could say was, "There's no real difference."

She fed a pile of twigs to the fire, ritually crisscrossing them in the flames. It had been charming. A quirk I'd cherished about her. I'd forgotten.

"Why did you really want us to come camping this weekend?" She looked up from the fire, her brown eyes demanding.

Something different. The script had changed. Irrationally, that scared me worse than knowing what was going to happen.

I opened my mouth, but my eyes tracked the movement of the enormous beast slinking toward her. Bigger than me as a lycanthrope. More than eight feet tall. The FBI had me registered as six-five in that form. His arm muscles as big as my thighs, too. No way to know if this was a real memory or my imagination. When they finally killed him, he'd been human. But this dream monster could tear me in two. Even if I'd already been a werewolf.

"Answer me, Mitch. What was the reason?" Her tone forced me to look at her. Anger. It was familiar, but not Jenny's. Littlewing's tone. Reality was bleeding through. Or memories getting mixed up.

"I wanted—." What had I wanted? I pressured her to go. She had said 'beach' but I insisted on camping. Why?

"Go ahead, do it." Not Jenny. I looked over my shoulder, unable to walk or turn completely away from my dead girlfriend and the monster that killed her. Grandma Adelaide Greyson suddenly stood there, holding her Bible. There was an expression of conviction on her plump features. What was she doing in this nightmare? I felt a tear well. A reaction I couldn't fight. I'd found a way to be more cruel to myself.

"Do what?" I pleaded, helpless and human. No weapon, no claws or fangs of my own.

The werewolf reached Jenny and I swung back around to face him. He didn't stop. One foot, then all of him passed her. He had always hurt her first, then came after me.

"Die of course," insisted my grandmother. "You know you want to."

The werewolf leapt at me, huge hands reaching out, digging sharp claws into my chest. I screamed and wept. But echoing in the background, the mocking laughter of the dead women I'd loved.

CHAPTER FIFTEEN

I woke sometime before the doctor was done. The smell of the hospital and blood were still strong in my nose. My blood. Reality and the dream overlapped, confusing me. I focused on the memory of the day I'd stopped being human, to drive away the dream. I'd asked a question, over and over. My mind still echoed with the awful answer. *She's dead.*

Only later did they tell me what I'd become. I would wish I'd died, too. Later I'd remember what had attacked us and I'd want to forget again. I never could. Ignoring it was as close as I came. Then the dream had begun. Worse than reality. Morphine had brought it back.

I heard the plink of metal hitting metal. Then a ball-bearing rolling in a pan. One piece of silver buckshot taken from my flesh. "He's coming out of it."

I blinked at the masked, black man to my left. I was completely naked, but I knew how fit I was. A werewolf metabolism gave me the definition of an athlete without having to work out. If it hadn't been for the fear of catching lycanthropy, I'd have had any woman I wanted. Instead, I went without.

"Why the hell did you lower the dose?" asked Dr. Walker. Frank's friend.

"I didn't. With most of the silver out of his body, he's breaking it down faster," replied the male nurse. Underneath my blood, they smelled of antiseptic, latex and talcum powder. I hated every bit of it.

I spoke without meaning to. My voice muffled by an oxygen mask. "How much is left?"

"I can't tell. We couldn't waste time X-raying you, so still digging through the blood. Problem is some of the smaller entry points have healed up and we're having to guess," replied Walker. She hated me, but not enough to ignore me. Or maybe she couldn't violate her Hippocratic Oath enough to disregard a patient's life. Either way, it was something.

"Won't matter if that Lyco-selenium doesn't get here from Birmingham soon," said the blonde nurse who had first dosed me with morphine. She came back into the O.R. and stood over me. "I don't suppose you carry a personal stash for cases of argyria?"

Argyria was the technical term for 'silver-poisoning.' It turned ordinary humans blue but didn't typically kill them. As a werewolf, my reaction was slightly more lethal. Forced to choose between being a Smurf and being dead, I wasn't sure which I'd have preferred. I looked at the blonde and blinked.

"Why didn't you ask Littlewing?" My voice was hoarse. Had I been screaming under the influence of morphine? Said anything about the dream? My guilt? I refused to ask. I didn't want to give any of them the satisfaction of confirming it had been more than a nightmare.

"Who? "The doctor dropped another piece of shot into the bed-pan.

"The sprite," replied the male nurse. "She's still out cold."

"What do you mean she's out cold?" I growled.

My mind was clearing. The pain was coming back fast, too. I didn't need the straps on my wrists and ankles to remind me of how weak I was. Even the tiniest amount of silver would poison a lycanthrope if it was in the system too long. It took a whole lot less for me to contract argyria than a normal human. I should have been worried about me, but all I could think about was my sexy little partner.

"She went crazy when Frank shot you. He got her in the temple with the butt of his gun," said the doctor. I heard a hint of remorse in her voice. She didn't pretend that Frank was completely innocent. The women in Resistance suffered less denial about their men than women in Los Angeles. I almost smiled until she asked, "Why'd he shoot you?"

"I told you!" I yelped as she dug into me less delicately, to make a point. "He just hates me for what I am. Even though I only came here to help the town."

"Is it true? Was there a vampire?" asked the blonde nurse. The doctor paused and scowled at her.

"The sheriff will tell us what we need to know." Walker resumed pulling silver out of me.

There were sirens and the sound of slamming doors. "What the devil is it now?" asked the doctor under her breath. She worked faster.

"You aren't the only doctor on call are you?" I asked.

"I wouldn't be working on you if I wasn't," she admitted. Another plunk of metal rolled around and joined its companions. I couldn't tell if she was working fast or not. But I knew it wasn't going to be fast enough at this rate.

The doors to the O.R. flew open and a red-headed teenage girl rushed in. There was horror in her eyes and not because of me. "Dr. Walker, we've got a serious problem!"

"Get the hell out of my O.R. without being suited up!"

"Not much chance of infecting him, is there?" stated the male nurse bluntly.

"Old Man Jackson got tore up by something," stammered the teeny-bopper nurse or candy striper or whatever she was. "Something like what killed Gabby."

"What!?" I tried to sit up but the restraints and Dr. Walker's elbow on my shoulder pushed me back down. "The same thing that killed Gabby killed someone else?"

"Something like it. Only Old Man Jackson is still alive. Barely, Doc," said the teenager. "There's blood everywhere. And the smell!"

"Damn it, I can't work on you both. Roy, you wanted hands-on experience. Keep digging out the silver and don't miss any. He's well enough. He doesn't need oxygen or a doctor. Like pulling splinters!"

"You can't just leave me," complained the black man but the doctor ignored him. She grabbed the blonde nurse and pushed the red-headed teen out the door in front of them.

Just us two big boys, all alone. And the nurse hadn't sounded very confident. Dr. Walker could claim that it was death by necessity. But would she be able to sleep at night if I died? I didn't think so. She'd regret the decision. So would I.

"Gosh darn it."

He stared at my exposed chest, but I raised a brow at him. "They never taught you how to swear properly?"

"It ain't polite to curse." Roy indignantly picked up long-handled tweezers and pressed his gloved fingers through the meat of my chest, just below the clavicle. "This is gonna hurt."

"I've been hurt worse," I said and it was true.

Steel knives. Bullets. Icepicks. Hell, a boulder had crushed my thigh once and that had been a bitch to heal. But this was my first experience with silver. And I didn't have any serum to deal with poisoning. If he missed even a single piece, I'd be dead in a couple of hours.

It wasn't that I didn't have any faith in Roy. I didn't have faith in any doctor or nurse. But faith in technology, yeah, that I had. "You guys have an MRI machine?"

"A portable one we share with all the neighboring county hospitals. Why?" He wiped the sweat from his brow and got a better grip on the surgical tweezers.

"Because I'm gonna save you hours of worry and self-doubt," I replied firmly.

His expression turned to surprise. "No, sir! That machine is expensive. If we use it on you with any metal inside? No way!"

"Better a broken MRI than a dead werewolf. Especially if there are still vampires in town. Or am I wrong?"

I'd used the plural. He didn't notice, but the sheriff would have. Erin, the dispatcher had killed one vampire. But there were still more victims popping up. It wasn't just an old-timer come back from the dead on its own. Or it was making fresh accomplices. I wasn't going to assume it was alone this time. Goodbye easy money. Killing a vampire was damned hard. But catching one for interrogation, that was a whole 'nother mess.

"That decision is above my pay grade," said the nurse with finality. He dug into my flesh for more nuggets of buckshot. "'Sides. Silver ain't affected by magnets."

"I'm betting old Frank couldn't afford pure silver and it has iron mixed up in the buckshot. It's worth a try!"

"Nope." But he did hold up one of the pieces of metal and examined it. "Even if there is iron."

"Fine. Then every murder-by-vampire you get from now onward is on your head." I gasped as he shoved the tweezers in hard. He wasn't trying to hurt me. I'd just rattled him that much with my comment.

"If you die because I try to get permission, that on my head, too?" he demanded, his eyes anxious.

"I'll make you a deal. If the mayor's wife won't pay for it, I will." My nerves were on fire as the morphine lost its effect. "I can't spend it if I'm dead. And I just know you're gonna miss one or more of these silver bastards."

Roy studied my haircut and tried to remember the clothes I'd been wearing. "You don't look like you could afford a beer, much less an MRI machine."

"How much do you think vampire hunters get paid?" I managed to make it a masculine grunt instead of the roar of agony I was feeling. If I couldn't convince this pansy-assed nurse to take a chance soon, it wouldn't matter.

"Alright, I'll do it. Only 'cause I figure a lawsuit by your family for letting you die is gonna be more than a new machine," he conceded.

The multitude of justifications he was lining up in his head weren't for his conscience. They were for his bosses. I didn't tell him that my family consisted of a dad and a sister, neither of whom would blame the hospital for my death. They'd see it as freedom for me from a curse. My sister would believe it out of compassion. My father out of hatred.

Roy unlocked the wheels on the gurney and pushed me out of the O.R., letting my bare feet bang the doors to open them without apology. He raced me to a nearby room and hit the light switch. It was a small room, barely room for the portable MRI machine and its controls. No room for the gurney.

With practiced skill, Roy removed the straps on my feet first. He lifted my legs up and onto the ceramic platform for the MRI and then freed my wrists. He watched me cautiously, but I was still too weak to try to make a break for it.

"I'm not a criminal. The straps were to keep me from thrashing," I reminded him.

That did the trick because he hefted me up by the shoulders and slid my upper body into position. While the machine warmed up, he took the gurney outside the room and inspected himself for bits of metal.

"No time to set this up proper and God help my soul if someone needs this thing to save a life tonight," muttered the nurse.

"You should be so lucky." I clenched my fists in agony. From there pain there were several bits of silver hidden under my skin. It was just as well that I wasn't able to hold onto him for support. I might have broken the bones from the sheer pain. "Hurry it up!"

"Almost there." He plopped onto a plastic chair at the controls. "Normally we set the controls outside the room. But the magnet will yank out any metal in you before it pulls this baby into it."

"Whatever!" I gritted my teeth. "Just do it!"

"It needs to calibrate." He looked at the door anxiously.

"For what? We want it to act like a magnet, not take pretty pictures."

He didn't bother to say 'oh' or make any apology. His eyes said it all. He hit a button and the whine of the magnet filled the room. It was like yanking off an assortment of Band-Aids, all at once. Every bit of buckshot was ripped out of my muscles. It hurt like heck, but it was over in a moment. Sparks flew from the metal striking the magnet's casing and Roy shut off the machine to avoid further damage.

"Let me take the buckshot out of the room and I'll give it another run." The nurse was acting much more sensibly now that he'd committed himself to destroying a very expensive piece of equipment.

I waited as he picked up all the silver-and-iron-mixed buckshot from where it had fallen in the room. He dumped the pellets out the door and then turned on the MRI again. This time, there was no pain. No more bits of metal torn out of me.

"Looks like I'm good."

"Can you really afford to buy a new one if the city doesn't cover it?" asked Roy with a look that said 'don't lie, I've already done the damage.'

"Yeah, but trust me. They'll pay for it." I earned a hell of a lot of money for my services, but I'd nearly died more than once, even as a werewolf. So my fees were justified. Just never had much reason to spend it. Travel for a werewolf was restricted. Sex was restricted. And I wasn't one of those guys that needed a fancy car to prove my virility or impress the ladies. So I spent it on food and a decent place to live, the occasional whore and replacement weapons.

I didn't pay much attention to my finances, but I figured I'd just hit the six zero range. Who'd have thought that Mitch Greyson, failure by his daddy's standards, would be a millionaire at thirty.

"How can you be so sure?" asked the nurse. Roy didn't mean how could I be sure I had enough money. He meant how could I be sure that the mayor's wife or the town would pay.

"Because otherwise I'll let the sheriff handle the vampires on his own." I stood up. The room swam and I knew I was still fucked. "Oh, shit. The poison."

"Kind of irresponsible to travel around the country without your own supply of Lyco-selenium." There was a sparkle of satisfaction in his eyes.

"You like that I'm probably gonna die?" My lack of faith in the medical community got a surge of confirmation.

That sobered him up. "No. But I did think that it was funny that a scary werewolf vampire-hunter was taken down by a crotchety old bartender and his decades old shotgun."

I grinned at him, letting my canines out just enough that he couldn't ignore them. "When you put it like that, it is kind of funny." The smile didn't hit my eyes. "How long before the serum gets here?"

Lyco-selenium serum was bioengineered for lycanthrope metabolisms. It was very different from ordinary selenium. It attached to silver particles in the blood, rendered them inert as far as werewolf physiology was concerned. It was expensive, but that wasn't the reason I didn't carry it. I'd just never been attacked by silver before. Dumb, but the truth. And if the locals would provide it, I didn't mind the miserly savings.

"Special courier. Maybe an hour." Roy was clearly guessing.

"Well, then! Let's see what I can do to cover your ass and find the vampire and or vampires before I die." I forced the room to stop spinning by sheer force of will. I could walk and see, but beyond that, nothing was certain.

"In an hour? Fucked up like you are?"

"I thought you didn't curse?" I asked him.

"I may have just trashed a machine worth half-a-million dollars," said the nurse. "I doubt the F-bomb once is gonna get me in much trouble."

That earned an honest smile from me. His gloved hands reached under an arm and offered me support to walk. "Where's my partner?"

"This way." A sprite injured in a bar-fight wouldn't be a big secret in a small-town hospital. "But Frank lied to the doc."

"What do you mean?" I stopped him in the hallway, my expression enough to make him stutter.

"He didn't hit her. I was the one who admitted her. The wing was an easy sew, but there wasn't a mark on her head and her eyes were unresponsive."

"Yeah, he drugged her before he pulled the gun on me," I confirmed.

"Darn it, Frank! You just don't know when to keep your bigotry to yourself," muttered the nurse.

"So it's not just werewolves he hates?" I watched Roy's dark eyes carefully. "And can you take off your mask? I'm not like an airborne pathogen or anything."

He yanked it down with one hand. "Sorry. Guess superstitious old wives' tales about how the Devil works still make me want to avoid your germs, even though I know better. But, heck, even the doc won't walk under a ladder, so it's not just me. The South loves living in the past."

"That your way of avoiding my question?" I asked as he led me to a door with a big glass window set into it.

"I don't gossip. But truthfully? Yeah. Frank isn't very enlightened. Let's just say that the man voted for our current president and leave it at that." Roy leaned me up against the wall to open the door with a key. "Do you know what drug he gave her? Labs are out, but they may take a while. Especially with her non-human physiology."

I shrugged. "It was in her tequila and smelled mediciny."

"Stupid, stupid Frank! He better pray that there's no reactivity with the booze," complained the nurse.

"If he's a bigot, why do you care if he gets in trouble or worse?"

Roy stared at me. "This is my town and like it or not, Frank's one of us. He may be a bigot, but I'm not. Even against people who hate me because of my color or my sexual orientation."

"You're gay?" I asked, surprised. Sure, the nurse thing should have sent off warning bells, but he just didn't give off the vibe. And the way he'd avoided looking at my exposed junk suggested he wasn't embarrassed by it, just not interested.

"No. I'm not. And for a straight black-man to be a nurse, you take one hell of a lot of shit. Gosh darn it, now I'm cussing without even thinking about it!" He made a face at me and I grinned.

"Can't win for losing, as my grandfather used to say," I said supportively, then pushed past him to get to Littlewing.

The sprite was in a full-sized bed, her entire body propped in the center of a large pillow. She didn't have an IV drip, but Roy had tried to attach her to a machine for reading vital statistics. As one of the fey, her pulse was either faster or slower than a human's, depending on the circumstances. And as for blood pressure, I'd never asked. But the way she lost her cool easily, I would have guessed it was off the charts.

Roy examined the lines which cycled on the monitor and the accompanying beeps seemed regular. He nodded as if it made sense to him. "She's doing better."

"How the fuck can you tell?" I asked. Just being in her presence made me want to be foul-mouthed.

"I'm not as stupid as you think," he said deadpan.

I approached the bed and ran a fingernail just above the sutures in Littlewing's damaged wing. Roy removed the lead to the machine from my partner. "She's not likely to come around. Best if you leave her here for now."

"Didn't anyone ask Frank what he gave her?" I stared at Roy suspiciously and maybe there was a flicker of amber in my eyes.

"I'm the only one who figured it out and I was kind of busy." His gaze went over my shoulder to the door. I turned to see Sheriff Williams standing in the hallway. "I think someone wants to talk to you."

"Fuck him." I focused on Littlewing. "If I find out what Frank dosed her with, that help?"

"Can't hurt. But if you ask me, he won't tell you. Better to let the Sheriff ask."

I couldn't figure out why Williams hadn't burst in yet. Something held him back. I went to the door and stepped outside. "What are you afraid of? Mine bigger n' yours?"

That pissed him off. "I'm not afraid of nothin'! What I am, however, is royally pissed off that I have two more victims on my hands. We still have a vampire problem here. And you need to put some damned clothes on."

"You were the one who fired me." An exaggeration, but close to the truth. "Roy, you get me my clothes?"

The black nurse glanced at my body with clinical detachment. He was looking for even a hint of scar or unhealed injury. "Just ain't fair. Full of buckshot."

"Better than being naked."

He nodded and disappeared.

"Well, I'm unfiring you." Williams looked past me at Littlewing, his expression not changing.

"Where were they attacked?"

"Different places. George Jackson was attacked behind the bank. Rebeccah Meyers was found on the road leading north to Fayetteville. No connection between the two other than they lived in town. Rebeccah has been dead since first dark. We've cleared the scene, but it's the only paved road that way. We couldn't block it off just for your nose." He slammed the wall. "I thought we got him!?"

"Well, it wasn't my fault your deputy cut off the vampire's head. We could have done a dental match to confirm." I staggered back against a wall as the room spun.

"What's wrong with you?"

"Silver poisoning. Thanks to your good-ol' boy, Frank." Two more victims. If George—that must have been Old Man Jackson—was here in the hospital, that meant the woman hadn't made it. That was good. Only one-in-three chance the sheriff would have to stake her, too. "Is Jackson related to Madeline?"

He shook his head. "I thought they got all the silver out."

"Doesn't stop the poison. I still might die if the serum doesn't get here in time," I explained. He scratched at his chin, trying to read my expression.

"What did you say to Frank?" I could hear doubt in his voice. He wanted to believe I'd started it.

"Nothing. He drugged Littlewing's tequila and shot at me from across the bar."

"Drugged? He said he knocked her out with the butt of his shotgun!" Williams wanted to place the blame for the lie at my feet, but he knew what Frank was. The whole town knew what Frank was and they tolerated him. They could stomach a liar and a bigot, but not a law-abiding werewolf. Yeah, I really loved the South. And all the rest of the fucking human population for their tolerance of their own kind.

"He lied. Roy figured it out though. Said if you get Frank to tell you what he knocked her out with, he might be able to help her faster," I said, calmly, though my face said I'd just as soon punch him as ask for that favor.

"No time. We have to find the vampire that's killing my townspeople!"

"No time? Really? So she can die to save more of the Franks in Resistance? Good luck on that. I guess I'll find Frank myself." I tried to take a step, but the room jerked sideways and I leaned against the wall.

"You stay the fuck away from him! I'm the law in this town and you're here for one reason and one reason only. To kill vampires." His threats grew more confident, probably because I looked weak.

"Actually, you released me from my obligations and told me to get out of town. I get paid either way. I don't have to help you if I don't want to."

"You sack of shit!" He jabbed at me with his finger. In my condition, I let it slide. "You want people to feel sorry for you. To think you aren't a monster. But look at you! Run away and leave people to die."

"Me, Sheriff? Who does that really sound like? Leaving a woman to die when you could save her?"

His gaze slid past me to stare through the glass in the door. Littlewing was a tiny golden figure on the pillow. His brows furrowed into a pained expression of hatred. "Fine, I did try to run you out of town. And I did suggest that her death wasn't as important as my town's welfare. Maybe I'm as big an asshole as you are. I'll talk to Frank. You find me that god-damned vampire. Deal?"

Roy returned with my clothes. I was surprised that the shirt hadn't been cut off of me, but except for the blood and buckshot holes, it was serviceable. My pants had taken few hits and were dark enough to hide some of the blood. The nurse helped me slide on my clothes because I could barely stand on my own.

"I'm already getting paid for what I've done. I don't do anything *pro bono*."

"You want more money?" His expression hardened.

"No, but I want *something*. Well, two things. One, Roy, here, had to use an MRI machine to get all the silver out of me. A single pellet would have guaranteed my death. I want Mrs. Cheswick to repair or replace it. Technically, if I'm still on the case, it counts as medical treatment. If you'd read the friggin' contract."

He stiffened, his hand going to the gun but he glanced at the nurse. Roy was trying to pull the shirt over my head but he paused to glance at the sheriff anxiously. Williams had bad self-control, but at least he didn't draw and point it at me. I'd warned him once. This time I would break all the bones in his gun-hand. "I can't speak for the woman and I'm the one who signed that shit piece of paper. What's the other thing?"

"If I stay and continue to help you, I want your help in return."

Some of his hatred turned to suspicion. "What for?" asked the sheriff.

I nodded at the bed. "It's for Littlewing. Someone's been fucking with the local fey. Promise that you'll help me resolve that matter when we're done. Arrest the mother-fuckers who are doing it and I'll stay till every last blood-sucking undead in this town is staked and ready for the Feds."

"They're just animals."

"Not to her. And even animals have rights. Federal cruelty laws or something will stick. Well?"

He wanted my help more than he hated me. A lot of people would have just to me to fuck off. I didn't like Williams at all, but he put his town above his own pride and ego. "Deal."

"Your word?" I pressed him. Roy knelt down and pulled on my socks. I'd never been dressed by a man before, it didn't feel right or natural. That last time a man had put socks on me, I'd been a child. Before my brother had died. I was grateful when Roy had my shoes on and stepped away from me.

"My word. Now let's stop all the crotch-stroking and take care of business!" He spun on his heel.

"You staying with Littlewing?" I asked. Roy nodded and I followed Williams like the good little werewolf I really, really wasn't. I had to keep one hand to the wall for balance, but I managed. Not that the sheriff would have stopped to help me if I'd fallen.

We reached the front of the hospital and he pointed me into a throng of chaos. Two deputies, along with several people in scrubs were dealing with a bloody mess down one hallway. The double-doors of the room were open and there was a trail of blood leading to them. That must have been Old Man Jackson.

"Call Mrs. Cheswick about the MRI." I could cover the price of the machine, but I hadn't realized just how expensive it was. Half-a-million dollars. Probably considerably less to repair it, if that was possible. But I had taken that buckshot for no reason. "Or I'll sue the town for being shot by everyone's favorite bartender."

"I'll go find Frank." The sheriff marched out of the building.

Frank should have been in the town's lock-up, but I'd remember that, too, if anything happened to Littlewing. If I didn't die of argyria first. I marched toward the vampire victim, wearing only my bloody jeans.

"Get the hell out of my O.R.!" shouted Dr. Walker when she saw me. "Someone get him back to his room." But Walker was also a woman. She eyed the sleek lines of my chest, belly and hips, and hated herself for liking what she saw.

"Sheriff William's orders, ma'am," said a muscular, red-headed deputy with a scar running down one cheek.

He was about the same age as the sheriff, but this guy looked broken. It wasn't just the scar. There was something in his eyes. Like he'd back down if there were a monster in the room. But he didn't act like I was that monster.

"This is my hospital. Not the sheriff's. If I say he's out, he's out!"

I hated medical people so much. They preferred to let people die. Sure, she wanted to try to save the man on the table. There wasn't any real chance of that. If he didn't die from the bite, he'd wake a vampire. But the other potential victims, she didn't care about them until they were wheeled through those doors. I liked her even less than Williams and that was saying something.

"You're wasting your time," I told them. The medical team turned from the grey-haired black man's body to stare at me. Even the doctor paused, her hands pressed firmly over a wound to keep the blood from spilling out.

"He's not dead," she said without any emotion.

"And that's a real shame," I replied. "Where was he found?"

The red-headed deputy took a step away from the dying man. "What are you saying?"

I looked at the deputy, sorry for him and for whatever had scarred him inside and out. But it was a fleeting emotion. He was in law-enforcement and they should have forced him out a long time ago. I was surprised that he wasn't dead. Maybe someone else had died because of him.

"If he survives the bites, he'll turn. Guaranteed. If he dies, he has a thirty-percent chance he'll turn. Zero if you do an immediate embalming. That what you wanted to hear?"

The red-head swallowed hard. I could smell his fear. See the sweat glistening on his brows. Too much of the whites of his eyes showed.

"I thought he had to die to turn?" asked the doctor. "Millie. Millie! Suction on that wound while Barry sews. Wake up, everyone! He's not dying on my watch!" She turned to stare at me, waiting for my reply.

"That's superstitious crap. Most vampires don't drink you to death. It's like any pathogen, they want it to spread. Too many vampires means not enough blood to go around, but they don't want to die out as a species."

"Isn't there a cure?" asked the redhead. The other deputy was too busy holding down the thrashing body parts of Old Man Jackson. He was a skinny black kid, maybe twenty and he kept to business instead of being afraid. Well, that wasn't exactly true. I could smell his fear, but he still did what he needed to do.

"Not if he was the first victim of the night, Red," I replied. Jackson wasn't the first, Rebeccah Meyers had been. But these people were the sort to latch onto any hope, so I didn't offer them any.

"Now you're just making stuff up." The doctor slowed in her movements. Her confidence had faltered at the facts about the fate of her victim. He stood a better chance of surviving if she let him die. If death could be considered surviving.

"Vampires are like poisonous snakes. The stuff that makes them contagious is like a snake's venom. The more bites, the less venom in their poison sacs to pass along. That's why you don't get vampires going around making armies. That's also why killing them quickly is such a high priority. Well, that's not exactly right. There's been a couple of cases of a vampire trying to build an army anyway, and both times were really nasty for everyone involved. Took a long time."

"That massacre over in New York last year?" asked one of the nurses, a pretty thing with mousy brown hair and big, coffee-colored eyes. She had those tiny ears that you wanted to nibble on while your hands explored other soft parts. I had to imagine her lips under the mask.

"Yeah. That was the most recent. And vampires don't wake up knowing stuff. Thought he was going to take over the city, so he bit twenty or thirty people. Didn't work, obviously. Only had enough venom for a couple at most. Problem was, the police couldn't tell which were first and which were later victims and they all had to be put down."

"Why didn't they wait?" asked the red-head, his fear escalating to horror.

"Ask our lovely president. Bachmann ordered a no-tolerance policy on vampire victims. Even if that man survives the bite, the Feds will come and stake him just to be sure." Even in Utah. "Unless someone foots the bill for a very expensive and time consuming blood test. Government won't pay."

"I wouldn't allow it! Sheriff Williams wouldn't allow it!" exclaimed the doctor outraged.

"And how would you stop them, Doc? Would you pick up a gun and shoot law abiding humans to protect a potential monster?"

I was not only weak from the silver poisoning, but wallowing in anger. Rather than trying to convince Walker that she was as much a monster as I was, I should have been hunting the vampire. My time was running out just like the town's.

"Where was he found?" I asked.

"East-side. Edge of town," said the skinny black deputy. His eyes were angry. "Go find the bastard that did this."

"At least one of you has their priorities straight." The room lurched and I hit the wall. "God damn it!"

"You aren't going to make it anywhere in your condition," the doctor barked.

I shrugged, acting tougher than I was. "Without that selenium serum, I don't have much choice."

"Wait, that Lyco-selenium stuff?" asked the skinny deputy.

"Yeah, why?"

"Shit. Why the hell don't you people communicate." He gave the doctor an apologetic look. "Sorry, Ma'am, but we got some of that stuff he needs. Down at the station."

The kid let one of the nurses take his place and he rushed over and grabbed me by the arm. "Boyd, help me get him outside."

"Why?" demanded the red-head, taking a step away.

"Because you do your job, or this time I'm gonna get your freckled ass fired!" He turned to me. "Name's 'Garvy,' but people call me 'Gar.' You wanna help me walk or do I have to carry your heavy carcass out of here?"

"I can walk." I shoved Boyd away when he reluctantly approached me. "And it's 'Mitch.'"

"Nice t' meet'cha, Mitch. Now move it." Garvy helped me with my direction but I used my own legs to hurry out of the hospital. He shuffled me into a patrol car, revved the engine and rushed me down the street.

"The new federal packets came a week or two ago," he explained. "Full of weird-ass shit in the preternatural kit. Stuff like wolfsbane injections and holy water vials."

"Stuff to kill me won't help me," I said through a surge of pain. I didn't elaborate on the uselessness of holy water for nearly everything they might encounter. Only thing it worked on were a couple of psychically-limited demon varieties because their victims believed it would hurt them.

"The kit includes one shot of the Lyco-selenium stuff. And something that cures iron-poisoning in elves." He glanced at me as he raced down the street. "You ever met an elf?"

"Yeah, once." I blinked, confused. "Why the hell would the government provide something to cure elves?"

"Are they like in the books?" he asked, wistfully.

I knew what he pictured. Handsome, regal and noble creatures, with magical powers that healed nature. And that could make you fall in love like with a god. Fantasy, not reality.

"No. They're nasty creatures. Make vampires look like children." Better to crush his hopes than let him wind up dead.

"Oh." He slammed on the brakes and veered around an old lady crossing the street. "Get new glasses, Mrs. Sloakum! Got more pride than brains that woman does."

"You aren't like the rest of the deputies. Even Deputy Jason's more like a puppy dog. You actually got common sense."

"You gotta have something extra to join an all-white sheriff's department with this skinny black slab of muscles." He grinned. "And I'm not just talking about what's in my pants."

"You've got something, alright." I liked Garvy more and more every minute. No way I was gonna leave a vampire alive to kill him or Jason or any of the other people of Resistance. Even if I hadn't made a deal with the sheriff. "What's wrong with the others?"

"You've seen Boyd, met Jason. One messed up, the other nice as sugar. But that's his problem, too. Life just ain't that nice." He skidded to a stop in front of the sheriff's office, stuck in a row of other buildings downtown.

"Why is it that the sheriff's department has a dose of Lyco-selenium but the hospital doesn't?" I shook my head.

"Dunno. Figured they would have a batch, as well. But I'm just a deputy. They don't tell me shit." He hopped out of the patrol car and went around the front to my side.

"You cuss a lot more than your colleagues, Gar," I said as he helped me out of the vehicle and toward the station door.

"I don't cuss!?" he replied startled.

"I've heard you say 'ass' like twenty times since we left the O.R.," I corrected him. "And just now, 'shit' as plain as day."

"That ain't cussing. Daddy didn't raise no disrespectful kids, so we don't cuss. But body-parts and waste-products, that's just science. Daddy was big on science." He grinned. "You get the respect you give in this world. Even if sometimes you gotta wait for it."

"That your daddy's philosophy?" I asked and Garvy nodded with a rueful shrug. "How long you gotta wait?"

The deputy pulled the building door open and shoved me through by my elbow. Then he steered me onto a desk, planting my ass hard on the edge. He grinned again. "Longer than you have to wait while I get that shot."

The room swam, then stabilized and I saw that the place was empty. Five desks, a private office behind glass, but all of the deputies were out. I wondered where the dispatch-console was, I couldn't see a communication system in the room. An unattended police facility. My opinion of Williams dropped again.

"As for waiting?" asked Garvy, coming back with a metal container. "Before Mrs. Bachmann, we had our first black president and my daddy never thought he'd live to see the day. He waited and it happened. Never saw my daddy cry before that day."

"Things swinging the other way with that nut-job in office."

"The people have spoken," intoned Garvy. He watched me from under disapproving eyelids. "And being religious don't make her a nut-job. Her parents did that. I'm religious. My whole family is. And none of them are nut-jobs." He stabbed me without warning, the injection like fire in my veins. "Says it's supposed to hurt, but you're a werewolf, right?"

"God damn it, Garvy! They only give it to werewolves!" I howled and thrashed around on the desk as my muscles convulsed involuntarily. It was all I could do not to accidentally kill the skinny black man.

"My bad," he said. Even in my pain, I could hear the humor in his voice. It wasn't malicious. More like when you spill a drink by playing basketball in the house. No one could be that happy all the time. I couldn't smell drugs on him. I'd figure it out later, after the pain finished. Whoever's desk I'd been sitting on wasn't gonna be happy. It was mostly splinters, only good for kindling now.

"Well that was about as nice as a kick in the head." I stood up and felt the strength begin to course back through my body. "And about as fast."

"Supposed to be instantaneous unless you're about to die," agreed the deputy. Suddenly he lost some of that cheerful confidence he'd displayed so far. "You aren't pissed at me or anything, are you?"

"For what?"

"Stabbing you with the needle? Thinking that it would hurt you less than one of us?" He was finally treating me like a potential danger. Not like a monster. Just a pissed off man.

"No. Rookie mistake. Mine was not carrying my own supply. It won't happen again." I looked around the sheriff's station thinking about all the loose ends. As if something in the room would trigger an epiphany. There were as many loose ends in this case as pieces of that broken desk.

"What's wrong?" Garvy kicked a piece of the shattered desk away from his feet.

"Too many things I can't figure out. The worst is that damned smell of embalming fluid. Neither mortuary reported anything odd. And I can't believe the vampire would have travelled out of the county and then back again, smelling of the stuff."

I grew uncomfortable having Garvy focus on me like I was some supercop. I was a werewolf who did some detective work while tracking the real monsters. Garvy's reaction was different from Jason's excitement. Jason thought it was cool that I was a werewolf. Garvy acted like I was a man who knew things that the sheriff in a Podunk town couldn't know. I hadn't been seen as just a man in so long, well, it felt dishonest.

"Never mind." I clenched and unclenched my fist, reveling in the steadiness of my muscles. "For now, take me to the scene of the latest attack."

"Old Man Jackson," said the skinny deputy with a grunt.

"No. The other one. The one who died on the spot," I corrected. "Rebeccah Something."

"Rebeccah Meyers? Ah, man, seriously?" I saw the hesitation in his intelligent brown eyes.

"What's the problem? I thought a black deputy in the South would want to prove himself? That nurse Roy put himself on the line for the town."

"What? All the brothers gotta agree?" he asked. The grin came back. "It's near the old Rail place. *Nobody* goes out there in the nighttime. Even before the mayor's death."

"Why not?" His reluctance surprised me.

"It's where that first bloodsucker's victims were found years ago. Where they found the bodies. Buried under the floorboards."

"The first—? You mean the one like sixty-three years ago?" I asked and he nodded. "I thought the vampire was found at the mine?"

"That's what the *official* file says." He lowered his voice. It was a secret, even though no one else was around. "Most people don't even know that the bodies were vampire victims. The mine owners said Rail was a serial killer. Law enforcement files don't go that far back, but stories get handed down to deputies to keep us alert. Like one of them urban legends. I wouldn't trust what's written down in the public records any more than town gossip. Rail wasn't no killer unless he was the vampire."

"That sounds like as a good a place to start. Come on, you drive."

"Well, sir, you're the one getting paid big bucks to save our little hole in the wall. I'm just a skinny black man in a white man's job. I'll drive you to your car, but I gotta be honest, Mitch, I'm not interested in being your back-up tonight." Garvy looked guilty, I didn't blame him. He waved at a map on the wall. "I'll point it out on a map and send you on your way. But I already done my good deed by giving you the Lyco-stuff."

"Fair enough." I might have done the same in his place.

It was completely dark outside, the middle of the night. I'd never fought a vampire at night. It was stupid to go without any back-up. But thinking about Garvy and Deputy Jason, I decided that I'd rather go alone than get someone else killed. Especially someone I liked. And I liked Garvy well enough that he'd die for sure.

CHAPTER SIXTEEN

Rebeccah Meyers had died on the side of the road, but the body had already been carted off. Police tape flapped in the breeze, but there was no other direct evidence that the cops had been there. Her car, a seventies model green Ford station-wagon, was on its side, the passenger side window smashed. Bits of glass were strewn inside the car and along the bloody road. Williams had left it for me, to use my nose to search for evidence. But my eyes noted some interesting facts as well.

She had been hauled up and out of that window while still alive. I smelled her residual fear despite the mask of the body fluids which came with the release of death. With it, the stench of decay, and a faint trace of apples. Definitely another vampire attack. But was it the original vampire? A fledgling made by the vampire the deputy killed? Or none-of-the-above? If the pathogen spread, my reputation would suffer and the Feds would swarm the place. Oh. And more people would die.

It didn't matter that very little traffic had come this way since she'd died. The emergency vehicles had obliterated any trail I could have followed. I detected the exhaust of at least three different engines. Williams had been here because I got a whiff of his cologne and Deputy Jason's *Irish Spring*.

If they had parked further away, I might have been able to follow the vampire's scent. Except I already knew where it led. To where Old Man Jackson had then been attacked, closer to town. Jackson had a better chance at surviving than I'd thought if he was the second victim of the night. But that assumed one vampire and a normal infection rate. This thing had a double row of teeth. Presumably any new vampires it made would as well. All bets were off. This new breed of vampire might carry more of the virus in its fangs than the old kind.

I listened and surveyed the countryside. A dark night. Country dark. No streetlights and just that sliver of a moon. The stars were especially bright and I took a minute to stare up at the sky without the usual angst about being a werewolf. Then, in my mind, Littlewing's memory nagged at me to get back to work.

I sighed and focused on the facts. Two victims tonight after they'd killed the janitor in the county records. The night before, only the mayor as far as we knew. A few nights earlier, the suit. The number of kills was escalating. Vampires had to drink every night. So where were the victims from before the mayor? And why so many extra kills tonight?

The Feds would have assumed extra vampires. My gut didn't agree. And something else bugged me. Why hadn't the original vampire fled this area? It had been staked and imprisoned in the mine for years. Most of the newly escaped undead would have left to find a new, safer territory after killing the suit. Why stay here? If I could uncover the vampire's connection to Resistance, I'd have a better chance of finding it.

I ruled out revenge. The victims were unrelated classes of citizens. I doubted that any of the Jacksons had been treated better than servants back in the fifties. Maybe one of them had been a worker in the mine, but would the vampire's revenge be that broad reaching? And Meyers hadn't even been born. My gut said it was something else. The pattern just didn't sit right for vengeance.

I glanced at the map, running my fingers over the creases to flatten it out. Garvy had used a thick felt marker to draw a line on the map leading to this place. He had also circled several times the Rail place where the first vampire's victims had been found. It was close. I'd have to ask the sheriff why this information was only passed along by word of mouth. I'd been so busy being a jerk I hadn't done my job as well as I should have.

I left my car parked on the side of the road a few yards from the police tape and hoofed it. If there were vampires somewhere on the property, I'd stand a better chance of finding them if they didn't hear me coming. I'd have no place to stash my guns or my clothes if I shifted into full wolf-form and I definitely wasn't in the mood to go hunting completely naked. So I ran as a human, listening and sniffing the cool, country air.

Cypress and eucalyptus and a slew of other plants helped wipe out the smell of death. But the overly-ripe scent of apples faded the moment I left the dead woman's car. If the vampire had returned to its old haunt, it hadn't come this way. But Rebeccah Meyers had been taken too close to the Rail homestead for coincidence. I kept moving.

It was frustrating, but I wasn't making the connection between the mine, the Rail place, and that occasional whiff of embalming fluid. I hoped I'd find my answers on the other side of these woods. A few more bodies and the Feds would decide it was time to take over. I wanted to be the one to find the bloodsucker. Otherwise it was just bad for business.

CHAPTER SEVENTEEN

Racial slurs and sexual graffiti marred the once pristine ranch-house. I smelled urine and years of fear, but surprisingly, no sex. People were drawn to have sex in places where violence had occurred. As if the two were inextricably linked. Here, fear had led only to minor vandalism. I could see in the dark with my lycanthropic vision as if it were new dawn.

I turned at every sound, breathing the air. I tasted it with a heightened alertness for that elusive, overripe apple-scent. It was stupid to be out at night, hunting a vampire without Littlewing at my side. Especially in an area that I hadn't checked-out thoroughly in the daytime. But if the Lyco-selenium had done its thing, I was as strong as a vampire. And nearly as a fast. Time was running out.

A quick survey of the terrain and I saw a cluster of long-neglected hickory trees that suggested the family plot was directly behind the house, a few hundred yards away. Close enough to be sentimental, far enough to avoid giving the former occupants the heebie-jeebies. I didn't expect to find anything useful there, because vampires weren't any more comfortable in cemeteries than the living. It was like inviting the ground to swallow you up forever. But a family mausoleum might paint a different picture.

The moon had moved below the horizon, which wasn't great for me. Even during a crescent moon, a little pulse of those silvery rays could boost my strength. And moonlight weakened a vampire because it was reflected sunlight. On a full moon, with no clouds in the sky and no lingering effects of argyria, I'd lay my money on a werewolf over a vampire. Tonight, well, I wasn't feeling quite so optimistic.

I walked quietly around the wreck of the house. I glanced up into the sky and then over my shoulder and then finally into the shadows I passed. I smelled rabbit and squirrel and the musky scent of skunk which suggested to me that this place rarely had visitors of the human kind. But even the animal smells were elusive. Nothing nested inside the ruined house. That was odd.

And no blood. Not human anyway. I'd wasted time. Vampires didn't hide in graves and this place didn't look like it had a secret basement or tunnels for a bloodsucker to lay low in. Still, I didn't make those kinds of assumptions. That skeptical nature had kept me alive so far. I would go inside the house and make sure that nothing was buried beneath the baseboards. Even though my nose told me it was free of recent death.

I thought about the chain of events again. Rebeccah's attack along the road and those bodies sixty-three years ago were the only two connections to this place. Was that original vampire a Rail? Or had he just chosen the house because it felt safe? Most importantly, what did that have to do with the present killings or the mine? Too many questions. No answers.

As the silky Alabama breeze ruffled my hair and carried the fragrance of eucalyptus and grass and a hundred other plants I knew by scent if not by name, I grew distinctly uncomfortable. Something was nearby. Watching.

"So you're the werewolf." It was a man's voice, youthful and curious.

I dropped into a crouch, spinning toward the house. My gun was in my hand without a second thought. A figure stood less than thirty feet away. My nose told me nothing about him, which made me even more cautious than I'd been a moment before. I could smell the leather of his knee-high boots and black, biker jacket. Even the worn cotton fibers of his denim pants and the polished silver of his belt buckle had a scent. But as far as my nose was concerned, the man didn't exist.

His sculpted features were masculine, but groomed. Graceful and muscular, like me. Like he relied on his appearance in life. He could have been an actor or newscaster. Maybe an athletic model. His skin was a soft brown, not tanned. Natural coloring. Because of the high cheeks, straight nose and the nearly black hair, I guessed Native American mixed with Caucasian features. It made his age hard to guess, but younger than me.

He had no body fat. Better-than-model perfect. Werewolf perfect. But I couldn't smell lycanthropy on him. His wide eyes were so dark that the irises blended in with the pupils. He didn't have a blemish or scar anywhere I could see. I'd never met a human without some kind of imperfections. Definitely not a werewolf. And *not* human.

"What are you?" I demanded, standing slowly. I glanced around to be sure I wasn't being ambushed.

"What? Can't you tell?" His dark eyes grew angry and mockingly playful all at once.

I studied him for weapons. No knives or guns ruined the outline of his skin-tight clothes. He didn't stand like someone who relied on external tools. He *was* the weapon.

"Not a vamp." No subtle apple-perfume of the undead. His lack of sweat told me nothing about his sex or health. It was like he didn't exist except for the clothes on his back.

"You the same hunter that took out the dryads below Seattle?" he asked.

That case had been misreported by the Feds, the real details internal. Washington law enforcement knew. A reporter might have uncovered the story. But to track me here afterwards?

I narrowed my gaze at him. "Yeah, that was me. What do you know about it?"

Dryads were nasty creatures. Far worse than elves. Like succubae that couldn't leave their trees for very long, which was their *only* saving grace. It limited the area of killing. There had been an infestation in a forest near Arlington, Washington, a town considerably larger than Resistance. Five dryads had sexually seduced, then mind-fucked several of the high-profile residents to make the area their own little harvest-garden. I'd been called in by the local law enforcement agency after they'd lost half their force.

Dryads were every straight man's version of an ideal woman. Full figured, smooth skin, long lashes, soft to the touch but tough enough to handle the roughest sex. Strong if they were in contact with their tree. Less the farther away they travelled. They'd die if they strayed too far or were gone too long. But they weren't completely human-looking. They had skin in shades of blues and browns not found among real women. And the texture of their dark hair was often interwoven with small leaves. Their nails tough as bark, pointed and deadly. And during the day, some part of them had to physically merge with their tree, sharing nutrients to stay alive.

None of that made them dangerous. The danger was in how they affected the mind. They gave off pheromones that made you think of nothing but pleasing them. Touching them. Fucking them. Even while they were driving a clawed hand through your heart or took your life's savings. Or both. That was the danger.

It was hard to kill something you were making love to, but I'd managed thanks to Littlewing. It had been our first case together. I'd lost too many men in the early days of Werewolf Incorporated. Human men. So I'd worked alone for several months, thinking it would save me money and lives. But even a werewolf couldn't do everything in a detective agency. Well, that's what I called myself at first. And it was damned lucky for me I hadn't given in to stubbornness and I'd hired the sprite. Sprites were immune to most bespelling magics, unlike a certain werewolf.

If she hadn't saved my ass by breaking their spell long enough for me to act, well, I owed her. If she died because of Frank, he might wind up dead himself. It would look like an accident. It wouldn't be.

"How'd you resist their charms?" The man's tone was curious but I still got that hostile vibe. I made sure that my .45 was pointing directly at his chest. Neither of us moved, unnaturally still.

"You an elf?" I wondered if I'd finally pissed off one of the most dangerous creatures that made it in our world through the holes in the universe. I wasn't going to mention my partner to him. Let him think I'd done it all on my own.

He didn't look like an elf. But that didn't mean anything. I had told Garvy the truth about meeting an elf before. Only, the creature had been locked in cold iron with a leather face mask which had covered his eyes so that he couldn't use certain magics. Elves could look like anyone if they were glamoured. I couldn't remember what the thing had smelled like. I'd been too overwhelmed by the fear given off by all the humans holding it captive. But it had had a smell.

He laughed, surprised by my question. It was a masculine, youthful sound. Full of a strange combination of emotions. Like he couldn't make up his mind what he felt. Made me think of psychotic, multiple personalities. Not that all multiple personalities were psychotic.

"Not an elf, then," I grumbled. "What do you want?"

He stopped laughing and his eyes hardened. "I was curious to see how you'd do against a vampire. But so far, you've been running around with your tail between your legs." The man picked at the wooden fence as he balanced effortlessly on the top rail and glanced at my body. "Speaking of tails, what pack do you belong to?"

My finger twitched on the trigger but I had better control than that. If he was asking about my affiliation with a werewolf pack, this might be a territorial challenge. Couldn't use a gun if that was the case, but didn't have time for it either. I avoided other werewolves for a reason. Too many rules and most of them about fighting. If I shot him over territory, it wouldn't be just his pack that came after me. No right to one-on-one combat, either. Or claim to self-defense.

I sniffed him again, but still only got his clothes. He couldn't be a lycanthrope, could he? All the ones I'd met during my rehabilitation after the bite had smelled like healthy, musky humans. Cleaner than ordinary humans and more alive. Pack dominants always counseled new werewolves, trying to get them to join their groups. Most werewolves, like most humans, wanted that social interaction.

Not me. Felt too much like the military. An overt ranking of authority and everyone having to obey whoever was above them. I'd seen enough of that with my father.

Maybe he was some other kind of lycanthrope. Werecats were the second most common form of lycanthropy. What did werecats smell like? Never met one face to face, but if they were as nasty as regular cats, I'd have known what he was. I was pretty sure all lycanthropes smelled of their animal. So he was something else.

"Why do you care?" I asked, growing impatient.

If I couldn't smell him, how many others like him might there be around the abandoned ranch? Was he a different type of undead? Vampires were hard enough to detect. So it was possible.

In other circumstances I'd kick myself for running off without Littlewing. Especially at night. But her present condition had given me no choice. I was on my own. And if the vampire was nearby watching, he could take advantage of my distracted state to attack. In fact, this mysterious stranger might be a tool for the vampire. I heightened my peripheral concentration and began to walk slowly past the man, toward the cemetery. The shadowy old ranch had gotten much, much creepier.

I'd come to depend on Littlewing for companionship, not just her ability to fight. Smell wasn't helping me this time. Maybe her fey senses could have told me something my nose couldn't. I know. Any excuse to wish she was with me, unharmed. Then her voice again in my head. *Keep your fucking mind on the job.*

"Don't rush off," complained the scentless man. He slipped off the fence with a graceful motion, nearly human. There was nothing vampiric or even lycanthropic about it. His balance on the post would have given a gymnast pause. His muscles didn't seem bothered at all. Smell or not, I would have known if he was human. He wasn't.

"I've got a job to do," I said.

When I didn't know who or what I was confronting, it was best to leave the unknown alone. A potential adversary might get bored and leave me alone. If not, the law would be on my side.

"Did you ever wonder how the dryads got to Washington?"

I froze. He had my attention.

"You know something about that?" He only stared. Waiting. Reluctantly, I answered his question. "I wondered. But it wasn't my job. The Feds handle that sort of thing."

"But you could kill them. Without knowing anything about them!"

His expression grew heated. He had a personal connection to the dryads or a fetish for the fey. And I had killed them. That still didn't explain how he found me half the country away from Washington or California.

"They were monsters. Killing people." I looked around but it was still just us.

"What do you care about *people*? You aren't human."

"We have that in common, do we?" I didn't expect a reply. "They tried to kill me. Almost succeeded."

He smiled, his eyes dangerous. "Only almost. I'd like to know how you managed that."

"Don't you know?" Still not about to tell him about Littlewing. Definitely not.

"I know their thorns aren't just decoration."

Thorns? I didn't have any idea what he was talking about. He seemed smug, like it mattered. But he could have just been baiting me. Distracting me. I'd ask Agent Hancock about it later. He was my contact with the FBI. Not my area. "Already wasted enough time."

I started to turn my back on him. Something about his expression gave me pause.

"I was planning on just watching. But you aren't at all what I was expecting." It reminded me of the sheriff's disappointment and I grew annoyed. He grinned at my reaction and cocked his head to one side. "How about we see what you're made of?"

I had to drop the gun or shoot him because he sprinted toward me without warning. And he was fast. When he was close to me, he threw himself at my hips and I had to make the choice immediately. Since I didn't know what or who he was, I opted not to kill him. I wasn't licensed to kill bystanders and my top priority was to catch the vampire alive. Staked, but not dust.

I still didn't think he was the vampire. But it was possible. If the vampire had a genetic mutation which allowed for double rows of teeth, it might not give off a smell either. Wouldn't explain how he knew about the dryads. Unless he'd fed on someone who was familiar with the case. My gut said he wasn't related to my vampire hunt. I had my own personal non-human stalker.

I dropped my gun onto the ground and reached around his chest as he tackled me. His shoulder dug into that region between my groin and my bellybutton as he carried me backwards fast and hard. He was stronger than I'd been expecting. His body firm with dense muscles. But I used my legs underneath him as I fell to kick upward, yanking hard with my arms at his chest to pull him away from me and threw him backwards over my head.

Or rather, that's what I *expected* to happen. But his arms were like steel grips. They stayed locked around my hips and I flipped us both up and over so that I crashed down onto my neck painfully hard, his weight driving the impact home.

I twisted and drove my knee up into his face. That, thankfully, broke his grip. Then I rolled and slipped to my feet, still in a crouch. He wiped his mouth, glancing down at his hand and smiled, angrily. There was no blood.

"Not bad," he said, no sarcasm. Another mood swing. It made him more dangerous, not less. "I'm surprised you didn't shoot."

"You *want* to die?" I held his gaze.

"It won't be at your hand." He grinned and ran at me again.

This time I leapt upwards and with one hand on the top of his head I pivoted over him. Unlike with the sheriff at Mrs. Cheswick's mansion, I did land on his back, hoping to break a few vertebrae. I felt the way his muscles resisted my blow, his whole body slamming downward onto the ground, no bones crunching. Unexpected and interesting. I was getting a picture of my adversary. He was strong as shit, and far tougher than a human. But I was faster.

I grabbed the back of his hair before he could stand and yanked his head toward me, my foot still on the small of his back. He arched backwards and I slammed my other fist into his lower back several times, aiming for the kidney. I didn't hold back. No need, considering his strength. He grunted but rolled sideways, forcing my foot off of him. He grabbed my arm on the next blow and yanked me toward him instead.

In the moment that I was off balance, he grabbed my head with his hands and pulled me off my feet and threw me into the air. I slammed against a cluster of branches in a tree before I could right myself. Several of its limbs cracked from the weight of me, but I was tangled in their broken embrace. It had hurt. He was stronger than me, but I managed not to cuss out loud.

"That's enough for now, I think." He was breathing hard, but no sweat on that tan face. His open-mouthed smile revealed ordinary white teeth. No fangs, single or double rows.

I elbowed free a branch as big as my thigh and as it fell to the ground, I was able to disentangle myself from the rest. I landed lightly on the compact soil facing the other man. Only, I pivoted twice, thinking that he must have slipped behind me. Gone.

I surveyed the overgrown yard and once more carefully checked the shadows for hidden shapes. He'd managed to disappear just as quietly as he had appeared. Angrily, I kicked the branch at my feet and it flew several yards, spinning in the air to come crashing down on part of the house.

"Next time, shoot first, ask questions later." I spoke to myself, but I hoped that if he could hear me, he'd take it for the warning that it was.

I searched the ground until I found my Glock. I relied mostly on smell and touch, because my eyes were scanning the yard for another attack. I shoved the gun angrily back into the holster, but didn't remove my hand from it. He had disappeared, but he might be back. This case was beginning to get more complicated and that didn't make me happy at all. I didn't get paid extra for complicated.

CHAPTER EIGHTEEN

I took a few minutes to catch my breath and listen with my preternatural hearing. No heartbeats, no footsteps in the woods. Only the sound of trees creaking in the breeze. Branches snapping from their own weight and falling lightly on the ground. Birds ruffled their feathers in nests, hidden in the trees after being disturbed by our brief battle. He was gone or a ghost. I didn't believe in ghosts, but there was something different about this place. Or maybe I was letting the place's history unsettle me. I was a tough werewolf, but my psyche was still human. I could experience horror. I had, several times. Not just the dream.

"Get a grip, Mitch." I moved toward the cemetery.

The intruder had interrupted me as I was going there. Was I onto something? When I reached the small, foot-high fence of decorative metal rods, there was nothing but headstones lost in an overgrowth of fragrant weeds. Well, not quite nothing. I walked around the private cemetery and could see that someone had recently pressed down the overgrown plants to look at the markers. Seeing if a particular family member was dead? Had the vampire wanted vengeance on the Rails for some reason? I wasn't finding answers, just questions. And I couldn't help myself. My encounter with the scentless stranger still distracted me.

I read the dates on the gravestones. All of them dead before the original vampire attack except for one. William Rail. He had died some years after. No indication why. Someone had cared enough to make sure he wound up in the family plot, but hadn't bothered to inscribe any personal sentiment.

I needed to hear my own voice again. "But no mausoleum."

Something moved through the tall grass at my words and I crouched. I balanced with one hand on the ground as I searched for the source with my eyes as much as ears or nose. It was only a mouse. The scurrying rodent worked its way through the vegetation in pursuit of food or sex at the far edge of the cemetery. I could smell and hear something that small, but my human-like visitor had been scentless and silent. For the first time since becoming a lycanthrope, I couldn't trust my senses. I was glad that Littlewing wasn't around to see me acting this way. She'd have never let me live it down.

I left the cemetery and moved back to the house. The door was nailed shut, but one of the glassless windows had been climbed through by vandals. They'd been kids from the size of the opening. Frustrated, I kicked the door inward, no longer concerned with stealth. I expected the old wood to splinter, but it was strong and thick. They didn't make doors like that these days. It ripped off the frame and skidded into the depths of the house.

Dust billowed up and there was mold and mildew mingled with it. Those were the first smells I expected to find in a long abandoned house. Finally something was what it should have been.

I covered my mouth, hoping the mold wouldn't cost me my nose. The urine stench was strong. Whoever had broken into the place over the years had made a game of peeing. But the urine was weeks old. It wouldn't mask the absent stench of dead, rotting flesh. But it did try to hide something.

I closed my eyes after a quick glance behind me, just to be sure I was still alone, and took a deep, slow breath. I filtered past the overlapping fragrances of decay. Past the rotting wood where the urine had eaten away at it. But the unfamiliar scent was more elusive than the smell of a vampire.

My phone rang and I flinched, slamming my back against a wall, a gun instantly in my hand. "What?"

"Where are you?" It was Sheriff Williams.

"The old Rail place."

"Find anything?" He sounded anxious. "I don't want another night of this, Greyson. People are scared and they think I screwed up letting you come into town. Adding to the monsters."

"Nothing worth mentioning." My heart still raced from the phone. I concentrated on the shadows in case my distraction had made me miss something or someone in the house. Williams wanted to blame me, but they'd done nothing but hamper my investigation. If even a single crime scene had been undisturbed, I'd have had a chance to track the vampire.

"Frank told me what he dosed her with. Doc Walker said your little pet would be fine by morning. Which is in a couple of hours."

"She's a person. Not a pet." I was looking for a fight to calm my nerves, but he was being an ass intentionally.

"Gar—Deputy Coleman. You met him. He found something we missed."

I hated when people baited a sentence. Made you ask. "Well, what the hell is it?"

"Crematorium. Out at the west-side of the county. So old that even I forgot about it. It's registered as active, but mostly used for disposing of animal carcasses. I doubt they have embalming stuff."

"You'll verify that, right?" I put sarcasm in my voice.

He let out an exhalation of anger before he spoke, calmly. "It's almost daylight. You can go alone if you want. I'm going to bed for a few hours. Hold on." The sheriff put his hand over the phone mouthpiece, but I could hear Garvy's voice in the background. When he came back on, Williams sounded actually happy. "Looks like I get to sleep in. Deputy Coleman wants to escort you to the Summerlin Crematorium, personally. But I want my men to be alert. Too tired, they'll be worthless if we get another attack tomorrow night. He'll pick you up at Miss Conklin's place at eight in the morning."

I looked at my watch. It was almost five. "Fine, I could use a couple hours sleep myself."

I hung up and walked carefully along the foundation beams. When they'd dug up the floor to find those bodies all those years ago, they hadn't replaced the lumber. I knelt at the largest opening and stuck my face down close to the soil. Nothing grew there and I knew why. They had poured lye or some other killing agent where the bodies had been. It had been done years ago. I almost missed it with the overlaid urine and that musky, pungent smell.

I smiled. Deputy Jason hadn't been that far off. A werewolf's nose, if trained properly, was like a chemistry lab. There just wasn't anyone to train my nose, so I'd had to learn it all myself. I'd spent a year in botanical gardens, at zoos, and in the local university lab taking a chemistry course so that I could memorize as many smells as possible. I couldn't remember them all, but I'd catalogued a pretty serious collection in my new werewolf brain.

The vampire wouldn't have come back here. The smell of pee alone was enough to make me sick of the place. But it felt uninviting. Most places where vampires chose to hide had some feeling of the homey. Maybe not after killing and depositing bodies. But their lairs usually started out that way. Safe if not homey. This place was neither.

I spent another ten minutes walking the entire house and except for a feeling of unpleasantness, I found nothing to suggest that a vampire had ever been here. Another night gone. Another bust. But I'd have Littlewing back the next day and the crematorium sounded like a promising lead.

I raced back to the car, darting through trees and bushes, wishing I could run naked under the stars in wolf-form. Sleep was my priority now. I reached the wreckage of Rebeccah Meyer's car and my legs had that feel-good twinge of being stretched after sitting too long. I hadn't run in a few days and even a short sprint cleared my head a bit.

My smile died, when I saw the words 'see you soon' scraped in the paint on the side of my car. My attacker had a personal grudge. One problem at a time.

I drove home breaking the speed limit, but thwarting the law didn't take my mind off of the ruined paint job. Nor the sun edging up over the horizon. This was going to be a bad day. I felt it in my bones.

CHAPTER NINETEEN

Deputy Coleman pulled up to Ruth Conklin's B&B and honked twice. I peered out of the bedroom window, annoyed. He was leaning on the horn like he was a guy from Los Angeles instead of the genteel South.

I trotted down to the vehicle, smelling the remnants of a breakfast I'd missed by two hours. Six a.m. or go hungry. Conklin's immutable rule. Not exactly hospitable, but staying up the extra thirty or forty minutes would have guaranteed one groggy werewolf. On two hours, I could function. And I hadn't been haunted by the dream, so it had been a sound sleep.

My stomach growled and I stuck my head in the kitchen. There was nothing sitting out waiting for me. My nose had told me that but I was hoping it had lied. There was no sign of Ruth, so I couldn't even ask for something cold. Not eating didn't just make me grumpy. My body needed food the way a vampire needed blood. I'd have to hope that despite the brief argyria, my metabolism would hold up until I could find something elsewhere.

Garvy wasn't alone in the Ford king-cab pick-up. Littlewing sat on the dash, laughing in that way she did when she wanted her breasts to jiggle just so. The deputy's uniform was pressed, his badge polished. He was showing more pride than I'd noticed the day before. And he flirted openly with the sprite. I scowled until I smelled marinated grilled meat.

"That wouldn't be for me would it?" I asked as I slid into the truck.

"As a matter-of-fact." He handed me a thick fold of aluminum foil. "Miss Conklin said you'd missed breakfast. Saw her in town when I was picking up your partner here."

"Thanks. Saves us time." I looked at Littlewing. Her color was off. And there were spots of blood on her clothes. But she looked happy. She had her gun in its holster, extra rounds on the other hip. Clearly ready to go. "You okay?"

"Peachy. You?"

Neither of us were big on mushy. She knew how I felt. I knew how she felt. Like a couple of guys, nothing else to say.

I grunted, biting into a tri-tip sandwich and wondering if food could be better than sex at that moment. Since I'd become a werewolf, I ate a lot. But I didn't get laid much. I chewed hard, pretending it was something else.

Garvy pushed in the parking brake and headed out of the drive. "Straight to the crematorium?"

"Yep." I was like a beast snuffling through a mouthful of food. Gone too fast. I rarely forgot that I needed to eat, but Resistance County had done nothing but make me forget the simple things.

"So, Mitch." Garvy glanced at me out of the corner of his eyes. "Can I ask you some questions?"

"About the case?" I licked the sauce off my fingers, looking around the interior for any other unclaimed food.

"About being a werewolf."

I sighed, my appetite gone. Littlewing grinned wickedly at me. "He's very enthusiastic."

"I noticed." I wiped my mouth on the back of my hand, across my tattoo instead of using the handful of napkins on the seat between us. "Fine. Shoot."

WEREWOLF INCORPORATED: THE FAMILY PLOT | **153**

"Bang." He laughed but when I scowled, he sobered up. "Does it hurt when you change? Like in them movies?"

I made myself comfortable on the bench-seat, pleased to have Littlewing settle onto my shoulder. "Werewolf 101. No, it's like flexing muscles. The movies do it for effect. Making it look messy or unnatural. That stretch of a muscle feels good, right? Releases endorphins. Pleasant even. That's what changing is like. It feels almost the same as that."

"Can you control yourself when you change? I mean, I read most werewolves wind up in prison for life. Can't keep from killing even their families. That happen to you?" The question took the edge off my good mood. I flashed to the dream, wondering what the changes in the plot had meant.

"No. I'm still a man inside. Any killing urges come from dealing with assholes." I turned to stare out the window.

"You mad, Mitch? I didn't mean nothin'." Garvy sounded upset.

"He wasn't yanking your chain, Mitch." Littlewing leaned forward, hanging onto my ear and she kissed me lightly on the cheek. "I'll yank your chain, though. If you want."

I chuckled and faced the thin deputy. "Not your fault. Better to understand lycanthropy in case you're ever in a situation." I winked at Littlewing. "You must be feeling better if you're talking about yanking things."

Garvy got a twinkle in his eyes and looked over at me a couple of times before he asked, "What about, you know. Does *everything* change?"

"What are you, twelve?" I asked, but I couldn't fight my grin. "Yeah, everything changes. Bigger, hairier."

He gripped the steering wheel and kept his eyes on the road, but I could see the smile of curiosity playing at his lips. "You got a werewolf girlfriend? You guys do it, you know, literally doggie-style?"

"Littlewing! You told him to ask that." She folded her arms and ignored me. Confirmation enough. "No, Gar. I don't have a girlfriend of any flavor. Werewolf females are few and far between and almost universally belong to some sort of pack. If they don't, well, it can lead to all sorts of messes for them socially." I remembered being pressured into joining a pack shortly after turning, but Garvy didn't need those details. "Don't get me wrong. If I ever found a single woman like me, I'd be interested. But then I'd have to fight every dominant werewolf we ever met. If you get beat, you lose the female."

"Don't be such a sexist pig, Mitch." Littlewing stomped on my shoulder to make her point. "If a dominant female wants your man, it can work that way, too."

"Fine. I'm a sexist pig." I added, "A sexless sexist pig."

Garvy practically shouted. "Seriously? You don't get laid?"

"Most women are afraid of getting what I got." I stared out the window as the countryside rolled by. "And the ones who have werewolf fetishes, well, they're freaks you wouldn't want to touch. Think Jerry Springer meets stalker chicks. They want the bite, which is not only stupid, it's illegal." Like vampire junkies.

That took me back to the missing suit for only a heartbeat before my mind flashed to the strange scentless man with the dryad interest. I needed to consult with Littlewing about him. Not in front of Garvy. No guarantee my assailant was related to the present case. And better to keep my private life private, even for a nice guy like Garvy. Hell, especially for a nice guy like Garvy.

"Shit! That's awful, Mitch. I can't imagine going a week without sex, much less months." Garvy slapped the steering wheel with one hand for emphasis.

"Yeah, well, I don't need you to pity me. I need your hyper-ass to focus on this case."

"Hey, I am!" He grew excited again. "I'm the one who found out about the Summerlin Crematorium."

"Williams told me." Littlewing yanked on my ear. I wasn't playing nice. Not fair to either of them. "I admit, glad someone in this town is doing their job."

"Another ten minutes till we're there."

"Last chance for dumb-ass questions," I offered in a moment of weakness.

"Do you like being a werewolf? I mean, ignore the sex thing. You like being superstrong and healthy as shit?"

"For all of its upsides, there are more things that I hate about being a werewolf. It's not a game, Gar. It's like having HIV. Worrying about your blood or intimate contacts all the time. Never being seen as just a man, but as a man with a disease. And it's not a sympathetic one like AIDS. Women and men both are scared shitless of me. At least, ones right in their minds." I stared at him but he didn't seem to get the hint. "Why are you so God-damned happy all the time?"

He turned to look at me. His brows furrowed and he tilted his head. "What do you mean, Mitch? I'm just normal."

"Then most people are cranky, messed up assholes." I always figured being a jerk was natural, but maybe the deputy was right. Maybe he was the normal one.

"Broken Record Greyson strikes again!" exclaimed Littlewing, her idea of subtle. "What about you Gar? Do you have a girlfriend?"

He stopped his werewolf questions then, more interested in the sprite's flirting. I stayed quiet, letting their warmth fill a dark hole in my heart.

Garvy's questions had been harmless, but they'd made me lonely. And they'd reminded me of the dream. Like the deputy, Jenny had been happy most of the time. It wasn't fair that she died and I lived. Except, lycanthropy was a curse. Maybe it *was* fair. She would never have survived becoming this.

Some of the dream made sense to me. I still blamed myself for her death. I'd insisted we go camping. Unlike the dream, the werewolf had bitten me first. Then it had tossed my infected body aside before he went for her. He'd torn her body to pieces in an act of sexual/killing rage. I'd been unable to move, watching it all. Seven years and the guilt hadn't died one bit. This most recent version of the dream proved that. But what had the changes meant? I mulled over the question dream-Jenny had asked me, but nothing came to me before we reached our destination.

We arrived at the Summerlin Crematorium around ten. I sat up and focused on the property before us. The crematorium was a large, rundown two-story Victorian. Loose shingles. Peeling paint. There was craftsmanship in the gingerbread details, but no sense of pride in its maintenance. Once upon a time, the whole building had been brightly painted to fight the association with death. Now it was the color of an aged skeleton, with scabby hints of what it had been.

I strode up to the entrance and knocked loudly on the wooden door. Garvy peered in through the closest window, but it was heavily shaded. He shook his head. He couldn't see anything. Then I could hear the footsteps approaching from deeper inside the old building. Garvy stepped back, hand on his gun when the door opened.

The man who answered wasn't young, but he wasn't old, either. With his hunched back I mentally called him 'Igor.' He wore a stained long-john shirt, smelling of his sweat and bits of food from at least a few meals clinging to it. Instead of trousers, he wore overalls held up by fraying suspenders. The Igor metaphor was nailed home because it was a crematorium and the wide smoke-stack resembled a bell-tower.

"May I help you? Viewings are limited to the church." I sniffed deeper. He also smelled of chemicals and corpses, stale sweat and pork-grease.

"We're here on official business." Deputy Garvy slipped into view, startling the man.

"My," said the man. He put his hand to his rounded mouth. "I didn't realize we'd reported the theft yet."

"Theft?" asked Littlewing, hovering above my shoulder. The man jumped back, stumbled over an umbrella stand and collapsed onto the floor.

"He's as edgy as my Aunt Maviss at a séance. Nice going." Garvy chided the sprite. "Let me help you up, sir." The black deputy was stronger than he looked. He practically picked up the short mortician with one hand. "You the owner of this establishment?"

"My brother and I." The man half-hid behind the deputy, peering at Littlewing. "What is that?"

"Sprite. Littlewing's my partner." No long-winded explanation. Daylight was precious. Any more deaths and my reputation would be over. Jackson and Meyers had died after I'd been taken off the case and shot with silver ore. Not my responsibility. Tonight, it would all be on me. "What theft?"

The man shuffled inside. "It was nothing really. We thought perhaps our nephew, Eddie. He likes to dress up sometimes. The follies of youth."

"A dress?" Littlewing stared at me. "You said it was a male."

"The vampire Erin took out was male," countered Garvy. Defending my honor. It almost made me blush. Not really.

"We know there's more than one now." I had to turn sideways to move through the narrow hallway. The man didn't seem to notice the vampire reference. His eyes were glued to Littlewing. "The body belonging to the dress already buried?"

"My, yes! Cremated. After the viewing at the Pentecost church on River Road. That was three or four days ago!" He frowned at me. No one was properly intimidated by a werewolf these days. At least, not with our clothes on. "We don't keep bodies longer than necessary. Miss Carter was burned the very next day."

"Was she definitely dead?" asked Littlewing.

The mortician turned again. "I beg your pardon?" He clutched at Garvy's arm. "Deputy! We are a respectable establishment. We've been here for nearly a hundred years. Our grandparents maintained a flawless record of service."

"No one was implying otherwise." Garvy looked at his notepad. "That would make you Maurice Summerlin? Or are you Clarence?"

"Seriously?" I asked Garvy. The deputy raised his brows. Cruel to give them those names.

"I'm Maurice. Clarence is picking up a body from the Reverend Epson. You know his congregation? Protestant. Near the county line?"

"I've never had the pleasure," grumbled Garvy. "We're Baptist, Mr. Summerlin."

He sighed. "Well, young man, no one is perfect. This way."

"Where are we going, Maurice." I tried to say his name without mocking, but it was hard.

The man trundled when he walked, but he glanced over his shoulder as if I should know better. "I have a picture of the dress, naturally. We get pictures of the deceased for make-up. Though, technically, we aren't an actual mortuary. We touch up the bodies for the family before we dispose of them. They usually like to watch their loved ones given over to the flames." He paused, clutching at his chest as if having a moment of ecstasy. "The young lady was wearing the dress before it went missing. She was so beautiful. If a bit liberal."

"Liberal?" Garvy and I asked in unison. I frowned at him. "Let me handle this, Gar."

"Race before beauty," he said with a wry grin.

"That's not what I meant. We just don't have a lot of time. Mr. Summerlin?" I stared at the mortician. Or would that be 'cremator?' No, 'mortician' sounded better.

"It was a rather short, tightfitting outfit. Not conservative at all. Liberal. Yes, well, here we are." We entered a large room with narrow windows along the top of the exterior wall. It held three metal tables, all of them empty at the moment. Sheets were piled in a canvas bin.

The smell of chemicals was overwhelming. Even Garvy wrinkled his nose.

"This where the dress was taken from?"

"Yes, Mr.—I'm sorry, I didn't catch your name?" Summerlin glanced at me, while his fingers were rummaging through the contents of a roll-top desk.

"I didn't give it."

"He's Mr. Greyson. Hired by the Resistance Township to help in a criminal matter." Garvy was more patient than I was. "The pretty little thing is Littlewing. I'm Deputy Coleman. Mr. Greyson's escort."

Littlewing tittered and Garvy frowned. His eyes were guarded, but not angry.

I shrugged and said, "She likes to make everything about sex."

"Oh." Garvy cocked his head to one side, his grin blossoming when he figured out why she'd laughed. "Gotta stay on my toes with you two."

"Wouldn't hurt, Deputy," I suggested.

Maurice ignored our banter, finding what he sought. "Here it is. Yes, a lovely, lovely girl."

He handed me the photo. Her red dress was practically painted on. I'd seen it before. "Shit."

"Hot for vampire much?" Littlewing peered over my shoulder and flicked my ear.

"How was I to know?"

"Vampire?" Maurice staggered against the desk, spilling papers everywhere. "That's not possible. She's dead."

"She?" asked Garvy, but I let it slide. Obviously he was referring to the girl in the photo. Cremated bodies didn't come back as vampires. No matter how new the variety.

"Oh, nothing. No, really, I have so much to do before Clarence gets back." The man was afraid. And not just of us.

"You're not going anywhere Mr. Summerlin." I grinned as Garvy played tough cop. He gripped the man by the shirt sleeve. "This is a multiple-murder inquiry and you are a material witness. If you have any information on the vamp that was staked sixty-some-odd years ago, it's your civic duty to share it."

"There are worse things than a vampire." I let my eyes turn amber and my fangs grew large. Maurice squeaked and collapsed. Garvy eased Maurice all the way to the cement floor. I was unsure whether to be pleased or annoyed. "Did he just faint?"

"I reckon he did." Garvy studied the man but let him lie. Then he glanced around the room. "Why'd she come here for clothes? The town would have made more sense."

I agreed. "But let's be sure she was here. Too many chemicals for my nose, but I'll try."

Three days had passed since the vampire had taken the dress. I smelled formaldehyde and other embalming fluids I couldn't name. And human death. I circled the gurneys, bent over the canvas bin to take a deep breath. Nothing.

Then I stared at the wall. "She was here."

"You can smell her?" Garvy was impressed.

"No. But that's her. There." I pointed at an old black-and-white picture on the wall. No mistaking that figure or face. My young woman in the red dress under the street-light was our vampire. And the Summerlins knew her.

CHAPTER TWENTY

I went through the entire house twice before Maurice Summerlin woke. He blinked and frowned with confusion. Then saw me and screamed. Garvy helped him into a chair despite his flailing arms.

"Oh, for Christ's sake, Summerlin," muttered Garvy. "He's a werewolf, not a monster."

I stared at Garvy and admired the kid for being true to his principles. He didn't want to be judged for being young, skinny or black. He treated me the same. He didn't need to know that some werewolves were monsters. But when they were, they wound up *dead* monsters. I hoped his interest in lycanthropy stopped short of wanting to be infected with it.

"A werewolf? Why?" stammered Maurice.

"Why?" I shouted and he flinched. I forced myself to calm down. "I'm here to find your great-whatever-she-is! The vampire." I waved at Littlewing who was near the man's fleshy neck. "We don't have a lot of time, so either cooperate or—!"

The sprite shot a burst of sunlight out of her hands against his skin and he yelped in pain. "It stings. Pure sunlight. But it doesn't leave a mark. Not like my gun."

Littlewing's ability to absorb light wasn't the same as absorbing heat. The sting came from the skin's reaction to UV rays in intense bursts. She couldn't light a match with it or start a fire, but her bursts of energy could hurt anything affected by sunlight. Not just vampires. Moonlight, on the other hand, wasn't nearly as useful.

"Stop!" Garvy hadn't known what I planned and looked bent out of shape. "You can't torture the guy."

"President Bachmann says that Mr. George W. was right. Enemies of the state should be tortured if it will save lives. I think Mr. Summerlin here fits that criterion."

"Please! She'll kill me." The short man cowered in his seat, seriously afraid.

"How will she know?" Littlewing let a spark of light pulse between her fingers.

"If you come after her, she'll know it was us." His head pivoted from Garvy to me and then back again. Reminded me of a demented mannequin. "We're the only family she has in these parts."

"Bull," I barked.

"Fine." Maurice sobbed as he spoke. "We're the only people in these parts who know the truth about what happened sixty years ago."

"Sixty-three," corrected Garvy and I frowned at him. He added, "My bad."

"Talk!" I took a step toward the mortician. Maurice pressed himself against the chair, his features pale. Finally! Someone was more afraid of me than a damned vampire.

"She was our father's cousin." Maurice's eyes never left my mouth, even though I'd put away my fangs. "You should wait till Clarence is here. He'll remember what I forget." Inbred much? Or playing dumb?

"Any chance it's written down anyplace?" I looked around the house meaningfully. "In case something happened to the rest of the family?"

"We were afraid to. It damaged our father."

"Mr. Summerlin, please." Garvy leaned over the man, but the deputy's expression wasn't threatening. He was playing good cop now. I'd bet good money that he wasn't acting though. "People are dying."

"Our father was six years younger than Reed. They grew up together. Here, in this house. Something bad happened when daddy was twelve. Reed died. At night, in her bed."

"No one guessed it was a vampire bite?" I asked.

Maurice shook his head. "No one really believed in vampires, Mr. Greyson." He paused and studied the back of my hands. He saw the tattoo. "Or werewolves."

"Ignore that." Littlewing let a little flash of light loose without stinging him. She liked to threaten people. The main reason she'd taken the job with me was citizenship, but the legalized bullying of bad people appealed to her.

"Back then, there were no rules about embalming. Oh, everyone did it. We did it. Most of the time." Guilt flooded his sagging features.

"You tried to save money?"

"Our grandfather did. Reed was family. We were going to cremate her anyway." He stole a glance at Garvy, worrying that he'd confessed to some still arrest-worthy crime. We were only interested in the vampire. The one in the here and now.

"Well, that would have done the trick. But she woke before you could."

He nodded, swallowing hard. "Daddy said they found our grandmother dead. Her throat torn out, blood everywhere. Right here in this room. They knew that Reed had done it."

"Go on," encouraged Garvy.

"A year went by. They never saw her again. But—people began disappearing. Daddy said Grandpa Summerlin knew. Became obsessed with vampires. Back then there was no internet. No computers. Daddy's library's still down in the basement. Weird books, old stuff, anything on the supernatural he could find. Me and Clarence don't go in there. Too many bad memories."

"The vampire who bit Reed. No one saw him or her?" I asked.

"Yeah, but not here. He was caught over in Mississippi. Left a trail of bodies." Maurice looked furtively at Garvy again. "That vampire, the corpses, they led in a direct line through Resistance County. So we were pretty sure it was the same one."

"The Feds didn't come check out Resistance?" Littlewing hovered close to his face suspiciously.

"We didn't report it." Maurice gulped. "Daddy said Grandpa wanted revenge for the death of Gran'. He wanted to keep the mine open and the town running. We had a grocery in town, not just this place. Our life's blood. Ironic really." His eyes glazed over and an unhappy smile played at his lips for a second before he shook off the past. "Plus there was some kind of deal with the owners of the mine. No one wanted it known."

"How'd you find Reed to stake her?"

"Someone was helping her. Hiding her. That's what Daddy said. Reed had a boyfriend. They found her at his place. Daddy was thirteen and Grandpa Summerlin made him watch as they staked her. He said they took her inside the mine and forced a collapse of one of the tunnels afterwards."

"She wasn't human any more, Mr. Summerlin." I glanced at Garvy. "That explains why she came here when they removed the stake. This was home."

"Mr. Greyson, Daddy said she threatened to come back and wipe out the Summerlin line. How do we protect ourselves?" His eyes pleaded with me. One monster to protect him from another monster. I wasn't feeling very sympathetic.

"She didn't kill you when she took the dress."

"No. But we weren't born until years after she was staked. I'm not sure she knew who we were."

"Did she take anything besides the dress?"

"Clarence thought that Eddie had maybe brought one of his friends down here. The desk was a mess, papers everywhere. You understand what I mean? We sanitized everything as best we could."

"Sex on the desk? A dress is stolen, someone rifles through your stuff, and you don't report it because you think a cross-dressing nephew had something to do with it?" He nodded at me frantically. If Maurice had reported the theft, we might have saved some lives.

Garvy stared at the wall to keep from saying anything harsh. His question was civil, but his face was angry. "Is there anything else that might help us find her? Who was the boyfriend?"

"Andrew Rail?" I asked, something clicking into place.

Maurice looked startled. "H—how did you know?"

"The bodies were found under his family's floorboards. If a human was helping them, he'd be the one. I don't suppose he's still alive?"

"Wouldn't know." The mortician rubbed the sweat off his brow, staring wide-eyed at us. He smelled of truth, but he'd soiled himself. It wasn't pretty, so I glanced at Garvy, hoping he'd know and we could get out of this place.

"Sorry, Mitch. I don't know the Rail family."

"Well, call it in! Time is running out." I looked around the room at the narrow windows and Victorian architecture. "Any place here where she might hole up? A large family mausoleum? Underground bunker? Anything like that?"

"Not that I know of." More truth, less fear now that he thought we were getting ready to leave. Most people told me what I wanted to know just to get rid of me. He'd reached that point.

"Littlewing, let's check it out. Gar, get me that information. If Rail's alive, she might have gone for him."

"But he'd be old." The deputy made a face. He was thinking about them having sex. One short drive with Littlewing and she'd already corrupted him.

"Yeah, well vampire bites are funny things. I'll explain later. Wing?" I didn't have to explain what I wanted, the sprite knew.

"On it, Boss."

She zipped out of the crematorium and I followed her. With any luck, we'd find evidence of Reed Summerlin's lair nearby and this case would be closed. Littlewing used her fey senses to detect things that I might miss, while I let my nose scour the garden which ran all around the building. The yard smelled stale, too. Full of old, discarded belongings largely eaten away by the elements. I smelled the gamey sweat of the two men and lingering smoke from the crematorium. And the bits of charcoal left over from the burned bodies.

There was little refuse. If it was burnable, the Summerlins didn't bother filling up trashbags. It blended with the smoke in a sickening combination. I could detect beneath that nastiness a variety of mature floral aromas, but no over-ripe apples.

She hadn't been back since she'd stolen the dress. Not near the house, anyway. I extended my search to the outlying areas. But after a frustrating fifteen minutes of running, I found nothing but farmland and woods surrounding the place.

"Zilch," I told Garvy back at the house.

"Andrew Rail is alive." He tapped the radio at his belt.

"Where?"

"The Resistance County Old Folks Home."

"Right next to where Mayor Cheswick was killed." Maybe the mayor had been a victim of chance and this wasn't about revenge. A hunch, not an assumption.

"You think it was coincidence?" Garvy's thoughts had followed the same lines as mine.

Of the three local deputies, he was the smartest. So why wasn't he the one keeping Sheriff Williams company, instead of Deputy Jason? It was okay for Williams to have sex with a black woman, but not to treat a deputy as equal? Was I reading too much into it?

"Is he still there?"

"They're checking on it now." Garvy stared as Littlewing settled onto my shoulder. He smiled, flirtatiously. "If you were more than eight inches."

"If you were only more than eight inches, too." I heard the smugness in her voice.

"How do you know I ain't?" Garvy adjusted his pants by the belt, grinning. I shoved him gently toward the car. "Where we going?" he complained good-naturedly.

"Back to town. I want to check out this Andrew Rail myself. If she's been there, I'll smell her."

"What about the Summerlins?" Garvy studied the big old Victorian with a frown.

"Leave 'em. If Clarence is anything like Maurice, they aren't worth much in this investigation."

"What if she comes back and kills 'em?" Garvy watched me closely. Trying to see what kind of man I was, underneath the monster.

"Fine. Send a squad car. *Before* dark. I can't waste time babysitting."

He got into the driver's seat and started up his pick-up. Littlewing tugged at my earlobe. "Why didn't she kill 'em when she took the dress? If I was that pissed at the family, I would have."

"He smelled like truth." It was the only answer I had.

"Something's not right, Mitch." She wasn't happy, but she dropped it as I got in the car.

On the drive back to town, Littlewing kept Garvy's keen mind busy with nonstop innuendo, which let me think about that skin-tight red dress. Reed Summerlin didn't look like a killer or a beast. Truth was, as a vampire, she was as much a victim as I was. Except that I didn't go around killing innocent people every night to stay alive.

But I *was* a killer. I had killed. How different were we really?

CHAPTER TWENTY-ONE

The old folk's home was busy with more old people than I would have expected in such a small town. Some watched TV. Some played chess or bingo. And some were tucked away in their rooms. Those in the common rooms turned as we walked by or when they heard our voices. Their eyes hungry were for conversation or companionship. Some were dead but didn't know it. I could smell it on them. Some more like zombies. And the home stank of the incontinent or sickly. This place was creepier than the vampire we were looking for as far as I was concerned. Littlewing sat on my shoulder, eyeing them cautiously, too.

It was just past noon. The day was slipping away and I had to wait on Williams. He didn't trust me to be delicate with the staff. And he'd ordered Garvy to return to the station before the deputy had learned much from the nurses. I could see why some werewolves had lost control. How could you not want to kill to get away from this place? They were all like human vampires needing to feed with a desperation. It was a loneliness worse than my own and I felt ashamed for feeling sorry for myself.

When the sheriff arrived, he stormed in, face flush with urgency. He knew time was running out. He skipped the pleasantries and walked past me, directly to the head nurse. I followed him, grateful to get away from the staring eyes of the old folks.

Garvy had already spoken with the woman, but Williams didn't trust anyone. Or maybe it was because Garvy was black. That question about his bigotry rose in my head again.

"What room?" demanded the sheriff. He didn't seem any more tactful than I would have been. I thought he was being downright pissy about it.

The head nurse was Veronica Stern, and the name fit her. She was big-boned, curly haired and unhappy. Her life hadn't been any better than her patients' and she still had years to go. "He's not here."

Sheriff Williams clutched at his gun. "When was the last time you saw Rail"

"I told your deputy, Louis. Don't bite my head off! I don't know."

"Don't you feed them regularly?" I asked, keeping the sheriff from sticking his foot in deeper.

She stared at me, wringing her hands unconsciously. "The family hired a private nurse. Felt bad for neglecting him all these years."

"When?" I glanced at the sheriff and he nodded. He understood why I'd asked that.

"Oh, a couple of days ago. Why?"

"What'd she look like, Ronnie?" The sheriff pulled out his pad and a pen.

"Not 'she,' Louis. He was about sixty I'd guess. Short. Chunky. Bald patch on top and funny little glasses."

"Did he have a name?" Williams seemed less angry than he'd been a moment ago, so I let him ask questions. Maybe Veronica would talk more openly if a werewolf wasn't around. I gave a subtle cue to Littlewing. She flitted into the air, my eyes and ears while I sneaked off to Andrew Rail's room.

I found it easily, they didn't just use numbers. There were names on nicely engraved placards on the doors. It wasn't locked, either. I slipped inside and left the door open me. But even so, it was dark inside his room. Too dark.

I pulled open the drapes. Someone had painted the window, black and thick. No sunlight came in to illuminate the single, narrow bed or the antique dresser against one wall. It was beyond Spartan, but from what the nurse had said, Rail was pretty much bedridden and suffering from dementia.

I took slow, careful breaths. The overly ripe scent of apples was stronger than I would have expected from a night visitor. Strong enough that maybe she had been sleeping here. Sleeping with him. But she wasn't here now. And no scent of embalming chemicals. Only her elusive undead fragrance.

"You can't be in here." An elderly woman on a walker stood in the open doorway. She frowned sternly at me. She was incredibly short, enhanced by a curved neck and spine. Half of her pale, withered face didn't move as much as the other. Stroke victim. The top of her thinning head only went up to my waist, but she looked up at me defiantly.

"I'm with the police, Ma'am." I was more polite than I'd been to anyone in years. She was old enough to be my great-grandmother. I couldn't help myself. "I promise not to mess with Mr. Rail's stuff."

"Andy don't got much. Why are you in here?" She clacked her walker once, hard enough to mean business. I fought a grin.

"Mr. Rail has gone missing. I want to help find him. That's all."

She snorted. "Missing. He's off with that granddaughter of his."

"How do you know this?"

"Insomnia. I watched 'em walk out the front door when it got dark last night." She stamped her walker again at me as if I had done something wrong. "'Bout time someone in his family took an interest. Not that I knew he had a family, mind you. Thought they was all dead and gone." She cleared her throat, an unpleasant, almost hideous sound. Then she spat phlegm into a cloth handkerchief wrapped tightly in one hand. "She's been here to visit every night since she got into town. He seemed to be perking up having her around so much. More company than a lot of these old geezers get. Should have packed more than one dress, though." She started to turn away, then craned her head painfully back to me. "Don't take his stuff."

"No, Ma'am."

Snorting again, the woman left. Clack. Shuffle. And clack of the walker again. There was no mistaking her slow, methodic progress down the hallway.

I returned to the sheriff and Littlewing. Veronica had returned to her duties and they were waiting for me with the same impatience I'd felt earlier. "She's got him. Took him last night."

"How the—? Never mind. Why?" demanded the sheriff.

"Love." Littlewing's voice was loud in my ear and she settled into her traditional place on my shoulder. "He was a young man when she was staked. They were in love. She came back for him."

"Sixty-three years later when he's a shriveled up old coot." Williams looked at me. He wanted to know more.

"The virus which creates a vampire will make an older person younger. But not a younger person older. Eventually, he'll become her age. Her age at being bitten." He needed to understand what would happen to Rail over time. "We need to figure out where they went."

"You checked out his family place last night. You sure they weren't there?" Williams looked skeptical.

"Yes, Sheriff. I'm sure. The Rail Place was too foul for a vampire to hide willingly." I left out the part about my encounter with the scentless man.

"Where else would they go?" His anger spilled out again. He was picturing more deaths, I could see it on his face.

"We'd waste too much time covering all the possible hiding places. If she waited around for him, they'd have no reason to stay."

"Mitch, you're forgetting the private nurse!" Littlewing zipped into the air and punched the tip of my nose to get my attention. "Maurice lied. The man's name was Summerlin."

"I tell you he wasn't lying." I sounded confident, but I suddenly wasn't. Werewolves could smell the changes in sweat and hear the heartbeat. But just like a lie-detector, I wasn't fool-proof. Not if Maurice had better control than I'd figured he had. Although, I *had* judged him based on how he looked. "Or there's Clarence."

"I'm guessing she's holed up at the crematorium and you just missed it with all them chemicals Gar said was there." The sheriff headed for the door, putting his radio to his mouth. He called for some of the local militia to go with him to the Summerlin place. When I stood in the doorway of the rest-home watching him go, he turned back to me. "Aren't you coming?"

"It's still daylight. You round up the brothers. Maybe we'll get lucky and Clarence will tell you what we need to know. Me, though, I want to keep checking out other possibilities."

The sheriff grunted and left. Littlewing, however, buzzed my face the moment he was out of sight. "You think you missed something."

"Maybe."

"Then what?"

I walked outside, ignoring the continued, hopeful stares of old people in need of companionship. They were the waiting-for-death and I was suddenly grateful that my grandmother had not suffered like that. In the reassuring warmth of the sun, shuddered and surveyed the town. "Why the recorder's office?"

"What?"

"Why the recorder's office? Gabby was collateral damage, not food. People didn't know there was a vampire on the loose. The streets weren't abandoned. Easier meals to be had."

"Away from witnesses?" The sprite played devil's advocate. It usually helped.

"Security cameras. Alarms. Too many more dangers inside but she risked it anyway." I began walking. "Okay, that's dumb. She's been locked away for more than sixty years. There weren't security cameras and the like. That's not relevant." I paused, giving Littlewing my attention and started over. "Two killings revolved around that building. I don't know how the mayor fits though. I mean, it makes more sense that he was just in the wrong place at the wrong time. In plain sight of the Old Folk's Home. Maybe he interrupted Reed. But Gabby was definitely killed because Reed wanted something inside. What's in the recorder's office? I mean, what kind of documents?"

"Deeds. Death certificates. Marriage certificates. Birth certificates." Littlewing stopped. "She was looking for something specific. To see if Rail was alive?"

I walked in silence for a time, wrinkling my nose at the unpleasant smells in the alleyway. My brain was putting pieces together, but it was like there were chunks missing. Surprisingly, Littlewing didn't interrupt. I finally shrugged.

"The timeline's wrong. The mayor and Gabby were both killed after Reed started visiting her old lover. In fact, I think the mayor was killed because she'd found Rail. I mean, look. If she was taking him on walks, they could have come out that gate there right into the alley. If the mayor caught them, she'd have killed him to hide that fact. So maybe she came here last night to make sure her cousin and uncle were dead. Find the certificates instead of looking for the people. Love first, revenge next."

"How does that help us?"

"I guess it doesn't. I've just been running around, thinking less than I should. I do this job because I'm smart, not just scary."

"You do this because no one'll hire you for regular work." She beamed at me smugly.

"Fuck you."

"I wish." She looked thoughtful. "You really think Gar's got more than eight inches?"

"Why the fuck would I care?" I fought a grin. She was in better spirits which was a good sign. I stopped walking and looked up at the

174 | M<small>ICHAEL</small> D<small>ON</small> A<small>NDERSON</small>

sky. Shit. Time was passing as we stood around thinking and talking. I needed to do something. I needed to sink my claws into something that would scream in pain. Preferably something non-human.

My cellphone went off and I answered it with a playful growl. "What?"

"Maurice Summerlin is dead." It was Williams' gruff voice. Damn they'd made good time.

"But it's daylight." I made eye-contact with Littlewing who zipped closer to press her head near my ear.

"Yeah. Wanna explain that?" asked the sheriff.

"Killed how?"

"Blow to the back of the head. Phone was underneath him. We figured he was stopped from calling someone."

"His brother?" I had a bad feeling about this.

"Not here." There were voices in the background and I could tell that the sheriff's men were still searching the grounds.

"I mean, could it have been his brother?"

"Why would he kill Maurice?" Williams hadn't gotten the same bad feeling about the murder I had, but I'd give him a few minutes. There were lots of reasons why someone might want to protect a vampire. Money was the number one reason. I was hoping it was just money.

I hesitated. "Reed needed a day-watcher. I'm guessing she made a deal with Clarence."

"Not Maurice?"

"I'm thinking not." Maurice was the submissive sibling. I should have thought more like a wolf and less like a condescending Californian.

"Shit, first the suit, the mayor and two government peons. It doesn't matter if Jackson and Summerlin are just plain residents. Every dead body is another nail in my ass."

"What do you mean, two government peons? Gabby the janitor and who?" Littlewing scowled because my suspicion was just about to be confirmed.

"Rebeccah Meyers. She worked in the recorder's office."

"Doing what?" If it wasn't about revenge, what else could it be?

"Family decree stuff. Marriages, divorces—."

"Adoptions?" Go with intuition when the facts didn't add up to anything else.

"Yeah, adoptions. Why?" Now Williams had that same tension in his voice that said his gut was trying to warn him. The same way mine had done. It was satisfying that I could leave him unfulfilled.

"I'll get back to you. But Clarence is working with Reed. Search that crematorium extra careful. And have someone look up all property in the Summerlin and Rail names."

"I know how to do my job." The sheriff hung up.

"I know that look, Mitch." Littlewing buzzed in line with my eyes. "What?"

"Give me a minute." I scrolled through my cellphone and pressed the number for my only FBI contact. "Mulder, it's Scully."

"Stop calling me 'Mulder,'" grumbled Peter Hancock of the FBI's Undead Prevention Unit. "I'm kinda in the middle of something, Greyson."

"Blowing your boss again? Look, I gotta know something. Can vampires give birth?"

There was silence on Peter's end. I could hear his heart jump a beat and his breathing grew shallow. "Don't know, Mitch. Why?"

"Bullshit. Is that a yes?"

"Two vampires can't mate, if that's what you mean." Not the whole-truth.

"What about if I fucked a vampire? Could I knock her up?" Two could play the word game.

"Can your little guys even swim?" We weren't friends, but we had an odd sort of respect for each other.

"So that's a yes!"

"Look, Greyson—*Mitch*, there are some things you aren't cleared to know. This is one of them." Hancock paused, changing the subject. "I hear the count's up to four. A few more and we're gonna have to move in."

"More like seven if you count a day-walker bashing in his brother's skull."

"Shit, really? We don't have the resources at the moment. But if you're up that high? If you don't get them tonight, I doubt you'll get a second chance." If the FBI came in, it was bad for business. Werewolf Incorporated couldn't get the job done, so the men-in-black had to come save my butt. Not going to happen!

"Thanks for the heads up. Maybe I can return the favor sometime."

"Stop calling me 'Mulder.' And stop calling us 'upa.' It's the 'U-P-U.' Do that, and we're even."

"Touchy, aren't we?" We wouldn't be even. I still owed him for a gunshot to my gut. It hadn't been silver, but it had still hurt.

"Yeah, well, I get it from my own kids, so yeah." He had three teenagers and they liked me more than their old man. Go figure. They'd learn the value of family loyalty when one of them eventually died. That's how it had worked in my family.

"Fine, Hancock. Maybe. I don't know. Gotta run." I hung up on him, but not before I heard the grinding of his teeth. "Well, Littlewing, I think I know why our vampire didn't take Mr. Rail and head for the hills."

"You honestly think she had a baby?" Right, she'd heard my half of the conversation. I could always dazzle the sheriff instead.

"Let's go check out the files she wanted so desperately to see. See if anything stands out from—what's sixty-three years ago?" I asked.

"1951."

"Should still be adoption records that far back."

I marched toward the government building. A sour-faced man stood at the back door, thin and scraggly, shotgun in his hands. The attitude reminded me of Frank Lynch, the bartender. I got ready for a fight, hoping he wasn't packing silver.

"Littlewing, hide under my jacket for now." She obeyed. I wasn't wearing my 'let's debate it' expression.

"Can't come in." The man shifted the muzzle of the shotgun so that it was aimed at my heart.

"I'm working with the sheriff. Or do I have to bother him in the middle of another crime scene?" If I smelled silver shot, it would be after he fired.

The man swallowed. I could smell his fear and I hadn't even flashed him fangs or amber-eyes. He moved out of the way and I relaxed. But when I started forward, he couldn't help himself. "You're a killer just like them undead."

"Yeah. I am." He'd expected me to argue. The color drained out of his face at my expression and he sidled further away as I went inside.

The smell of blood and other body fluids was still strong. Soured from the passage of time. I could see places where Gabby had been smeared against the wall and dragged along the floor. I was glad that I'd never met the man. It had been a horrible way to die.

The first room was empty. I listened and heard the sound of papers being shuffled. It was daytime, so either Clarence was doing Reed's dirty work because she hadn't found what she wanted, or someone was cleaning up. There was still yellow police tape. It wasn't cleaning.

"Wait," I told the sprite. Her pump bottom pressed erotically against my nipple. I knew she was doing it intentionally, although it was the best place to hide between my jacket and shirt. The pocket on the outside masked her movement.

Following the sound of paper, I smelled a familiar perfume before I saw the skinny, boyish build of a woman. She wore a classic secretary's skirt and dress jacket, arranging documents in the recorder's office. It was the same perfume from the morgue. She screamed and I put both hands in the air. "Calm down, I'm not gonna hurt you."

"What are you doing here!? How did you get past the militia?" Fear mingled with her perfume, but there was something hard in her eyes. I didn't need to be a werewolf not to trust her.

"I'm working with the sheriff. Who are you?"

"This is my office. I'm Anne Holland, the county clerk." I smelled truth, but something else. Her heart raced with a kind of impatience.

"You were at the morgue after the mayor was killed. Why?"

"I was not!" The fear was unmistakable in her eyes.

"I have the nose of the finest hunting dog. You were there. Snuck in without ol' Harv seeing you. Why?" This time I flashed some fang, saving the amber eyes for backup.

"You really are a werewolf?"

"You know that. You scrubbed real hard, but the smell of a person doesn't just come off." She was involved in something, stalling. Did she know what the vampire had been looking for?

Holland edged around the counter, setting down the stack of papers. Much of it was splattered with the janitor's dried blood.

"I know the mayor and his wife very well. I just had to see what had been done to him."

Truth. Some anyways. "That's not all."

She glanced around, looking for a weapon and I tapped my jacket. The woman screamed again when Littlewing popped up in front of her face, gun drawn. "Answer the man! We ain't got all day."

I took a step toward the counter, not needing to go around to catch Ms. Holland if she ran. I could leap the wood and snatch her off the ground before she made it two feet. She reacted to my step by stumbling backwards against a bookcase.

"Well?" I prompted.

"How do I know you don't work for *them*?"

"Who?" I was getting bored and annoyed. Bad combination.

"The Silver Earth Consortium."

"What about them?" Not so bored anymore. Was there a connection between the mine and the vampire after all? Had the mysterious, scentless man been part of their organization? It would explain how he had tracked me to Alabama.

"The deal with the mayor and his wife. I assumed that when he died and Mr. Vittani left town, that something went wrong with their deal." Less truth than lies.

"That doesn't explain why you visited the mayor." Or why she was afraid of the Silver Earth Consortium.

She hesitated and so I gave her the full werewolf hint of change. My eyes grew amber, my fangs as large as they could get. My ears lengthened and got pointy, and my growl, well, Ms. Holland peed herself.

"Please don't kill me!"

"Answer my question."

"The mayor was trying to cut into the Consortium's profits. Pressure them into giving him a bigger percentage. He had a document. Thought it would protect him." The skinny woman was holding her stomach, trying not to throw up. The wetness between her legs spreading along the fabric of her skirt, stinking of unhealthy piss. "I went to the morgue to find the document. He kept it on him at all times."

"Did you find it?"

"No. It wasn't in his things." She seemed more desperate than afraid now that she was used to my transformed features. More afraid of the consortium than me.

"What kind of document is it?" asked Littlewing, reminding us both she was there.

"I don't know. He didn't trust me enough to tell me." She looked for a way to escape, furtively glancing at the doors and windows as she edged sideways along the bookcase.

"He trusted you enough to know he was trying to blackmail someone? But not how?" I smelled only fear and piss. It made it hard to hear the truth of her words.

"The mayor didn't trust anyone completely. Not even Mrs. Cheswick."

"Why here? Now?"

"I really am the county clerk."

"Why *now*, I asked?"

She frowned, as if something unexpected were happening, then threw up on the floor. She soiled the papers she hadn't picked up. Blood and vomit. Nice.

Littlewing made a noise of disgust and flittered out of range. When Ms. Holland stood up, she had a gun in her hand and her expression was cold. She didn't give me any warning or make protestations of innocence. She just fired.

The slug hit my shoulder and spun me around. A high caliber gun. Probably a .45 like my Glock or Rutger. I leapt aside in case she fired again, but I heard her scream of rage.

I heard the militia coming in from the street, responding to the gunfire. I spun toward Holland, knowing they'd choose her over me. She was clutching her forehead, blood dripping into her eye. The sprite hovered in the air between us, out of line of fire.

"You do that?" I asked Littlewing.

She only grinned, shaking her head. "Recoil. Gun flew up and caught her on the brow. Surprised she was able to hit you."

"My lucky day."

Two men rushed in. The thin guy from the back-door, the other an out-of-shape man with glasses and a button-up shirt. Out of work desk-jockey. They aimed their weapons at me. Either or both guns could have silver buckshot in them.

"Put those away!" I barked at them. "This woman fired at me! She needs to be held for the sheriff."

"That's Miss Holland. She works here. Looks to me like self-defense." The thin man raised his shotgun from my midsection to my head. If it wasn't silver shot, it wouldn't kill me. Probably. But it would take a long time to heal and it would hurt bad. If it was silver, Littlewing would probably kill him for me.

I moved werewolf fast, slipping under the barrel of the shotgun. I was so much closer to him than I had been to Frank when he shot me in the bar. The thin man squeezed the trigger as I yanked the gun out of his hands, spraying buckshot over my shoulder. He stood there, astonished at my speed. Then he was unconscious as the butt of his own gun crashed against his head. I made sure it hadn't been hard enough to kill him.

The desk-jockey dropped his gun and ran back out the door. I could have caught him, but I didn't care about him. I faced Miss Holland. The woman had crumpled onto the ground. Buckshot riddled her face and chest.

"She's dead, Mitch." Littlewing hovered over the dead clerk, glancing up anxiously at me.

"Shit."

"How are we gonna find what the mayor stashed in all of this crap?" The sprite pointed with her gun at all the papers scattered on the floor and piled on the countertop.

"We aren't. That isn't our case and she isn't our mess. He'll be back with more of the militia. They can clean it up. The sheriff can investigate if he wants. We're here to track a vampire."

"You don't think they're related?" She seemed dubious.

"How? A business deal gone wrong? It started all of this. What did she call him? Vittani? He released the vampire and it came back to bit the mayor on the ass."

Littlewing stared at me for several whole seconds. "You've been waiting two days to say that haven't you?"

I grinned.

"So what are we looking for?" She zipped around the room, peering at stacks of papers before hovering like a hummingbird in front of me.

"I already said. Adoption records from 1951."

"In this mess?" Littlewing eyed me skeptically.

"We're not going through a page at a time. Sort of see if there's any order to the dates. And look for family law records. We don't care about deeds and stuff."

"What if she already took the adoption record?"

"Then we're wasting our time. You got a problem with that?"

"As long as I get paid." She began sorting through the papers on the ground, peeling them back where blood and vomit had stuck them together.

I took another side of the room.

"Aren't you gonna call a doctor for the dead woman?" asked Littlewing. The body wasn't making her uncomfortable. It was my disrespect for the dead. Sometimes that offended her.

"A doctor for the dead woman?"

"You know what I mean. The coroner or something." Her discomfort was becoming annoyance.

"Oh, he'll hear about it soon enough. I figure ol' desk jockey'll have the police up in arms in about five minutes. By the time one of the deputies gets here, hopefully we'll be done."

"Optimistic? Where's my Mitch?"

"Shut up and look at the papers."

We searched the recorder's office, ignoring clumps of papers which had been filed recently. The only adoptions files we found were in a small stack of folders which covered the entire nineteenth century. Adoptions weren't big in Resistance County.

"They're numbered pretty simply." Littlewing shook her head. "Nothing's missing."

"So not a legal adoption."

"Then no birth certificate."

"Not a standard one." I smiled at Littlewing. "That's it. The baby wasn't born in the hospital. Which means when the adoptive parents needed a birth-certificate, they'd have to have done one of those midwife affidavit things."

"You're making stuff up now." Littlewing always told me that when I mentioned something about human culture which sounded bizarre. Sometimes, I *did* make stuff up to annoy her. This time I was serious.

"If the baby was born at home, it'll have a different record than hospital-born babies. There can't be that many between 1950 and 1951, can there?"

"They don't look computerized yet. And the clerk is dead." Deadpan sarcasm. She really was feeling better.

"Alright. So, yeah. It's not the best use of our time. But if we could find out who the child was, maybe we could beat the vampire to her next victim."

"If she knew who the child was, why not take the kid last night after killing everyone?"

"I don't know. Good point." I surveyed the chaos. "I think she didn't have time. Maybe Gabby surprised her. Surprised them. She escapes while her creation fights the cops."

"Lot of assuming there for someone who doesn't believe in it."

"What's your thought, then?" I raised one brow at the sprite. It was hard to keep my eyes up on her face with her jiggling around angry. It wasn't about size. It was about proportions.

"I didn't say I disagreed. You just get pissed off if I make that many assumptions."

I was about to reply when several armed men charged into the room. Five of the local militia, but no deputies. Shit. "Easy, boys."

"Check Brody. He dead?" ordered a woman who was clearly not batting for my team.

She was stocky with muscles, pants sagging at her wide hips. They revealed men's boxers with the word 'queer' repeated around the waistband. She wore camouflage pants and a matching hoodie, with a tight, wife-beater underneath. Her face was boyish, heart-shaped. Almost cute. If you were into boys.

One of the others, a man about my age moved cautiously to the unconscious Brody in the middle of the room. He kept his eyes on me as he checked Brody's pulse. "Strong and steady."

"Camouflage went out with the nineties." I kept my hands in the air, but locked gazes with the lesbian. Clearly she was in charge. Made me want to test her.

"I don't follow fashion trends." She saw the bullet hole in my shirt, where Holland had shot me. The wound had healed, but the damage was still obvious. "Who did that?"

"Her." I nodded at the dead woman. "Recoil smacked her on the head. Then Prince Charming there came in and got ready to shoot me."

"You killed her."

"No. He did."

"Liar!" shouted desk-jockey, hiding at the back of the other four. "He was trying to shoot you!"

"I never said he wasn't. I just said he shot her." A couple of the others looked twitchy and I needed to figure out a way to keep from getting another bullet lodged under my skin. "Did you call the sheriff? Didn't he tell you that I was working a case with him?"

A blonde man, maybe ex-military but too old to still serve, spat on the ground. "The whole town knows after the bar-fight. They also know you crushed Frank's leg. Might never walk again."

"Good. He tried to kill me and my partner. Maybe that'll teach him not to break the law." I locked stares with the blonde instead of the woman. She seemed more rational. It was safer to deal with the emotional types first.

"Frank's a lot of things, but he don't break the law." Another fan of the bartender. What was wrong with these people?

"Really? Poisoning Littlewing? Shooting silver buckshot at me for coming into his bar? That on the books as legal in this Podunk town?"

"Listen you piece of filth—!" The Lesbian slammed the butt of her shotgun into the wall behind her. It silenced the blonde, but startled one of the twitchier militia. A stream of buckshot grazed the air near my head.

"You mind?" I growled at her, but I was relieved. It wasn't silver.

"Put your guns down. All of you. Jasper, we ain't the law. We're here to help support the sheriff's department. I got a call into him. We wait. No more fuckin' shooting!"

"You ain't in charge, Charlotte," complained desk-jockey.

"You got bigger balls than me?" She took a step toward him and he stumbled back. "I didn't think so." Her phone rang and another of the men shot into the molded copper ceiling. Original and worth a pretty penny. Too bad, but better it than me or Littlewing.

"Yeah, sheriff. That werewolf feller was in the records room with Anne Holland. Brody shot Anne, but he was trying to shoot the werewolf. Because he was threatening Anne. Yup. Yup." She handed me the phone. "Wants to talk to you."

"Sheriff?"

"What the hell are you doing?" He was pissed alright.

"Holland and the mayor were involved in something not-above-board with the Silver Earth Consortium. She shot me, then your little

Gomer Pyles came running in and tried to kill me for just standing there bleeding."

"Why are you even in the hall of records?"

"I think I know why the vampire is hanging around." I glanced at the militia. "But it requires governmental clearance to share."

"If I find out you're lying, I will do more than kill you." He sounded like he was looked forward to it.

"Yeah, you'll slice my throat and piss in it."

"That's disgusting!" Clearly the sheriff was a lot more wholesome than I was. "I'll skin you alive is what I'll do. Then see how long it takes for silver buckshot to kill you if they leave it in."

"No imagination. So can you tell these over-zealous Rambos to leave me the fuck alone so I can keep working?"

"When are you getting your ass up here to sniff around the Summerlin place?"

"Did that once already! If it's like any of the other crime scenes, it won't help much after your people have paraded around with cologne and deodorant and an army of vehicles. I almost think you don't want me to find her. Because you sure as heck aren't helping." He didn't argue, he couldn't. It took some of the venom out of my attitude. "Let me finish up here and I'll get up there when I'm done. We still have a few hours till the sun sets. I need to play this smart."

"Put her back on."

I handed Charlotte the phone. She listened for a moment and nodded as if Williams could see her. "I'm probably the only one willing, Sheriff. Yup. 'Kay." She flipped the phone closed and looked at the men behind her. "Sheriff says get your asses back to watching the street."

"What about that murdering beast?" asked Jasper. He gripped his gun so tightly that I thought he'd break the stock.

"Give him your full cooperation. Like he was Williams hisself."

"Bullshit." The blonde was crazy enough that he might fight her no matter what the sheriff had said.

"Git!" Charlotte slammed the butt of her gun against the wall again. "And take Brody with you." The men collected the unconscious Brody and shuffled out of the room. We waited until they had disappeared down the hall. Then Charlotte glanced at me. "I'm supposed to help."

"Is there a way to find out homebirth records from 1951?" I waved at the massive piles of papers scattered around the room.

"Doc Walker would have those. Her old man was the town doctor before her." Another person who knew something useful. Things were looking up.

"What happened to him?"

"Smoked hisself to death. Could give advice better n' he took it. What'cha need it for?"

"Help me track the vampire."

"You think she's going after someone born back then? Revenge killing?" I liked the way she thought. It reminded me of Littlewing, without the sexy figure. Well, it was probably sexy to someone Just not me.

"Need to know, I'm afraid." Clichés could be useful. This was one of those times. "Charlotte, I'm Mitch. The buxom beauty is Littlewing."

The woman looked in the direction I pointed and smiled. "I heard you had one 'em with you. Sprite ain't'cha?" That won Charlotte points with my partner. Most humans didn't differentiate between all the small winged creatures. But the fey really cared.

"Yes. But you don't look like a Charlotte. I bet you're a Chuck."

The woman beamed at Littlewing. "Damned straight. Well, so to speak. C'mon, let's go over to the doc's." Charlotte paused. "You can't grow bigger by any chance?"

Littlewing giggled and her breasts jiggled more than usual. Flirting. Sex was sex as far as she was concerned, although she preferred men from what she always said. "Now why does everyone always ask me that?"

CHAPTER TWENTY-TWO

I wanted to draw a gun as I moved through the sterile, silent corridors of the hospital. Not as creepy as the Rail place or the old folks home, but suspicious. "Where is everyone?"

"After last night? Seriously? Sleeping." Charlotte strutted toward a set of offices with Littlewing perched on her shoulder. Bosom buddies now. Littlewing had been grumpy since she'd discovered the lobotomized fairies. At least until she'd nearly died of poisoning and survived. If this kept her distracted, well, all the better.

"Not much excitement here usually?" asked Littlewing.

"Oh, we get our hunting accidents. Or tractor accidents. Hell, we even get domestic accidents. But murder an' such? This town was sleepy before the mayor was killed. Plain boring."

"You actually hang out in the *Broken Record*?" I asked.

"Hell no! I drive to Birmingham on weekends to party with the girls." She craned her neck to look at Littlewing. "What about you? You like to party with the girls?"

"I just like to party!" Littlewing fluttered her wings, excited. "Chuck, why are we here if the doc's sleeping?"

"Because her main squeeze is in the hospital." The woman gave me a hard look. "They're sending a specialist to try and reconstruct his ankle bones."

"That sounds expensive." The bastard had deserved it. Charlotte's angry stares weren't going to make me feel guilty.

"It is. Mrs. Cheswick is picking up the tab. Along with repairing a certain MRI machine. You're lucky Roy still has his job. Doc Walker was pretty pissed off."

"Why? Something between them? Between Cheswick and Frank I mean?"

"Hell no!" Charlotte rapped on the door which had the single word 'office' on it. "She's being responsible for bringing you here. Cleaning up your mess. That's the kind of lady she is."

"He started it."

"Stop whining, Mitch. It ain't attractive."

I wouldn't look at Littlewing. "I'm not whining. It's true."

The door opened and a very haggard Dr. Gwen Walker stood there. She held my gaze and I knew she'd heard us speaking. "Yes, it is."

"Pardon?" Her agreement caught me off guard.

"Frank admitted that he did what you said." She was still angry at me. "You know that man survived two active combat rotations?"

"So?" My father was career military. I'd seen what happened to soldiers who took too much action for the human mind to deal with. Frank wasn't messed up like them. She wasn't helping his case.

"He earned a right to live in peace." Not where I thought she was going.

"Then he ought to leave people in peace. Look, Doc, we don't have time for this. You want me to catch the vampire before the Feds come in and lock this town down, I need to know about any homebirths from 1950 to 1951."

"Those are confidential!" Clearly the doctor was not going to cooperate. Even after learning that her little boyfriend had been the bad guy in our conflict.

"Yeah, well, under the Anti-Vampire Act of 2013, signed by your President on her very first day in office, warrants are not required in direct pursuit of proven acts of vampirism. Her words, Doc. You wanna argue, argue with Bachmann. Me, I want to save lives."

"This way." She spoke through gritted teeth, but led us further down the hall. She paused at a room that said 'files.' I loved the simplicity of the place, but I suspected it was going to make finding the documents harder. I was wrong. Again.

"Computers!" Littlewing grew excited and fluttered around in the small room. She gave off a few pulses of sunlight.

"Conserve that!" My growl made the doctor jump, but Charlotte actually smiled at me.

"Can you teach me that?"

"Comes with too much baggage." I let her see a flash of amber and she nodded, disappointed. She thought it was sexy. Most people wet themselves. Or maybe that's what she wanted.

"Just those two years?" Dr. Walker sat on the vinyl upholstered chair, exhausted. Her eyes were bloodshot and she looked twenty years older than when I'd met her. She took her job seriously. That sparked a twinge of guilt in me.

"Yeah. Please."

Littlewing glanced at me. She was hovering behind the doctor, near an antique filing cabinet. She mouthed the word 'please' with brows raised.

"What exactly are you looking for?" asked the doctor while she slowly typed at the machine. "It might help me speed this up."

I scratched my chin, considering her question. "I think a baby was given away during one of those two years. The mother died."

"What's the name?"

"Let's just assume they used an alias. That'll keep us from limiting the search in the wrong fashion."

"So the father recorded the birth? No. You said 'given away.' You think the adoptive parents claimed the baby as their own?" Walker looked up at me. "My father was the GP. He would have known."

"Why? I get knocked up. I'm ashamed or from hardy farm stock. Stay home for nine-months. Drop the baby. Come into town to register it."

"That's what I'd do, Doc," agreed Charlotte.

Walker scowled at us both. "That's not my point. You won't find anything in the official records. About thirty percent of deliveries back then were homebirths. But my father's personal medical notes would have mentioned any irregularities."

"Why not the medical files?" asked Littlewing.

"Because he only put facts in the files. Medical facts. Any conjecture or personal concerns or historical details he logged separately for his own use."

"Can we check anyway? Give us a list of names to compare in his journal?" I looked at her hopefully.

"Would be faster just to check the journal. But—." She squinted at the computer monitor. "Live births in those two years? Twenty-eight county-wide."

"How many homebirths?"

"That's what I mean, Mr. Greyson. Twenty-eight homebirths those two years."

"Any of them Summerlins?" I needed to narrow that list considerably or it would be dark and more people would be dead. "Rails?"

She looked at me startled. "Why does that sound familiar? The Summerlins. They ran an old mortuary on the far side of the county."

"Crematorium, actually."

"Wait! Now I remember. Rail was the psycho who killed all those people and buried them under his floorboards."

"Your father have notes on that, too?" We might have a solid lead. Finally.

"He might. I've read most of his journals, but not all of them. Seems to me, though, I'd remember seeing something about that."

"Can we go look at his journals?" I pressed. "Daylight won't last forever."

"A lot of that stuff is confidential and there's more than one skeleton in his notes. Infidelities. Medical peculiarities. Stuff I don't want to get out."

"I trusted you with why I wanted the information. You need to trust me to keep it private." I held her gaze for longer than most people.

The doctor turned to the younger woman. "Chuck, I can't let you read any of it."

"Figures. Anything juicy about my family?"

"My point exactly." The doctor hit a button and a printer started rattling away out of sight.

"Dot matrix? Seriously?" asked Littlewing.

"Mrs. Cheswick gives enough to this town. We make do till things don't work no more and can't be fixed. America could learn a few things about conservation." Dr. Walker stood up and went to a cabinet. She opened the door and tore off a strip of paper. It had perforations between the pages and holes along edges which were for feeding it through the printer. I hadn't known that they still made that stuff. "You'll have to drive. I can barely keep my eyes open."

"Not a problem."

"And Chuck, check in on Frank for me, will you?" Her voice gentled with compassion and worry. It made her seem human for the first time.

"Sure, Aunt Gwen." Great. Of course everyone would be related. It made it harder to learn the truth. And while I was good at my job, it just might take longer than we had.

CHAPTER TWENTY-THREE

The doc was a stern, austere workaholic, but her house was a four-bedroom museum to femininity. Laces were affixed to everything. On the window-coverings. On the lampshades. Even on the numerous pillows which covered two large couches and an overstuffed chair. Floral prints dominated, matching the multitude of vases with fresh cut flowers. It smelled impressively clean, although the perfume from the flowers helped mask a few traces of unavoidable mold in a house this old.

"You have a maid?" I wondered aloud.

"I'm a type-A personality. What do you think?" She closed the door behind us and headed for the back of the house.

"You have time to clean? Or do you just not need sleep?"

"What you saw in the O.R. yesterday, last night, is not normal around here, Mr. Greyson. I have more time on my hands than you might think." She approached a solid wooden door, original to the house. She pulled out a ring of large, iron keys to unlock it. "My father's study. No matter how long he left it, he always locked it. The people deserved their privacy, he said."

"You sound like you really admired him." Littlewing fluttered between the doc and me.

"He was a great man. When times were hard, he didn't even charge his patients. It was a calling. Not a job."

"Another of his pithy sayings?" She frowned at me and I waved at the air. "Let's just do this."

Walker pressed her hip against the door, studying me sternly. "I don't know what you believe in, Mr. Greyson. But I want you to swear by the lives of your parents and God, that you'll not betray any of the confidences in here."

"Except to find the vampire," I amended.

She hesitated, then jerked her head in agreement. "Except to find the vampire."

"Fine. I swear by the lives of my parents and to God, that I will not betray any confidences." I'd testified in court, so I'd gotten in the habit of repeating things verbatim. I'd learned early on that it kept people happier. Happy people cooperated better and I got paid faster. "Satisfied?"

She grunted and pushed the door open. Inside, I smiled at the smell of real leather, hand-waxed using with something that had lemon in it. Then the rich wholesome scent of expensive wood blended with the musty smell of aging books. It was a real man's dream study. Dark woods. Supple leather chairs. And an impressive antique desk with brass fittings. All it needed for my perfect room was a French maid in a peek-a-boo bra and panties, fishnet stockings and bright red-lipstick that would get smeared all over my naked chest and lower down.

"Mitch!" Littlewing shouted at me. But at least she didn't hit me with her gun to get my attention. "You're drooling."

I touched the corners of my mouth, just to be sure she was being metaphorical. She pointed down at my crotch with her drawn gun. Oh, that kind of drooling. Maybe we'd grown too close in the year we'd worked together if she could tell what I was thinking that easily. "So where do we start, Doc?"

"It's arranged chronologically. I guess we can make sure I didn't miss anything on the bodies. But if he wanted to be sure that certain facts remained lost to time, he'd have hidden them in the Pile."

"The Pile?" asked Littlewing.

"It's what I call the stacks of unsorted manuscripts he had stored in the basement. I've been trying to put them on shelves, but there are quite a few."

"Why so meticulous here and a pile in the basement?"

"We had a flood. Water damage. Everything was rotted through and through and it all came crashing down. He hated to go down there, even before that."

"Why?" I didn't think that the doc was involved, but I was suspicious by nature. People had secrets. Everyone did. Some of them were ordinary. Like sexual perversions or incest. But some of them were dangerous.

The woman stared at the tidy shelves and ran a hand along the back of the overstuffed leather chair which was the focal point of the room. "My mother. She was—she was mentally disturbed."

"Genetic?" I asked, implying that the doctor might be unhinged herself.

To my surprise, she only shook her head sadly. "No. An accident affected her brain chemistry. Daddy spent years trying to cure her. His journals on her were kept even more private that these. Locked in the basement and out of sight after she died."

"As sad as all that is, does it help save lives now?" I tried to be warm, but I didn't like the woman, sob story or not.

"No, Mr. Greyson. It won't. My point was, that if he wanted to keep something truly secret, it would be down there." She looked troubled. "The flood made a lot of it illegible."

"It's better than a sharp stick in the eye." I glanced at Littlewing.

"Poke in the eye, dumbass."

"Here's the journals for 1950 and 1951." She handed me two thin, hand-bound sets of papers, covered with cloth-covered cardboard.

"Just in case, you got 1949 there, too?" I wasn't interested in just the baby. I was interested in the victim and her family. Reed Summerlin might have been of interest to the man for other reasons.

"This is it." Dr. Walker pressed a third journal into my hand, reverently. "I'll look in the basement on my own. Even for your vampire, I will not put my mother's madness out on the table."

"We need to know." She didn't reply, but left the room. "Alright, Littlewing, which year you want?"

"This is an unhappy place." She was grumpy again. I glanced at the wall and saw a painting of a fairy at a large, yellow sunflower, plucking the seeds. Figured.

"Then the sooner we find the vampires and kill them, the sooner we can get our butts back to a real city." I tossed 1951 onto the desk for the sprite. "Look for any reference to babies or deaths that the doc's father—Daddy Doc—found unusual. Or outright references to vampires or the supernatural."

"Whatever." She flitted over to the desk and used both hands to heave open the journal. I began to skim through 1950. The man's handwriting wasn't awful, but a few words were nearly impossible to cipher without context. I don't know how much time passed before I reached an interesting paragraph. I read it aloud for Littlewing.

"'The Summerlins came by asking odd questions. Makes me wonder at the disappearance of the women-folk at their place. Sheriff busy with other people gone missing, doesn't see a connection.'"

I read some more, but it was ordinary stuff. Affairs and sexually transmitted diseases. Erectile dysfunction. The stuff we took for granted these days because it appeared even in commercials.

"Mitch. This is interesting." Littlewing hovered above the pages. "'The Rail boy's been asking about babies. He ain't been the same since his girl disappeared almost a year ago. If he's got one of the girls in town pregnant, I worry that his father'll do more than tan his hide. The man's abusive. More than a father ought to be.' *Charming.* I guess you were on the right track after all."

"But it doesn't help find her. Keep reading. I thought I had something, but so far it's just conjecture."

We read in silence until I came across another paragraph, a few weeks later. "This was thought out. Listen to this, 'One of the country boys, William Rail's eldest came in today. Asked about how to kill a blood disease. He became distressed when I said that some diseases of the blood can't be cured. Worse, he got excited when I said that the stuff strong enough to kill the disease almost nearly always killed the host. He looked bad. I prescribed a sedative—' Blah, blah, blah. So that explains why the victims under the floorboards didn't rise at night. Must have tried embalming them with chemicals from the crematorium."

"Still doesn't help, does it?"

"No. Keep reading."

There were snippets of related materials. 'So and so went missing.' 'The town was growing terrified of itself.' 'The sheriff tried to get the FBI to come help, but they turned him down.' 'They resumed local militia.' The picture was growing, but I still needed the corner pieces. Where would the vampires hide?

"Here's something." Littlewing buzzed her wings excitedly. "Let's see—it's about Rail. 'The Rail boy was carrying baby food and diapers in his bicycle basket today. There was blood on his sleeves, too. I called the sheriff and the Summerlins. I believe he's got the missing Summerlin girl at his place. It's a horrible thought. The boy seems sincere, but I've known men to do worse to satisfy sexual urges. He might have more than just his former girlfriend. I began tracking the disappearances and the Rail place is in the center. I can't reach William Rail by phone. It's in the hands of the police, now.' So the doc's father set things in motion."

I glanced at the door into the study. "Seems to me like he wanted to be Sherlock Holmes as much as Marcus Welby, M.D." I walked over and looked at her journal, flipping to the next page.

"Alright, so we know what happened. The sheriff staked the vampire and left her in the mine. The boy gets away with the baby and gives it up for adoption. The boy's father gets blamed for the bodies under the house. And eventually, Andrew gets put in an old age home, his life destroyed by the past. Movie of the week. Still not helpful!"

"Yeah, but there's something strange. There's mention of going to see the bodies. Then it skips to some teenager getting a vacuum stuck on his privates. The vacuum incident's almost a month later." I skimmed the rest of the ledger but there was no more discussion of the Rail boy and no pages torn out.

My cellphone rang. I folded up Littlewing's journal and tapped on the 1949 one for her to read as I answered it. "Hello?"

"I'm sitting on my ass waiting for you." The sheriff sounded calm. Not a good sign.

"I told you I was chasing a lead. Why are you waiting? Can't you keep a deputy on hand?"

"The FBI says 'no.'"

"You called them?" I looked at a clock on the desk. It was already half-past three. Not much daylight left.

"They showed up. Says you told them the number was near to ten."

"That fucking Hancock!" I saw Littlewing roll her eyes at me. She hated the FBI because they locked up the fey. "So then why are you waiting for me?"

"Something about a conditional license to hunt vampires?"

I frowned. Because I was a werewolf, the government had placed certain tags on my operations. If I was freelance, I could do whatever I wanted within the law. Once the Feds took over, I was obligated to assist. They had to pay me, but that wasn't the point.

"They want me to sniff the scene."

"Right in one." He was talking pretty abbreviated. I wondered if he was holding something back from the Feds or from me. I decided on the direct approach.

"Is there something you aren't telling me?"

"There's a lot I wouldn't tell an unchristian animal like you." There was the secret message in those words. He'd made sure I was marginally a Christian before he'd allowed me to join the investigation. By calling me unchristian, he was telling me that it was a lie. So there was something he didn't want the Feds to know.

"They pissing on your parade?" Littlewing gave me a thumbs up.

"Oh, just holding me responsible for the death of Anne Holland because it was our local militia that killed her."

"Ouch." I actually felt bad for the man. "Tell them I'm on my way."

"Can you stop by dispatch and pick up Deputy Coleman. I sent him in for some supplies."

"Got it. Anything else? Lunch? Coffee? Donuts?"

"Get the hell over here, Greyson!" That voice shouted from near Williams. I hung up on the sheriff and Hancock's boss, Dexter Lawrence.

"Something stinks," I growled. Littlewing sniffed under an armpit. "Not you. The sheriff was being cryptic and sneaky."

"Hiding something from us?"

"From the Feds."

"Well, he's not all bad, then is he?" She had a point.

"Lawrence is with him."

"Fuck me."

"Let's go tell the doc we're leaving." We found her in the basement, weeping over a journal. She looked up startled, but from shame. "Doc, we have to run. Can you keep looking?"

"Yes, I'll—I'll do my best." She seemed defeated. Nothing like the ballsy woman who had threatened to let a werewolf die on the operating table. Sure, that had been bluff, but reading about her mother had devastated her. She wasn't going to find what we needed. Not that it mattered. The Feds had taken over.

"Come on, 'Wing." We left the doctor's residence and drove over to the sheriff's office. The sooner we got Garvy, the sooner I could wash my hands of the whole vampire mess. Even my deal with the sheriff was off and Littlewing would have to live with lobotomized fairies. The FBI always screwed up my cases. For once, I'd like to screw up one of theirs, instead.

202 | <small>MICHAEL DON ANDERSON</small>

CHAPTER TWENTY-FOUR

Inside the sheriff's office, Garvy was pacing back and forth. "Mitch!" He grabbed me by the shoulders, relieved. "We got a problem."

"I heard. Can they really hold Williams responsible for that shooting?"

"To heck with Anne Holland. I never liked that old biddy from day one. This is about the case. The Feds are taking over our department and putting all their resources into searching the Summerlin crematorium." Littlewing landed on the deputy's shoulder.

"Hi, Littlewing." He didn't waste time flirting with the sprite. This was business. Something had rattled his cage and she wasn't about to distract him from it.

"We already looked. The sheriff already looked." I stared at him confused.

"Exactly. But the Feds are sure they've got some secret chamber in that old creepy building."

"It'll take hours to tear it apart if that's the case."

"Now you're catching on. It'll be dark long before they finish." Garvy looked grim.

"And if the vampires aren't there, they go on to kill again." It wasn't like the Feds to be that sloppy. If my nose couldn't pick Reed Summerlin's scent out of that place, she wasn't there.

"So what do we do?" The man looked to me for guidance. I hadn't lost any of my own team in a while. It felt bad to let Garvy help, because I believed in statistics. I was due for some worse luck.

"You stay here and coordinate. Littlewing and I—!"

"Are trying to ditch my skinny black ass because you think I'm a kid!" Garvy let go of my arms and glared at me. I wasn't intimidated. It made him look younger. Especially with the sprite perched on his shoulder like some doll.

"I don't want you dead." I put it out there, plain and simple. "I like you, so I want you to live."

"To hell with you! I'm just as dead if I'm stuck on the sidelines! Why be a cop? Why do anything if you live afraid to put yourself out there?" He held up a piece of paper. "Sheriff Williams said you'd need my help."

"For what?" I snatched the paper out of his hands. It had two sentences. 'The Feds want to take old Frank's approach to hunting. Greyson needs to use his nose to figure this out.' "What's this?"

Littlewing buzzed over and read the paper while I stared at Garvy.

"Sheriff said to tell you verbatim. Sounded pissed off. More n' usual." The young deputy stared at me defiantly. If I left him behind, he'd come on his own and then he'd get killed for sure.

"He already told me this. Why tell you?"

"Why mention Frank?" asked Littlewing. "The only thing he was interested in hunting was us."

Williams was smarter than I'd thought. "That's what he means. He thinks the Feds want to kill us. But that's insane." I pulled out my cellphone and autodialed Peter Hancock's number. It picked up on the third ring.

"What'dya want, Greyson?" He sounded busy and unhappy, but he had picked it up despite caller-ID.

"Why the fuck did you send your people in on my case? You said I'd have till tomorrow."

"What're you talking about?" His breath was ragged and I could hear screams in the background. "I'm kind of in the middle of something."

"Your boss is here taking over the vampire killings." If he could pick up the phone, he wasn't in that much danger. If the phone went dead, I wouldn't call back. That actually might distract him and get him killed.

"My boss? Kelly is here with me."

"Not Kelly. Dexter Lawrence."

There was a confused pause. "Lawrence quit the Bureau over suspicions of misconduct." His voice grew anxious. "Wait. You're saying he's there?"

"With men claiming to be FBI."

"Oh, shit. We so do not need this right now. There's been a new rip. Swarms of goblins are eating their way through lower Manhattan. We have all the available men here." He covered the phone, habit from before the days of mute buttons. A moment later he removed his hand. "Mitch, we can't send anyone for a few hours at best. You aren't sanctioned to take human lives in this hunt unless they've been bitten, but—."

"Stay alive anyway." I added the only other bit of useful information I had. "They have the local sheriff."

"You don't make anything easy, do you? I've gotta go. Make it work." Seriously? He hung up with a quote from *Project Runway*?

I stared at Garvy. No way he'd back down. "Alright Gar, I will need your help. We need to take out a bunch of phony Feds without killing anyone. Ideas?"

He grinned but that just pissed me off more. He was excited about this. All I could do was picture his body riddled with bullets, lying on the ground. That bad feeling ate at my gut, but either way, Garvy would come. This way, at least, maybe I could keep him alive.

CHAPTER TWENTY-FIVE

We reached the Summerlin crematorium after a couple of detours. I pulled into the gravel driveway in a borrowed black van. Garvy and Littlewing were in Garvy's official sheriff's vehicle, but parked further away. If I couldn't hear my back up, Lawrence and his people wouldn't be able to.

I left the van running in the middle of the driveway and took a quick slip through the woods to the crematorium, staying hidden. I counted five men outside, Lawrence not one of them. They had rifles and hand-guns, clearly non-government issue. They wore black suits and sunglasses but their shoes were too expensive for most FBI agents to wear in the field. I couldn't tell how many people were inside, but I didn't see the sheriff and his local militia. Had to be inside with the bad guys. Or dead.

I listened for human heartbeats. But even as a werewolf, there was too much background noise and I was too far away. Two of the black sedans used by the fake Feds were running. Lawrence knew enough to mask sounds from my heightened senses. He would probably use silver-infused tear gas if he got the chance, knowing that it would slowly kill me if his bullets didn't. I went back to the van and drove the rest of the way to the crematorium, parking beside one of the running sedans.

"Where's Lawrence?" I asked as I stepped out of the van, smiling.

Anyone who knew me would recognize the smile as a bad sign. I glanced at the van, feeling bad about taking it. But my 1963 Mustang was too precious to risk in a fire-fight. This thing with Lawrence, not good. He had FBI training and money behind him. Whatever he wanted would end in a lot of destruction. I'd apologize later to *Barry's Breads* if anything happened to the van. Otherwise I'd return it to the parking-lot I'd stolen it from, possibly without his knowledge.

"Inside." The men stiffened out of reflex and the grips on their guns tightened. Just enough. They were professionals, because I almost didn't notice the change. Money. Guns. Professional killers and an ex-FBI chief. What the hell had I gotten mixed up with?

I went up the steps casually and didn't bother knocking. The moment I pulled open the door, I could smell the tension and Dexter Lawrence inside. He had a peptic ulcer and he tried to mask the stench of his sickness with Ralph Lauren's *Polo Black*. He'd worn it every day since the first time I'd met him. It made him easier to identify now. About a year ago, Hancock had taken my advice and switched to fragrance free toiletries during cases with me. His boss, Lawrence had just doubled his usual dabbing as a non-verbal 'fuck you' to me. He'd regret that decision. The chemicals in it made my nose itch and I fought a sneeze.

"Greyson. About time!"

Lawrence stood in the foyer, his arms folded across his chest. He was mid-fifties. Tall and lanky, but fit. He'd have been distinguished looking if his thin lips hadn't been a constant sneer. There was grim cunning in his eyes, which seemed ominous knowing that he was impersonating a Fed instead of being one. His clothing, like the men outside, was too expensive for an FBI agent. Someone was paying him a lot of money to break the law. The same someone who had gotten him in trouble with the Bureau no doubt. Who, and what did it have to do with the vampire situation?

I didn't shake his hand. He didn't offer. Mutual dislike worked in my favor. Instead, I took a deep breath, masked it as a sigh. No sign of the sheriff or Deputy Jason, but they'd been there. I smelled the sweat of a lot of men. Very little blood. A good sign.

Lawrence motioned to a nearby door. "Start in the basement. That's where the body is."

"Good to see you, too, Agent Lawrence." I glanced around the darkened crematorium and sensed rather than saw two or three men hiding in other rooms. Not any smarter than Lawrence. I could smell their gels and soaped bodies. Hancock would have had his men use something to neutralize the smell because I was a werewolf. I was glad it was his boss that had gone rogue instead of him. Dexter Lawrence believed that pure humans were superior to anything else. My chance to prove him wrong.

"Wait. Where's that sprite?" Lawrence had never used her name. In his mind, the fey were monsters or exotic pets, dangerous. He was right about the dangerous part.

"She's back in town. You interrupted us doing research on the history of the vampire." It was a lie. Littlewing should be somewhere just outside. Our plan was a little loose, but that's how we played best. "Oh, and William's deputy—what's his name, Coleman—said that he got a call from one of your agents. The Manhattan problem is under control and they've got twenty additional agents in the air." Bigger lie.

I saw Lawrence flinch mentally as I walked toward the basement door. Hopefully it would make him act rashly, giving me a chance to get the upper hand. I needed to find the sheriff and his men before I took any action, in case I endangered them needlessly. I could be an ass, but I wasn't reckless.

"Good. We can use the help." I expected it to happen in the basement, but a gun went off as my feet touched the landing. It hit me in the middle of my back, right at the heart. I was knocked forward, onto my belly and down the stairs. I skidded a few steps face-first and came to a painful stop.

"Don't bother. He's as weak as a baby now," I heard Lawrence tell one of his men. "The silver will kill him nice and painful. The fire will take care of the rest."

They closed the door and I heard it lock, an angry jerking sound. My nose picked up the overwhelming stench of gasoline. The fumes overwhelmed me as I stood, but hands clutched at me, hefting me upright. I didn't fight them off.

"Not as smart as I hoped." It was the sheriff.

"Smart enough." I took off the borrowed hoodie, ripping it off my shoulders. The Kevlar underneath was harder to remove.

"You understood my message then."

He helped me unfasten the buckles with practiced skill. I saw that all of the deputies and several of the town militia were there, clustered together in the small space. And they were pissed. The body of Maurice Summerlin had been carefully laid out on the cement floor. Blood had splattered his clothes, but not the area around him.

"He killed down here?" Not important, just something to focus on while I waited for Lawrence to think I was dead or dying.

"Upstairs. They tossed him down. We had time on our hands." Williams handed the Kevlar to Deputy Jason. "What's the plan?"

"What happened?" I tilted my head, listening to the sounds of footsteps upstairs heading away from the basement. A door slammed. Give them another minute.

"After I called you, they locked us down here. Revealed that much of their plan. Shooting you with silver. Pretty confident we wouldn't live to tell. I couldn't warn you." He looked uncomfortably guilty for falling into their trap. "Who are these guys?"

"Lawrence really is FBI. Make that 'was.' I met him a few times. Bigger ass than you. My source at the Bureau says he quit under suspicious circumstances. I guess this confirms it." Freed of the bullet-

210 | Michael Don Anderson

proof jacket, I flexed my muscles. The impact from the gunshot had hurt less than the tumble down the steps onto the cement floor, but I was a werewolf.

"So, what? Your plan was to get caught, just not shot?" The sheriff peered up the stairs.

"Yep. That's smoke. They've set the house on fire to get rid of their witnesses. When it hits the gasoline down here—barbequed law enforcement." I went to one of the storm windows, too narrow for a grown man to climb through. The cinder-block walls would be lined with heavy rebar. It would take too long to punch my way through. We'd be dead. "That ain't gonna work."

I trotted up the steps and listened at the door. The fire was blazing already, which meant that they'd used an accelerant upstairs. But at least they would have cleared the house. I smashed through the door, tearing it off the frame. If I'd been exposed to silver, there would have been no way the heavy wood would have budged.

Lawrence had assumed the silver had penetrated my skin. It was an object lesson in assumption to rub in Littlewing's face when I saw her again. But I planned on teaching Lawrence a more painful lesson when I caught up with him.

"What about Summerlin?" Deputy Jason watched me with trust in his eyes. That I would tell him what to do. It kept me from saying to leave the bastard behind.

"Bring him up. But if you have to make a choice, save yourself. Not a body already dead."

Jason nodded and disappeared back down the stairs. A couple of the men followed him. Guess it was the Christian thing to do. Not smart, but I understood. Arguing would have cost us valuable time. Only a few minutes to get these men out of the burning building or we'd all be dead.

The fire roared along the walls on both sides of the basement doorway. The smoke burned my lungs, but they would heal. Too much fire wouldn't and the blaze would make its way down fast. I motioned for the men to follow me and headed toward a window. It wasn't the best place to get them out, but it was the closest. We had less time than I thought. The accelerant was doing its job. The curtains were on fire around the window, while the wall on both sides blazed. It was like walking into a furnace, because the carpet was burning underneath and the ceiling above.

I knew that Lawrence had made one mistake thinking I was going to die. He might not make the same mistake about witnesses. If there was someone watching the house, we might be killed coming out. I'd have to trust that Littlewing and Garvy would do their part.

I grabbed a lounge chair and smashed it through the window. Hopefully it sounded like the fire had broken more of the glass. I grabbed the nearest man and threw him outside. One after another I got the men out, without hearing any corresponding gunfire. Another good sign. I got the last of them through the window but the fire had become a curtain of flames. The men cursed, their clothes or hair catching fire. Nothing to do about it. I hefted Maurice Summerlin's ahead of me as I leapt through the flames. They'd have to drop and roll, because I had to keep them alive in other ways.

I landed in a crouch, searching through the billowing smoke but all I could see were our people. I slipped along the burning building, looking for the five men patrolling the grounds. No one, not even Littlewing was in sight. I moved to the corner, flinching away from an explosion of fire. Dust billowed above the drive as the last of the vehicles disappeared.

Lawrence's people had fled without making sure everyone had died. Sloppy. Something that Hancock would never have done. Not that I'd ever give him that compliment. He might think he was good enough to boss me around.

"Littlewing?" I shouted. There were no flashes of gold light or that annoying buzz of her wings. "Littlewing!"

The sheriff and his men came hobbling around the corner after me. "All this just to kill you?"

I started to answer and bit my lip. The crematorium was completely engulfed in flames, chemicals for embalming combined with gasoline and old, old wood. Small explosions sent glass and wood spraying into the yard, drew my attention to how low the sun was behind the flames. "No, I was just an added bonus."

"A pain in the ass you mean."

"Yeah, actually. That's exactly what I mean. Whatever Lawrence wants, I'd only get in his way. I'd be happy to prove him right."

"Louis!" Boyd, the broken, red-headed deputy was at one of the sheriff's vehicles. "Coleman's on the radio." I followed the sheriff over to the SUV. "Sounds pretty excited."

"Where you at, Coleman?" The sheriff was watching me as he spoke.

"I'm following the Feds."

I grabbed the radio out of Williams' hands. "That wasn't the plan! And they aren't Feds."

He didn't even pause to reply. "Your plan sucked. Littlewing said they was wearing charms. She couldn't zap 'em. She said you two could handle the fire, so I'm following the bad guys."

"Give me that." The sheriff took back the radio and put his back to me. "Give us your 10-20."

"Looks like we're heading to the old Rail place. Damn. Mitch got me out there after all." I heard the nervous laughter as he tried to reassure himself. Didn't seem to be working.

"Where's Littlewing?" I asked the sheriff.

"Deputy Coleman, where's the sprite?"

"She's right here!" Littlewing zipped into my chest and I caught her reflexively. "Did anyone get the license of the truck that hit me?"

"A truck hit her?" asked Boyd, looking surprised.

"They grow 'em big and dumb, like a Julie Brown song." Littlewing sat up. "Some kind of hex. The same kind the Feds use when hunting fey. I fucking hate that Lawrence! Fake Fed or not!"

"Leave it." I held Littlewing up to my face. "For now. You okay?"

"Will be. But Lawrence won't when I get my hands on him. If you hadn't made me promise not to shoot them!" She waved her gun in my direction, I used a finger to point it away.

"Only in self-defense," I reminded her. "We aren't sanctioned for killing humans. Not even day-watchers or assholes like Lawrence."

"You need time to blow her or can we get moving?" demanded Williams.

He looked worried. I agreed. Garvy wasn't up to dealing with whatever Lawrence and his people were planning. I'd brought him along to keep him safe. But he'd gone off on his own after all. Damn it all to hell!

And it would be dark soon. Too soon. Lawrence had bought the vampires more time. But was that an accident? Or part of the plan?

I shook my head at Williams. "I had to go in cautiously because they had you as hostages. If we go into the Rail place with your deputies and their friends, that's more bodies I have to protect. Let me have a twenty-minute head-start. If I can't take 'em out that fast, then I'll *need* your help."

He stared at me, playing with the talk button on the radio still in his hand. "Fine. Take Boyd's car and stay in touch by radio."

"Guess Boyd can return the *Barry's Breads* truck." I tossed him the keys. "Yours?"

Angry, the red-head dug around in his navy-colored trousers and threw his keys on the ground. I picked them up without taking my eyes off of him. He wanted to hit me, but he wouldn't do it in front of witnesses. That would be stupid. Witnesses might keep him alive.

Littlewing zipped in through the passenger window which Boyd had left partially open. The days were growing warmer, but it wasn't the season for air-conditioning. Tonight, it would be more than warm. Things were going to get hot. I slipped behind the wheel, took a minute to figure out all the gizmos associated with a law enforcement vehicle and peeled out.

After I'd driven about five minutes, Littlewing spoke. "How does this thing work?" She hovered at the radio and pressed a button. Now we could hear Garvy's voice.

"They've turned onto the road toward the old Rail place. God damn, got me out here at night even! You there, Mitch? Shit, shit, shit. I'm gonna park and follow them on foot. I'm gonna have to turn my hand-radio down to keep from giving myself away. Over and out."

I grabbed for the handset and Littlewing shrieked indignantly. "Gar? Deputy Coleman, respond!"

The sheriff's voice echoed mine on the channel. "Coleman, do not follow! Answer me!"

We heard silence as I drove. I waited for Garvy to come back on the air, unhappy, but obedient. The sheriff waited, too. Too much time passed. "God damn him!" was the sheriff's only comment. He meant for me to hear.

"Drive faster." Littlewing wasn't the only one with a bad feeling about this.

I put my foot to the floor, relying on werewolf reflexes and superstrength to keep myself from crashing or getting thrown through a window. The next ten minutes passed without even a squawk from the radio. The sheriff, like me, was listening. Waiting for Garvy.

I watched the sun grow close to the ground. Less than an hour of light. A lot less. Fake Feds and a vampire. Maybe I'd luck out and the vampire would attack Lawrence and his people. Yeah, and maybe Littlewing would finally suck my dick. Not a chance in Hell.

"Turn here!" shouted Littlewing as I strained to hear something in the deadness of the channel.

I jerked the wheel around and the car spun twice, so that we were almost facing the same direction again. Littlewing bounced against the front window, then the seat and she slammed into the steering wheel before falling into my lap.

"Now I know what a pinball feels like." She fluttered off of my crotch and grabbed the lapel of my jacket.

"You okay?" She'd pass up a chance to stroke my lap. Garvy worried her as much as he worried me.

She nodded, her expression grim. "Keep driving."

Another ten minutes down the road and I recognized the roof of the Rail house across a stretch of countryside. I didn't know where the actual driveway was, so I made a new one. I drove through some overgrown plants, hit something buried over the years and bounced up onto two wheels before the car slammed hard onto a patch of tangled grass and bushes. The engine stalled and died.

"Quiet!" demanded Littlewing before I could say anything. She was listening. So I listened. There was nothing. "Fucking shit."

"What? 'Shit' wasn't good enough?"

"Not this time." She started to flit out of the window but stopped. She glanced back at me. "You get out of the car first."

She was afraid. I couldn't recall ever seeing her truly afraid before. Sure, dogs made her nervous and she didn't like them. But she wasn't afraid of them. This was 'boogeyman in the dark' kind of scared. If she wasn't afraid of vampires or werewolves, what *was* she afraid of?

"What?" I whispered, because it seemed like the thing to do.

She moaned angrily. "What's the most nasty thing you've ever faced?"

The djinn was the most powerful thing I'd faced. But nastiest? "The dryads."

"Then you'll love this." She still hadn't left the car. "Hurry up."

I slipped out of the car and walked around to the front. I could see the fake FBI cars at the back of the house, but no movement in the dusky light. I could smell Littlewing hovering at my ear, felt the buzz of her wings against my hair. "Tell me what it is."

"Elf." Her big eyes were even wider as she scanned the woods around the house.

"How do you know?" I'd only seen that iron-bound elf and even with a Hannibal Lecter leather face-mask muzzling his mouth, he'd looked like a nasty piece of work. Very few people survived their encounters with the elusive creatures. So we knew very little about them. Usually, leave them alone and they left you alone.

"I can hear it." Littlewing's voice was a taut whisper wanting to become a scream.

I listened again, straining to capture some sound that wasn't natural. There were twigs falling through trees to hit the ground. The house settling from time. There was even the sound of the wind rattling through grass. But I couldn't hear anything out of the ordinary. It was as quiet as the night I had come looking for the vampire. Maybe more so.

"I don't hear anything."

"Exactly," she said. "But it's there. The sound a predator makes when it's not moving. Waiting to strike if you look into its eyes."

"I'll take your word for it."

"It's there." She sounded terrified. "Wait for back-up."

"And if Lawrence gets Gar because I waited? Or we give the vampire a chance to wake? Because let's face it, we're screwed for daylight."

She was silent for a moment and I turned to stare at her. "I don't want to die, Mitch."

"Then stay here."

I raced across the yard, stealthy as no human could be. I watched and listened for human heartbeats or footsteps. There was nothing. The cars creaked and moaned as their engines cooled down, but the men who'd been driving them were as quiet as ghosts. Or the dead.

Littlewing's fear started to crawl along my skin, making my human hair stand up on end.

I moved quietly around the building. My nose could tell that the fake Feds and Deputy Coleman had been here. But—it was like a cloying spice had been released into the air. It ate away even those remnant traces of humans from the creepy abandoned dwelling.

At the back of the house, near the cars, I discovered that a hole had been dug. It was tall enough to walk through hunched over. Wide enough that Williams could have joined me. Shovels had been tossed aside near the hole. The opening had been dug by human hands. Lawrence's men.

That meant they'd been at it some time. Digging while the others had waited for me at the Summerlin Crematorium. Lawrence believed something was down there. The vampire? Buried treasure? I was betting on the latter.

I scooped up a handful of soil, smelling the rich scent of earth and clay, but there was something else too. Strange, fey scents. Littlewing had said 'elf.' Whatever it was, it almost completely masked the smell of anything human. It was a cloying, unidentifiable weight in the air.

Beneath that strange musk, there were familiar smells. Not 'good' familiar, just recognizable. There was death in that hole. And if pain could have a smell, it was there, too. I circled the opening, listening, but I couldn't hear anything.

"Leave it, Mitch." Littlewing actually pulled at my ear, trying to hold me back. "Can't you smell it?"

"Garvy?" I was wrong. There was a hint of something human. The deputy had come this way. Down into that. He hadn't just overcome his fear of the Rail place. He had wanted to prove himself to me. Impress the fucking werewolf. But he hadn't been the first to go down there. My nose was struggling. Lawrence's men had gone first. So whose death did I smell?

"If he's in there, he's already dead." Littlewing was somber, not exaggerating or threatening me. If she was afraid, I should be, too. But I was the only hope Garvy had.

"I'm not gonna leave him just on your say so."

"You'll see." She sounded like she was in shock.

She'd face a murder of vampires, but she wouldn't confront one miserable elf. I had thought that the Feds were just being overly cautious with that iron-bound elf I'd seen. I remembered laughing at the years-hardened agents who'd been spooked just being in the same room with the helpless creature. Now Littlewing was petrified with terror.

Sure, I'd been disconcerted by the elf's strange eyes, but that was all. So then, what made elves so scary? Guess I was about to find out.

I slipped inside the opening, my eyes adjusting until the darkness of the tunnel became discernible shapes. The opening had been dug by Lawrence's men. But the passage inside had been carved out by magic. The walls were so smooth that I doubted even a machine could have created the passage. I ran a hand along the soil, noting that no pebble or root broke the compact perfection. No loose dirt fell at my probing, as if something unseen held it in place. The precision of the curvature was indicative of madness. I liked mess.

For moments I didn't move. I just watched and listened. And used my nose. Down here, I could smell a lot of blood, freshly spilt. And that complex mixture of excruciating pain and death. I realized then that the smell of death wasn't because of the bodies that I knew I'd find further in. It was because of the creature which had done that killing.

There was no noise. No sound of a fey heartbeat. If an elf could be preternaturally silent, I'd have to rely on my eyes. If it could be invisible, then I was as good as dead myself. As far as I knew, their glamours weren't that good. I hoped I was right.

I looked over my shoulder, but Littlewing hadn't followed me. More than claustrophobia stopped her this time. I moved further into the tunnel. After a few yards, a wall of plant roots dangled down from the ceiling of the passage. They had been woven into a series of perfectly symmetrical braids. They were so perfect, that they belonged on a young girl's head. Not buried underground.

Were all elves this obsessed with symmetry or was it unique to the creature in this burrow? I pushed through the roots. I tensed up, expecting them to grip me when I touched them, but they were just decorations. Curtains to separate rooms.

On the other side of them, I literally stumbled on the first body. One of the fake FBI. His face had been ripped away to reveal white bone and strips of distended muscle. A gun was in his hand. I could smell the ozone and nitrogen dioxide. Two of the more obvious gasses associated with a fired weapon. And there was heated silver, all over the bouquet of blood and gore.

Firing his gun had done him no good. The silver, meant for me, had worked against him. Iron. Not silver. Not even steel did much damage against what he'd faced. He had needed iron.

A few feet deeper was another body. Make that two other bodies. One was missing its stomach. The elf had scooped out his intestines and left the ribcage like a flesh-covered bowl exposed to the world.

The man's eyes were gone. I glanced at the other body. Its eyes were missing, too. Their mouths were twisted in agony or fear or both. I'd never seen such fear. It looked like the kind someone could die from. Fear that came from seeing something horrific. The eyes had been plucked out after death. Definitely.

I heard a whimpering ahead. Too faint for normal ears. I rushed down the tunnel. There were more bodies and I stepped over those corpses quickly. If Garvy was in this passage—if that was his whimper, it might not be too late to save him. I mentally cursed his bravery at continuing down the tunnel after seeing these dead men. I'd happily cuss him to his face if I only found him alive.

I reached a section of the burrow that was infused with unexpected light. It seeped out of strange, bulbous plants growing in neat spirals from the walls. The light revealed another bend, but the smell of death was replaced by something sweet, flowery. It reminded me of the velvet texture of rose-petals or a woman's intimate flesh. Seductive and dangerous. A glamour of the senses, meant to distract. I was close, Garvy's whimper confirmed it.

I pressed my back to the wall, still moving silently. Still unable to hear anything except that helpless, horrible noise. I held my gun firmly, two handed as I sidled around the bend. I heard movement and a visceral wet sound. Meat being played with.

Just past that curve, I saw Garvy's mouth move, accompanied by another whimper. My gaze followed the line of a pale, bony arm coming out of the black man's back. The arm was attached to a creature which was the source of the whimpering. It animated the deputy's mouth like Garvy was a sock puppet. But the once cheerful and likeable young man was dead. His eyes were missing and his mouth was twisted into the same kind of terror that the other bodies had revealed.

I must have growled, outraged and horrified, because the elf spun, startled. I saw it in all of its unmasked terribleness. It was pale, like a vampire and had straggly hair. The hair was a green so dark it was almost black, like it's large eyes. No whites, just black ovals that blinked at me as it hissed. The sound came from a wide mouth full of nearly human-like teeth, and a long tongue, split at the end. No glamour. This was the creature's true form.

The elf was nothing like the Danish or Irish fairy tales of fey princes come to choose gleeful human maidens. Stories that blessed their offspring as desirable changelings. Or maybe the fairy tales had been incomplete. They'd left off the part about the cruel torture of the maidens once they saw their husbands as they truly were. Not that I was an expert on Western European mythology. But this thing was as nasty as I'd ever met.

The creature pulled its hand out of Garvy's back, making a slurping noise that sickened me. It waved the bloody hand at me, slowly. Like it was happy to see me. But the eyes were alien and whatever thoughts the monster had were not meant to be understood by humans. Or anyone sane at least.

Waving at me with Garvy's blood on its clawed hand was a mistake. It enraged me so that the world became white light and nothing but the elf existed. But it wasn't the elf's mistake. It was mine. My fury at seeing Garvy's corpse being used like a toy made me stupid. I didn't sense the movement behind me until heavy and powerful symmetrical braids grappled my arms. More of those perfectly woven roots. These sprang directly out of the earthen ceiling, commanded by that innocent waving to coil about me.

I tore myself free instantly, cracking the living wood with my anger-strengthened muscles. The startled creature did a little hop, shivering with some alien emotion. But the madness underneath its innocent gesture was plain.

I felt a press of force against my chest, then inside my body. Not roots this time. It used magic to crush the life out of me directly. It scurried like a chimp toward me, using its knuckles to pull itself toward me. I understood in a flash of despondent humor why the Feds had called the fey apes.

When the elf reached me, it didn't stop. It raised a long, clawed hand and swiped downward. I struggled against its power in the only way I knew how. I changed. As a human, I was strong. My wolfman form was even stronger. My skin darkened and hair covered it. I felt the muscles ripple where the elf's magic threatened to crush my heart and felt a moment's joy. The pressure eased as the body it held turned into something else. I was almost free.

But then I stared too long into its eyes and I blinked, confused. I blinked again but my memory cleared. I'd almost forgot what I was doing. Shit. If it drained my mind of any ability to think, I would end up just another dead werewolf. Whatever it was doing to my mind made it lessen its attack on my body. I shoved myself backwards just in time to feel the tips of its claws tear through my shirt but not my flesh.

I tasted the cloying weight of the elf's scent and bared a mouthful of fangs at my enemy, hardly aware of my actions. More roots came out of the burrow from above. These were thicker and stronger. It had finally realized that I wasn't any more human than it was. The fey vegetation coiled around my arms, lifting me so that my clawed toes barely touched the floor of the tunnel. Other roots curled about my neck, squeezing painfully, but not enough to break my neck. Only my legs were free but I had no leverage.

The elf spoke, a crooning, shrill sound that made me tremble with alien discomfort. The sound, never meant to be heard by a human mind, not even a werewolf's, filled me with a wave of madness. My body shifted wildly, patches of involuntary human skin visible next to the dark brown hair I tried to summon. Every sense was a weapon it could turn against me, but I wasn't a quitter. I was Werewolf Incorporated!

But my defiance didn't stop my descent into darkness. The roots became fingers of a strange, magnificent lover. Their embrace didn't threaten me. They reassured. As their grip tightened, I knew that I wanted to be pulled into the earth. Deeply and completely, so that I was buried in its comforting weight. I gave up my wolf, forgetting that I had ever wanted to fight.

A gun fired across my shoulder. The smell of ozone was a powerful trigger and I snapped out of the dysphoria which had taken me. "Sorry, Mitch."

I'd never been happier to see the sprite. "Better late than never."

I grimaced, which was the only kind of smile I could manage as the elf turned its startled attention to Littlewing. The fey monster came to life, violently animated. It flailed its arms in the air and hopped about as if its favorite food had been set before it. The gaunt, insane elf smacked its thin, wide lips and waved again in the air.

I understood then. Littlewing's fear had been too personal, too intimate. This elf had come from the same universe as the sprite. Littlewing's terror was based on personal knowledge of elves, not just a bad reaction to a dangerous creature. Elves were the predators there. Sprites the prey. She really was food. And she'd followed me into its lair!

Garvy had died. Littlewing wouldn't. I went full werewolf, with claws and fangs and the wild yellow of my wolf-eyes. Or at least, that was the plan. My body resisted the change and I felt a moment's panic. I figured it was because I was underneath the ground, shielded from any trace of moonlight but I could still sense the moon above me. It was more than that. The elf's power dampened my access to the wolf in me. That fey, cloying weight in the air was affecting my curse. It had to be something unique to elves, acting on werewolves. The way that the dryad pheromones had affected me. A natural part of the creature's biology, not a spell or conscious manipulation. It had probably evolved for elf survival, to mask them in shadows or forgetfulness.

Littlewing fired another two rounds into the elf. That was all her miniature gun held of the larger caliber shells. I saw the monster jerk back and didn't waste the time she bought me. The flesh of the roots cracked, then shattered as I tore myself free and leapt at the elf.

It shrieked, surprised at my strength and willingness to attack it. I was betting nothing else had ever come closer than a few yards to the fey monster without being rendered helpless by its voice or eyes. I was a different kind of monster. And I had the pleasure of seeing it grow worried.

It glanced past me at Littlewing and the madness became avarice. It wanted her. Wanted to eat her. That hunger in its eyes, that desperation could be nothing else.

The elf struck out as my leap put me on top of it, stiff-arming me. I felt its claws dig into my flesh with such strength that it was like pressing knives into butter. I screamed in pain, which brought a smile of pleasure to its wide mouth, but I didn't look away. I didn't dare.

The wild elven eyes grew shrewd. I knew that I had underestimated it. Its fear had been feigned, to make me overconfident. And it had worked.

With its other hand, it grabbed me by the throat, yanking downward with the claws in my chest. It raked the skin off my chest, shredding my shirt and ripping the muscles along my belly. My blood sprayed the elf and seeped into the soil at his feet.

I screamed, then roared in fury. I could heal fast, but I was afraid. If the elf's power slowed all my abilities, those wounds might kill me. Then my partner would die. "Littlewing, get out of here!"

That alien voice spoke again, sending waves of confusion and madness into my brain. Littlewing fired again. Part of my brain realized that she must have reloaded. We didn't rely on her gun normally, so three rounds in the chamber and two backup rounds strapped to her hips were it. I was betting that she knew what its voice did to humans. Only firing her gun could break that effect over me.

I took the opening, again. Despite the pain and my blood pooling at my feet. I drove my fist upward, the index and middle fingers extended like blades, and shoved them under its chin. I continued through its mouth to tap up into its brain.

The elf dropped me, screaming so shrilly that the sound seized my nerves. It sent pain into my body that drove me to my knees. Blood trickled from my nose and ears and I could tell other bad things were happening to my internal organs. Littlewing flew forward as the elf clutched at its head and wailed. There was no feigning the shocked expression of pain on its features. It couldn't even swipe at her.

She pressed her gun up to its forehead and pulled the trigger. Her last round, right where she needed it. "Fuck you."

The elf's brains splattered out the back of its head and sprayed the tunnel. Where it struck Garvy's corpse, strange non-Earthly plants unfurled. They had mossy bases, pale yellow-green leaves and flowers as black as the shadows.

"Those things dangerous?" The tunnel spun a bit, a residual effect of the elf's voice on my brain.

"Elf Death." Littlewing didn't look at me. She watched the unmoving creature, her now empty gun still aimed at it. As if it were Jason about to reanimate after his umpteenth death. But this wasn't a horror film. The elf stayed dead. "It's a powerful narcotic. Probably should burn it."

"You come from the same place as the elf?" Just because I'd guessed it, that didn't mean I assumed I was right.

Littlewing nodded, her lips pressed together in silence. She frowned at the Elf Death sprouting from Garvy's disfigured body and shivered.

"What's it for?" I started to sense the power of the moonlight again. Aware of it for the first time as a force always touching my body, influencing my mind. The cloying power of the elf was fading. No wonder Littlewing had been so terrified. But she'd saved my butt anyway.

"Part of the reproductive cycle."

"Like semen?" I made a face.

"Fish cast their seed into the water near female eggs. This isn't unnatural, Mitch." She was in shock, terrified even of the elf's corpse, but she defended its biology. Another of those times I wished she could grow to full human size. But then she wouldn't have to settle for me as a lover. Or even as a partner. A no win situation, I realized suddenly.

"Are there eggs around for it to fertilize?" I asked, annoyed by my self-pity. I looked everywhere but at Garvy's eyeless face.

"The flowers give off a scent. It attracts females if any are around. If they get here before the flowers go to seed, there's a chance they'll reproduce. If not, it's like masturbation. Wasted effort."

"Masturbation is never a wasted effort." I watched her turn to me, blinking. There was a twitch of a smile as she holstered her gun. She'd be okay. Looking at Garvy, maybe I wouldn't.

I went to the plants and pulled one from Garvy's body, but I tore his flesh, yanked out with the roots. Withered and drained in just those short minutes. I never threw up around death and dismemberment, but I had to cover my mouth for a moment and swallow down the bile. "Damn it."

"Just pinch off the flowers. Leave the roots in his body. They won't regrow."

Littlewing's voice was faint, lost. Her gaze was locked on Garvy and I couldn't bear the sadness in her eyes. I was already filled with guilt and self-loathing. If she cried, I didn't know how I'd react. I made myself look away from her. I concentrated on the plants that defiled his body. Pinched off every black flower until I had an armful. I'd put them in the car and burn them later. No way I was gonna let this fucker reproduce.

I saw the dark-brown hair on my hands and shifted back to human. The shirt was torn from the fight, my flesh completely healed underneath. At least elven damage didn't last like silver.

"No sign of Lawrence. Where do you think he went?" I wanted to pull Littlewing out of her shock.

"Who the fuck cares?" Not much of a reaction, but something.

"People died down here. What did he want? How valuable is an elf?" I studied the shadows. There were no hidden piles of gold or treasure. Just insane symmetry.

"Who the fuck cares, Mitch!?" She shouted at me. Good, finally.

"I'm gonna make him pay." Not for her. This was all about me. "Didn't even have the balls to come down here himself."

If he had, he'd be dead like those other men. Part of me was glad. It would give me a chance to kill him myself. Slowly, painfully.

"Gar did. Do you know how fucking brave that was?" She looked at me, her eyes damp. She never cried. Garvy had gotten to her. Couldn't afford it in our line of work. Proof in the pudding. Where was Bill Cosby when you needed him? Drugging some helpless woman probably.

"Do not fucking cry," I growled. Damn it, I'd said 'fuck.' "You are such a bad influence."

"Suck my dick." She'd lost some of her anger, falling back into despair.

I gave up. "Let's go call the sheriff. I don't look forward to telling him about Garvy."

I shouldn't feel guilty. I'd told him to stay out of the fight. But it was an ugly feeling nonetheless. I pictured growing old, stopping by and having a beer or three with Sheriff Coleman, him greying at the temples. A friend in a world where I didn't have many. Call me a selfish bastard to think that way. But thinking of him as a young intelligent deputy, gutted and terrified was a whole lot worse.

228 | MICHAEL DON ANDERSON

CHAPTER TWENTY-SIX

The sheriff arrived with a fleet of vehicles just after first dark. Lights blazing. Sirens wailing. It cut through the country quiet in a way that put me on edge. He'd called out the entire militia from the looks of it and there were more deputies. Charlotte nodded to me, but even in the glare of headlights used to light up the Rail place, her eyes were hard. They knew that Garvy was dead. I'd radioed the sheriff so that he'd have time to work through the worst of the grief before he was standing face to face with me. I wasn't in the mood to fight. Not against a human after witnessing the madness of that monstrous elf. I figured the damage to my clothes spoke for itself.

"Where?" Williams wouldn't even make eye-contact, trying to contain his rage.

I pointed at the entrance to the burrow and they wheeled in huge portable flood lights. The kind used for power outages. Then and only then did Williams and his men go quietly into the black tunnel. I watched them, handguns and shotguns gripped tightly, afraid of what they would find. The elf was dead. But that wasn't what they were anxious about.

I knew they'd found the first bodies when three of the men raced back, retching before they could clear the lip of the tunnel. Their curses were muted. They would have nightmares for the rest of their lives by the time they reached the end of that tunnel. If seeing the dead bad guys didn't affect them, Garvy's body would. And I wasn't going to tell them about the puppet thing. Nobody deserved to know about that. Not even me.

Boyd came up from the tunnel. The red-headed deputy looked around and stopped when he saw me. He came over looking grim, but otherwise unaffected. Seeing Garvy's body should have left him weeping or horrified. But he was just—broken. No different than before. He didn't even give Littlewing more than a passing glance.

"Sheriff wants you out of here before he comes back up with Coleman. Said to remind you that there's a vampire still out there."

I stared up at the night sky, seeing the first visible stars without any hint of romance. Garvy would never see those stars again. "Those his words?"

Boyd grunted, turned and went back to the tunnel. He hadn't asked for his keys back, so I glanced over and his vehicle had a clear passage out of here. Williams wanted to be sure that I had no excuse not to leave.

"Let's go, Mitch."

I studied the men standing around the burrow entrance. They studied the darkened woods furtively. If I didn't leave, I'd be associated with Garvy's body and be blamed. I was already being blamed by some. Besides, Williams was right. Night had come, the vampire was awake.

"Yeah, I'm going."

I drove Littlewing and myself back to the Mustang and left Boyd's keys in his car. After changing into a spare shirt from the trunk, I sat in the driver's seat of the Ford and stared up at the sky again. I had no leads, just more corpses. For a change, Littlewing left me in silence with my thoughts, but only because she was just as bothered by Garvy's death and our confrontation with the elf as I was. If it had just been me down in the dumps, she would have tried to cheer me up. Neither one of us had any cheer in us.

Twenty minutes passed but I was still in a foul mood when the phone rang. I'd never had such a hard time tracking vampires before and I hated failing. I wanted to blame it on Williams and his inexperienced deputies, but it was me. I'd been reacting badly to Resistance from the moment I'd entered the city limits. Getting hung up on the past. Garvy's death had been the icing on the grumpy cake.

"What's wrong?" Littlewing rode on my shoulder. She felt the tension.

"Nothing." I answered the phone, slamming back against the leather seat of my Ford Mustang. "Greyson here."

"Mr. Greyson, this is Dr. Walker."

My heart pounded at the excitement in her voice. "You found something."

"I think so. My father's journals say that one of the bodies wasn't found at the Rail place." Paper rustled on her end and I heard the clacking of a keyboard. "I'm looking at an online aerial map. There's a bunker next to an old warehouse about fifteen miles outside of town. A hunter and his bloodhound came across a dead boy. Thought he'd fallen and broken his neck."

Another victim. "When? This evening?"

"No. The one in my father's journal. Pay attention!" Garvy's voice echoed 'my bad' in my brain. Only it was my mistake this time, not his. Even dead, his good-natured attitude haunted me. "My father did an autopsy after dealing with the other bodies. He found two tentative puncture marks. The boy hadn't been drained, but Daddy figured it was related. The property had been purchased by the Summerlins about the time of the first victim. I checked. It was never recorded in their name. The County reclaimed it some years ago because of unpaid taxes. I found the deed in his journal. He must have uncovered it during his personal investigation into the murders. But—but I can't believe he didn't turn it over to the authorities or back to the Summerlins."

I didn't have time for her daddy-issues. "What's the address?"

"Head north along Aikman Lane till you hit Fawn. Turn right and go to 23235."

I hung up. "Come on Littlewing, we might have caught a break."

"We gonna bring back up?" Her question had an edge of doubt to it. Going in alone, after dark, not very smart. But Garvy had been our back-up and he was dead.

I just turned the key and hit the pedal with a heavy foot. I wasn't about to leave town without finding that vamp. "Navigate with the GPS."

"That's very 21st century of you, Mitch." She kicked open the glove-box and pulled out the device that she'd given me the previous Christmas. I'd ignored it in favor of paper maps, but tonight I'd swallow my pride rather than waste time. "What's the address?"

I repeated it and she tapped it into the GPS. "It's only two streets." She was miffed that we didn't actually need the high-tech marvel. Anything to take her mind off of Garvy's death.

"I know. But I want you to let me know the second we hit that address. The numbers won't be easy to see on the mailboxes and this place has probably been abandoned for about sixty-three years."

With my foot heavy on the accelerator and my werewolf quick reflexes, we made it in less than eight minutes. "Stop!" shouted the sprite without warning.

Littlewing braced the GPS between her body and the seat, clutching at the seatbelt as I slammed on the brakes. The dark shape of a warehouse was visible over tall bushes, behind a wooden fence that looked like it had been there since the turn of the previous century. No lights. Not inhabited. Good.

"This is the place. There aren't any cars or deputies to mask the scents, so we do this right. If this is her nest, I'll track Reed from here to wherever she's gone. It might be our only shot at finding her and any other vampires she's made. Rail wasn't food. But we don't know if he was being forced to give up the location of their child, or if she wanted him, too. So we treat it as a hostage situation."

"Not an all-night stakeout!?" complained the sprite.

I needed something to laugh at, but only managed a grin as I loaded my .45 with hollow-points. No sense in taking chances with regular ammunition. Something was going to die tonight. At my hands. It might not bring Garvy back, but I was too angry to believe otherwise.

"You can always fly back into town for coffee." I shut the door quietly and slipped into the vegetation. "Did you reload?"

She cursed and I waited a moment. The road was overgrown. I couldn't drive my car up to the warehouse, even if I'd wanted to. Her gun sorted out, Littlewing flittered behind me, her fear of the elf gone. In its place, a determination and the need for a fight. The angry buzz of her wings was a reassuring sound. I hadn't forgotten that this was a new type of vampire we were hunting. Reed Summerlin had been able to feed in the daytime, so that made her doubly dangerous.

I paused at the edge of the building, still hidden in the bushes like a wild animal. Unlike the Rail place, there was nothing heavy or eerie to mark the presence of the fey. The air was clean, except for a touch of decaying flesh. Something had died or been brought here dead. I was guessing we'd found our missing vampire lair.

Vampires had exceptional hearing, but not as good as werewolves. I motioned to Littlewing to fly close to my lips. She brushed me with the soft fabric of her wings and I had mildly erotic thoughts for half-a-second. It was my reaction to danger, a little heightened sexual arousal. I'd never get a chance to shoot my own Elf-Death equivalent with the sprite.

"We're looking for a bunker. The warehouse is full of holes. Sunlight everywhere during the day. There enough light for you to see?" Sprites were daytime creatures. Littlewing said she could see fine at dusk and dawn, but this was full-on dark. Again, not normally stupid enough to tackle vampires at night, but we had no choice.

She nodded and rose higher into the sky. I waited while she did a quick fly around. When she came back she was excited. "Follow me."

She zipped back into the air but I was fast on her tail. Regardless of my shape, I moved with more stealth than a real wolf. My mind automatically found places to step where there were no dried branches or noisy clumps of undergrowth. On the far side of the warehouse, there was a massive clustering of shrubs and vines centered around a pair of citrus trees, old and gnarled. They'd been there a long time.

I was halfway to the bunker when a body fell out of the sky in front of me. Littlewing, some distance ahead, didn't notice. I jumped sideways, startled, but my fangs extended and I crouched for an attack, digging clawed fingers into the ground for traction.

The body bounced from the impact before becoming still. As in *dead*. I felt the brush of air a moment before strong, clearly feminine arms curled around my neck and chest. Fangs sank into my shoulder and I roared with pain.

I reacted by flipping onto my back, but delicate ankles wrapped around my hips like I was on the receiving end of unwanted sex. An obviously female body pressed against my back with superhuman strength. Was she stronger than me?

There was a burst of sunlight. Littlewing doing what she did best. The vampire shrieked and involuntarily loosened her grip. I took advantage of the moment and spun so fast that I was facing her while we were still on the ground, her ankles loosely clutching my buttocks now. Reed Summerlin, the beautiful woman in the red dress. Our original vampire

I grabbed her by the throat and by one arm, before she could respond. I hurled her toward the warehouse with all my strength. That was another thing the movies got wrong. Vampires couldn't fly. Reed had only jumped down from the roof to attack me. The corpse had been a mere distraction.

She crashed into the building with enough noise to wake the dead. If there were any more around. The corpse suggested that her return to the bunker had just been accidental.

"Thanks." I glanced at Littlewing who chased after the vampire. "Careful, there are tw—!"

I didn't finish my word because another set of arms grappled me from behind. These arms weren't as strong and I broke the grip easily. I got a whiff of maleness, rotting blood, and the remnants of advanced age.

I yanked the second vampire around to face me. Then slammed him onto the ground, my arm extended to hold his neck like a metal bar. He struggled to bite my hand, but his rheumy eyes were almost animalistic. Wrinkled flesh. Flakes of dried blood around his mouth. It had to be Andrew Rail.

"Leave us!" Reed ran toward me from the building. Her skin-tight dress had been torn by the thin corrugated metal of the warehouse, and one breast half sagged out of it. It was the creamiest, whitest piece of female flesh I'd ever seen. I almost wished she'd been a real woman. Maybe even more than Littlewing. If vampires weren't always bad guys, they would have been a good sexual match for a randy werewolf. If she'd have been willing.

"You're a killer." It was an inane comment, but I was slightly distracted by the feeble man in my grip.

His teeth were slightly askew in his mouth. New hair was starting to come back in next to the long strands of white, sparse old-man hair. His eyes weren't completely aware, as if he were senile or drugged. He wouldn't regress to her age for a couple of weeks, give or take.

"They tried to kill me!" screamed Reed, coming close. I saw another flash of light behind her, but it was dim. Littlewing hadn't taken the time to recharge and her glow was too weak to kill. She probably only had a flash or two left. "I only want my family back."

"The man who freed you at the mine? He wanted to kill you?"

She hesitated, not expecting me to know that. "All the living want to kill me!"

I used my free hand to slap at Rail's fangs and saw them fall out of his nearly toothless mouth. Nubs of fangs had started to sprout from his upper gums, but they couldn't have torn their way through a baby's tender skin.

"Dentures?" I stared at the woman, distracted by her exposed breast. "Vampire dentures?"

"He's so old. It will take time for his to grow." She hissed but Littlewing drew her gun and shot near Reed's feet. The vampire paused a few feet away from me, but her eyes went to Littlewing. "What manner of thing are you?"

I stared at Reed Summerlin. "I thought vampires get memories from their victims. You should know what she is. What I am."

Reed moved fast then, acting without warning. Something flew from her hand and struck Littlewing. It knocked her from the air.

I snarled, but Littlewing moaned, so I knew she was still alive. "You're gonna pay for that."

"Only the strongest memories." The vampire took a step toward me, but her frantic eyes went to my hand around Rail's neck.

"Stop right there, or I'll tear his throat out."

"You'll kill us both anyway." She stared at Rail with a desperation that I found peculiar in an undead bloodsucker. A flash of perfect white skin peeked through at her hip and I could not ignore how well-formed she was as a woman. It wasn't the obsession that a dryad's pheromones inflicted. But I was a single guy and she was hot.

"A stake will render you lifeless, but not dead." I was fudging the truth.

For vampires, under Bachmann's laws, there'd be no prison. Just a guaranteed, almost immediate death-sentence. Everywhere but Utah. Beheading after any doctor confirmed what they were.

Would that be my fate? She'd bitten me. Not her first victim of the night, so the odds were in my favor. But there was a chance.

"He's an innocent. His mind is so jumbled. So confused." She sounded almost piteous. "I've been asleep so many years."

I figured I'd play the only card I had to throw her off-guard. To see if I was right. "You have a child, don't you?"

Her expression grew hard and hateful. She would kill me, there was no doubt. She wanted to escape and a desperate mother was a fierce warrior. Her eyes drifted back to Andrew Rail's face. He still struggled to bite the hand that held him. "He gave her up. I almost killed him for that."

"You love him, but you'd kill him?" I didn't mean to goad her. I wanted answers. What kind of creature was she? How did she think? And I was buying Littlewing time to regain consciousness. It was the first time I'd try to confront a vampire in the night time. The first time alone.

"He must not have loved me because he gave away our child. A miracle after I'd been made into this—this *thing*." She hated being a vampire. And she'd made him into one. A new definition of love-hate relationships.

"How did you feed? That first feeding, when the suit pulled the stake out of you? It was daylight wasn't it?"

It was probably my stare, but she was suddenly aware that her breast was exposed. She tugged at the dress and covered herself. "Why do you care?"

"Humor me and I might let him go." Vampires couldn't smell the truth on people. I had no qualms about lying to a killer to get what I wanted. The moment I staked one of them, the other would probably flee. She was the one I wanted to get first. Rail couldn't feed himself in his current state.

"Truthfully? I don't know." Her confusion seemed genuine. She wanted to talk about it. After the elf, having a conversation with a vampire didn't seem as surreal. "It was like fire poured into me. I reached out and my fangs clamped onto the nearest living thing. Like waking from a nightmare without knowing it. You sit up or scream before you are even awake. Then I fell into the same darkness that takes me every morning since I was bitten by that beast."

"The double fangs?" I was trying to see her teeth, but there was only the one row that I could tell.

She actually laughed. "Cousin Clarence suggested the false teeth. They were made like mine, only larger. Andrew cannot bite well enough on his own. I would take a bite, and then place his mouth around the blood. His mind may be frail, but his hunger is strong." She grew serious. "Give us two days and we'll leave this place forever. I'll give you whatever you want."

She did something with her torso and the breast slipped back out through the hole. It wasn't accidental. She was offering me sex. Sex for her life. For two days and two more nights of killing innocent residents of Resistance County. The sex was tempting. The trade-off wasn't.

"Why two days?"

She looked at Andrew Rail, forlornly. "He will be well enough by then. I'll take my family and go."

I thought about it. "Where is Clarence? He part of that family?"

She shrugged. "In hiding now that I no longer need him."

Maybe the pale-white breast was distracting me more than I'd been admitting. She was there, on top of me so fast that I almost didn't see her. She knocked me off of Rail but this time she didn't bite me.

I watched her fight the instinct to sink her three-inch long canines into my flesh. Something about my blood disagreed with her, and she didn't want to experience it again. What would her venom do to me? I'd been thinking of myself as invulnerable until the elf had nearly consumed me with madness. Not her first victim tonight, I reminded myself.

Reed clawed at my face, trying to blind me but I turned my head and punched her under the chin hard. I heard her bones crack as she was thrown backwards onto her butt in the dirt. Her skirt rode up, but there was nothing sexy about the flash of her mound. Her cool undead flesh was like dry plastic, waiting to suck the moisture from anything still alive.

Andrew Rail leapt at me. Hungry. Protecting the love of his life. Didn't matter. I slipped my gun from the back of my pants and shot him point blank in the gut. I sent another one a little higher, closer to his heart. A stake would render a vampire inert, dead for all practical purposes, but a bullet to the heart would kill him slowly and for real if enough of the heart were blown out of his chest. Those hollow points did serious damage. Rail didn't have long to live.

"No!" Reed raced to Andrew.

I had a chance to stand and put the gun away. I took a stake out of my jacket but paused, disturbed by what I saw. Reed Summerlin cradled Rail's withered body as darkened blood and other bits of viscera spilled out of his chest. Then she sank her fangs into his throat. It was such an intimate, tender act that I couldn't move. I was mesmerized by the way he tried to reach out to caress her hair, at his tears of blood which trickled down into his opened mouth. He groaned, years of frustration in that incomprehensible sound. He'd found his love and lost her before he was young enough to be more than a burden. That much of the man's mind had returned before I had killed him for good.

Reed looked up at me, a glint of hatred mingled with hope. I braced for another attack, poising the stake for a jab straight into her heart. But when she leapt to her feet, she pivoted and raced into the woods. I hesitated to chase her. I was afraid to leave Rail alone in case he wasn't dead. And I wouldn't leave Littlewing. In case she needed medical care. Of course I chose the sprite over the vampire.

"Littlewing?" I knelt beside her. There was blood at the corner of her mouth and when I picked her up, her body was limp. The stitches in her wing had torn open and sunlight was trickling out from behind her eyes. "Wake up. Stop lollygagging!"

There was a flutter of her eyelids and I smiled, relieved. The sunlight faded and she blinked, raising a hand to her lip. "Did you get the license plate of that truck?"

My one-hit wonder. "Yeah, driven only once by a little old lady gone undead." She sat up and tested her wings. "Can you fly with that?"

"It'll need stitches again to heal properly. Better carry me." She hated being helpless, so I didn't make any smart-assed comments.

"We got one of the two." I held her so that she could see Rail as he withered up, the last of his fluids draining into the soil. When the final death hit him, he exploded in a burst of dust.

"Fuck. Nothing sucks worse than inhaling undead remains." She leaned back in my hand. "Did you let her go because of me?"

I shrugged and headed toward the car. "She's gone. That's all. Back to the B&B. I'll stitch you up myself."

"Do a better job than you did on that woman in Jackson." But she grinned, pleased that I had offered to take care of her. We played at being hard-asses. "You can still track her. My wing will wait. We don't want any more of them being made."

"Oh, shit." I stopped and turned back to the bunker. "Gotta check the bodies."

I went to the building, remembering not to squeeze her in one hand as I used my other hand to lift the heavy steel hatch. It had grown stiff over the years and was heavy enough that I wondered whether an ordinary man or woman could open it. The smell inside was strong with decay. When I dropped to the floor of the cement structure, the hatch only closed partway. That explained why I hadn't heard Rail crawl out of it to attack me.

Three bodies were piled together in the corner. Two teenage boys, country-types with blonde hair and muscles. Vampires tended to favor victims they were attracted to. The third was a plump black woman in her sixties. She had a crucifix around her neck, covered in dried blood. She had been dead the longest of the three.

No trace of Clarence Summerlin, but then, I was pretty sure he was still human. He could hide anywhere and move about in the daytime.

"Stake 'em and let's get out of here," complained Littlewing. I didn't argue.

With one hand, I drove a stake into each of their hearts. They were dry and dead and it was easier than staking a living human or an actual vampire. Rules said to stake all victims. Andrew Rail had been an exception. But two vampires attacking at once were grounds for self-defense. Maybe I could have reached a stake as quickly as my gun. And maybe I had reacted badly after the elf-business. Either way, the facts couldn't be changed. Let the sheriff or the FBI clean up the mess.

When I picked up the woman's body to leave her with a bit of dignity before the authorities came, I heard a ping of wire snapping and recognized the trap too late. A balloon filled with liquid fell from where it had been tied. It struck the cement floor and splattered its contents everywhere. I raced for the opening and threw myself out, but not before I was covered with the unmistakable aroma of skunk musk.

"That bitch," cursed Littlewing, coughing madly. "Can you track her now?"

"Not a freakin' chance." I rushed away from the bunker. The smell billowed out of the opening, blown toward the dilapidated warehouse.

Reed had escaped. It would take too long for the smell to stop clinging to my clothes and hair. The subtle aroma of a vampire was difficult under the best of circumstances and she'd figured that out. She was making me look bad as a vampire hunter. And as a man.

My foot hit something hard in the heavy growth. I stopped, tore at the vegetation to reveal a broken headstone. I looked around and realized that I was standing in an unkempt family plot. The name on the headstone read, *Reed Summerlin*. Born 1931, died 1950. But the grave had never been filled. I walked in a short circle, covering my mouth and nose with a hand against the skunk stench. I found three intact and upright stones with 1950 death dates. Reed's victims. Or her maker's. Or both.

Buried and unregistered because of how they had died. A family secret and a secret cemetery. If the Summerlins hadn't tried to hide their shame, so many other lives could have been saved. The past rarely stayed in the past.

In the car, with both windows rolled all the way down, I set Littlewing onto my lap for the drive back to the B&B. She snuggled against the stiff bulge of my jeans, trying to arouse me. I'd let the vampire get away. Anyone Reed killed after this would be on my head. I wasn't going to sleep very well as it was. The last thing I needed was a cock tease.

CHAPTER TWENTY-SEVEN

As we pulled into Misty Lake House, I heard the scream before the motor had settled. "Sorry 'Wing." I scooped her up and dropped her roughly onto the seat before opening the door and I headed for the sound of Ruth Conklin's voice.

"Let go of me!" Conklin sounded more angry than afraid.

"Do you know what I've endured to find you?" It was Reed Summerlin. I put two and two together before I rounded the corner. When the vampire saw me, she snarled. "You!?"

Miss Conklin was leaning away from the vampire. Reed still had a breast hanging out exposed. That told me more about the vampire's mental state than anything else she said or did. She may have looked and spoke like a woman, but Reed wasn't completely human. Ruth Conklin was her daughter. A real mother would have made herself presentable before seeing a long-lost child.

"Do you know what this woman told me?" demanded the old woman, staring at me with horror in her eyes. "That she's a vampire!"

Reed hadn't dropped the bomb of her relationship on the old woman. "She is a vampire." Hope turned to fear in the B&B owner's eyes. "Let her go, Reed."

"I don't know how you found me, but I'm not leaving without her." She released her daughter and ran toward me, hands extended.

Another grapple-fest. All we needed was mud for a pay-per-view special on cable.

I shifted, into my manwolf form. The extra muscle mass ripped my shirt and my thighs filled the baggy legs of my jeans, but it helped me block the impact of her attack. I swung an elbow into her face as she grabbed my ear and yanked down hard. We both cried out and blood sprayed the air.

She held a bit of flesh and stared down at it. The ear had turned human in her hand and she threw it down disgusted. I was bleeding but it would stop soon.

I had cut her lip on one of her fangs and her nose dripped with blood. It was oddly sexy in a hind-brain kind of way. Except I remembered the feel of her dry flesh and the way her cool hands had seemed to suck at my living warmth. Not to mention a second chance of vampire infection.

"You won't survive this, monster!" Reed didn't wipe the blood from her face. Instead, she glanced around, suspiciously.

"If you're looking for my partner, that rock you hit her with damaged her wing." I crouched and moved to the right. I edged around in a wide circle to distract her from thinking too much. "You gotta know, that pissed me off."

"You're as strong as me. And fast." She studied the shape of my body. "Too bad your blood tastes foul."

"It's not too late to give up. You saw what happens if you don't." I cocked my head. "Do you really want her to wind up like that?"

"Young and beautiful you mean?" She smiled. That couldn't be good. "I did learn one useful thing from the clerk I killed by Andrew's home."

She rushed me and there was a flash of white metal in her hands. She had found a silver letter-opener somewhere. I reached back to draw my gun, but with my extra muscling, I couldn't tug it free of my waistband fast enough. I rarely used my gun in this form, so this was an unexpected problem. She was almost on me when I slammed my arms together and stopped the blade from piercing my eye by a hair's breadth as she knocked me onto my back.

"Die, you monster!" She put all of her rage into her well-shaped body, pressing the blade so fiercely that I imagined it scraping my cornea.

I heard a gunshot and she let out a shriek of startled pain. It was enough to push her back. Another gunshot staggered her backwards. I could see Littlewing fluttering painfully towards me. If she had remembered to reload, that meant three rounds. If not, she was empty.

"Get away from him!" shouted Miss Conklin. Reed risked a glance at her daughter. Ruth held a pitchfork in both hands, aimed at Reed. Hatred on her elderly face.

"You belong to me! All I thought about since the moment I awoke!" Reed's eyes were wild with desperation. She'd lost the man she'd loved after all her years of sleep. Now her own daughter was rejecting her.

"I don't know why you want my blood, vampire. I'll make you earn every drop!" Miss Conklin's arms trembled. I didn't need to smell her fear. To her credit, she didn't lower the pitchfork.

I leapt to my feet but Reed was expecting that. She turned to face me. "She'll change her mind when she's like me."

I charged the beautiful vampire, digging my claws into her shoulders as I drove her backwards. We thudded against something, jarring her free of my grip. A shaft of wood burst from her chest, just at the exposed breast. I moved away from the point and Reed's scream was cut off like a switch had been flicked. She sagged, her lifeless body propped up by the broken handle of the pitchfork. The force of my body hitting hers had driven Reed onto the wood.

"Die, you monster." Ruth meant the vampire, not me. She turned to me. "Why did she want me so much?"

I hesitated, but she needed to know the truth. "She was your mother."

The old woman stared at Reed's body, blinking like I had spoken a foreign language. "Pardon?"

"She was Reed Summerlin. Your mother."

"My mother is Barbara Conklin. She and my father are buried in upstate New York." She shook her head.

"Your biological mother." I wasn't trying to be shitty. I wanted to make sure the old woman knew what she'd done. Lying to her wasn't a kindness.

"That creature—she *isn't* my mother. Even if she gave birth to me. She wanted to kill me. To make me a monster just like her." Her mouth was a snarl and it was more than hatred. It was a hysterical loathing for the undead woman in a torn red dress.

"Mitch?" Littlewing's voice was weak. I reached her just in time to keep her from falling to the ground. "Don't forget your promise."

It took me a minute to remember. Right. Lobotomized fairies. Reed was staked. Technically. I was pretty confident that she was the last vampire. But first I had a wing to stitch up.

"Can you call the sheriff?" I asked Ruth. It wasn't really a question. Littlewing had saved my butt again. It was about time I repaid the favor.

CHAPTER TWENTY-EIGHT

Littlewing refused to sit out the raid on the Cheswick house, but she had to ride my shoulder until her wing healed. I slunk past the windows of the conservatory, peering inside the brightly lighted room. Roses in pots filled the place like a massive greenhouse. I wasn't happy. I knew our culprit had to be Madeline Jackson, the sheriff's woman. The question was whether she was doing it on her own or at Mrs. Cheswick's instructions.

"Stop moving." I froze. But the voice had come from inside. I stood and saw a figure moving through the rose bushes.

"Mitch, let me go in first."

"Your wing!"

"Will be fine for now. This is my show." Littlewing's tone brooked no arguments.

"Fine. I guess you've earned your due." I lifted her up toward the top of the closest window. Like all of the others, it was vented at a fifteen degree angle. Wide enough for her to flit inside. Once she was inside, I headed toward the doorway at the far end.

A shape appeared between me and the doorway. I froze, growling menacingly. In reply I heard Mr. Bixby's whimper and saw him wag his cropped-tail along with the rest of his rear-end. "Good boy."

The dog followed me, hoping for attention. But I was busy. I found the door unlocked. Something you didn't find in California or most big cities.

As I slipped inside, I gave the Rottweiler a gesture that made it sit and cock its head. I shut the glass door behind me, hoping he'd stay. I could hear a woman's humming, but I couldn't tell if it was Madeline or not. The acoustics of the conservatory were exaggerated and one southern drawl sounded pretty much like any other.

"You!" It was a shout of delighted exclamation. "You will make a perfect addition to my collection."

Littlewing's curses told me all I needed to know. She'd gotten caught. I stepped onto the path between the potted roses and let the gravel crunch under my step. A woman stood up from her workstation. She wore strange, magnifying lenses on her glasses and had a scalpel in one hand. Mrs. Cheswick, not Madeline. My reluctance became relief.

"You are trespassing." Cheswick glanced at her other hand, acting surprised that she held Littlewing in a tight grip. "Both of you. I should call the sheriff."

"No need, Mrs. Cheswick." Williams came in from the other end of the conservatory, having come through the house. I wondered how he'd gotten inside until I saw Madeline pressed close to his back. She stared with dismay at her plump employer. Deputy Jason came in the same unlocked door I'd entered, followed by Mr. Bixby.

"I see. You've thrown away your career in my employ, Madeline." Mrs. Cheswick removed the special glasses and set them on the counter. I could see a tiny figure taped to the table, writhing and squealing in fear. A second scalpel lay nearby. And there was some kind of liquid. A local anesthetic probably. "And you, Sheriff, will not be reelected for this violation of the law."

"Why, Mrs. Cheswick? You give everything to this town. Why hurt these tiny creatures?" The sheriff sounded like a little boy who'd discovered there was no Santa Claus.

"They keep my roses in perfect condition!" exclaimed the mayor's wife. "I'm the envy of all the nation because of them!"

"They are innocent creatures!" shouted Littlewing. "You butchered them! You were gonna butcher me!"

"They aren't any more than insects. I've done nothing wrong." She hadn't put the scalpel down, but none of us expected her to stab Littlewing with it. The movement was fast and precise despite her plump frame. The sprite fell to the ground, her blood on the blade. "I can kill them with impunity!"

I snarled, transforming again to my wolfman shape when a gun went off. Mrs. Cheswick screamed and clutched at her arm. It was the only thing that stopped me from slashing through her fatty breasts with my claws.

"Don't move, Mrs. Cheswick. Or next time I won't just shoot the arm." The sheriff strode down the narrow pathway between the roses, his gun tracking her as he moved. "Mr. Greyson, make sure Littlewing is alright. Jason hold that dog away from here."

"There is no law against what I'm doing!" screeched the woman, her Southern Lady persona cracking under the attack on her superiority. Mr. Bixby barked, but Madeline came and took him outside.

"Actually, Mrs. Cheswick, there are several." The sheriff shoved her none-too-gently so that she turned her back to him and he handcuffed her. "But I'll let your attorney explain that all to you down at the station." He holstered his gun and stared at Littlewing in my cupped hands. "Well?"

"She's alive. The blade tore open the other wing though."

"Maybe your reaction to my town wasn't unjustified, Mr. Greyson. Frank poisons her and shoots you. Dr. Walker doesn't want to treat you. Said some pretty unladylike things about you after you left the hospital. And now this. But personality, if I were you? I'd take it as a sign that you aren't really welcome." His eyes were full of pain as he motioned to Jason. I saw the dark circles under the deputy's eyes. They weren't so innocent anymore. "My deputies can attest to that." He really meant Garvy.

"What about Lawrence?" The fake FBI agent had disappeared without a trace.

"We're leaving that to the Feds. They're sending agents sometime in the next twelve hours."

"They get the goblins taken care of?" I didn't really care. I was just curious how much they'd told the sheriff."

"Not my concern." Tight lipped and unhappy. We were back where we had started.

"Don't you want help finding Clarence Summerlin? Be faster with my nose." If they didn't drive over all the evidence I could pick up the scent. I didn't offer because I liked Williams. I felt I owed Garvy something.

"You need to leave." Williams stepped aside as Boyd came in and hauled Mrs. Cheswick past us out to the waiting cars.

After I'd stopped the vampires and Littlewing had gotten injured, the sheriff was still warning us out of town. That pissed me off. "I was planning on staying for Garvy's funeral."

Sheriff Williams only stared at me.

It was Deputy Jason who replied. "We don't want you there." He hadn't called me 'Mitch.' He blamed me for Garvy's death. That affected me more than anything Williams felt.

"Fine. But he died a real cop," I growled with my own anger. "Something you never let him be."

Deputy Jason put himself between Williams and me. The sheriff had raised a fist, but he let the younger man restrain him. I got the satisfaction of seeing doubt in his eyes again.

I took Littlewing and left the Cheswick mansion without another word. I didn't even regret not saying goodbye to Madeline. Not with Garvy dead. Littlewing and I would spend one last night at the B&B, but I looked forward to the long, quiet drive back to Los Angeles. I so hated the South.

CHAPTER TWENTY-NINE

Littlewing was gone when I woke to the sound of my cellphone alarm. Six a.m. Breakfast time. I sat up, naked and tangled in the silky sheet. I was anxious that the sprite had been taken against her will, but I heard her giggling from outside. I walked to the window and stared down into the yard. A storm of winged creatures filled the well-manicured vegetable garden.

Miss Conklin sat at a round, wrought iron table, surrounded by the creatures. She glanced up and I casually moved a hand to cover my crotch, but I didn't back away. I wasn't ashamed of my body. The hand gesture was for her modesty, not mine.

She stood and came inside the house. I dressed, slipping on my jeans commando-style, and a clean t-shirt from my bag. Down the stairs, I heard the whuff of gas flames lighting and saw Miss Conklin at the stove, cracking eggs.

"Your partner said you prefer them over hard."

"Yeah." Like my women, I added in my head. "Thanks."

She stared at the pan. "Remember that uneasy feeling I mentioned? It was gone this morning."

"You asking me a question?"

"Am I? Was I *tainted* by what she was?" She looked up, spatula in her hand. "I believe I felt her when she escaped the mine." Littlewing had been talking. "How could I sense her nearby if I'm not like her?"

"She was pregnant with you as a vampire. But you're human. I think it just made you sensitive to her." I smiled, a real one. "You showed some real gumption. You aren't anything like her." She nodded, but didn't move. "What's for breakfast?"

That broke her trance. "I'll bring it out to the garden. Bacon and sliced tomato."

"Very English of you." She smiled at my comment and I went outside.

Littlewing stood on the table, holding court with a host of the local fairies. But she was waiting for me. I nodded inside, indicating Ruth. Littlewing shrugged. "She's handling it."

"Has it sunk in that she killed her own mother?"

"Yeah. She's a tough old bird." Littlewing accepted a double-handful of something from one of the fairies and licked at it. "Tribute."

"Tribute?"

"They're trying to convince me to be their queen."

"But they're half your size. And a different species. What happened to not being interested in pencil dicks?" From what I could tell, they were all male. I took a second look. Every color I could imagine. But yep, a total sausage-fest.

"It wouldn't be about making babies." She giggled as one of the fairies did a little provocative dance in front of her, rubbing his crotch suggestively. His black skin glowed faintly, his wings dusky blue, and his eyes a golden that remind me of Littlewing when sunlight shined out of them. "And they aren't small where it counts after all."

"How long have you been celibate?" I hadn't really pried into her private life, but because of her size and libido, sex was a common enough topic between us. Celibate didn't mean voluntary in our cases.

"Almost as long as you." She grabbed the dancing male by the back of his head. His eyes rolled up in delight as she forced his head back and bit gently around his exposed nipple. There was a pulse of light from him, and the other fairies grew more agitated. Not magic, I reminded myself, biology. She sighed. "But I'm not sure I'm up for a week-long orgy."

"Excuse me?" I blinked but she was serious.

"The queen of a hive has sex with all the males. Not all the time or they'd get nothing done. So they have a weeklong fuck-fest every few months."

"All of them?" I searched the garden, trying to estimate how many of them there were.

"Yes. Not one at a time, Mitch. And not all in the same way. A hand on the breast, a finger in the mouth, a toe in the butt. Any physical contact while the queen climaxes. I've seen it once and I won't lie, Mitch. I was envious."

"But what about their old queen?"

"She wouldn't move the nest. She let them become zombies. They killed her last night after Mrs. Cheswick was arrested." Littlewing didn't sound sympathetic. "Don't worry, partner. I won't make you stay here a week."

"Where are the females? These are all guys. Even the pink ones."

"This species only has a single sexually mature female at a time. There are juvenile females tending the eggs of the old queen, but they aren't really suited. After a while, one of the unhatched eggs will come out fully adult in the absence of another queen. But they don't want to wait." She sounded wistful. "Even if I wanted to be their queen, I couldn't stop that from happening. Wrong biology to suppress another queen."

She wanted more from her life than hunting monsters and flirting with human men. Not much I could do about that. Normally.

"Aren't there any sprite men you can, you know, date?"

She grew somber and let go of the male she'd been holding by the hair. He didn't seem upset that she was done with him. In fact, he buzzed off in a manner which suggested he was swaggering. "I've told you before. I don't want to talk about it."

"Whatever." I heard the sound of dishes clanking inside and took a seat at the table, brushing away the fairies before I slammed my ass onto the metal chair. "What happens if you don't accept?"

"That's the problem. I know they won't pick one of the immature females in the nursery. The fey don't have the same arbitrary age issues that you humans do. Biological age matters. There aren't any other females to choose from and without sex, I dunno." She shrugged and shooed off a couple more suitors. "They aren't fully intelligent. I mean, they are but—."

"Not smart enough for more than sex?" I prompted.

"Yeah."

"Can you even manage it with your wing messed up?" I peered more closely at her. The wings looked completely undamaged. "How the hell'd you manage that?"

"Fairy magic. Apparently it works across species."

She buzzed her wings but didn't leave the table. She was just showing off. She watched a particularly muscular fairy with red skin, pale wings and bright green eyes pause in front of her. He shyly offering a white petal, plucked from a rose in Mrs. Cheswick's garden. I recognized the very unique fragrance.

I saw that most of the creatures had petals gathered in their hands and wondered what those rose gardens look liked now. Had they stripped it bare? I would have, but I knew I was a vengeful ass.

"We'd have to stay out here at the B&B the whole week. If Miss Conklin doesn't mind," I said.

I watched Littlewing slowly process what I meant. She blinked several times, then her face lighted up. She startled the muscular fairy when she zipped up to my face and planted a kiss on my cheek. Her breasts pressed up against my skin in a way that wasn't accidental either. "Thank you, Mitch!"

"But don't expect me to spend all week watching you have sex." I owed her, but not that much.

"Oh no, Mitch." She giggled and flew over to accept the petal from the male. "Though you could join us."

"I'll pass. But thanks for askin'."

"Suit yourself." Another giggle and she took the red male's chin in her hand and kissed him on the mouth. He pulsed with green light like a star in the daylight. She glowed in response, a burst of absorbed sunlight and the entire mass of male fairies reacted to the signal. They pressed their aroused bodies against her and each other, forming a ball of giggling, erotically writhing fey. The entire group flew off into the woods, Littlewing at the center.

I watched until they were out of sight, then wondered what I was going to do for a week. Besides staying out of the town to avoid the locals. I could read, but there was no TV in the room. My mood started to drop when the smell of breakfast overwhelmed me. Miss Conklin came out with two plates of southern cooking. In addition to the bacon and tomatoes, she'd also piled on biscuits and gravy, fried pork chops and perfectly battered okra.

My stomach spoke for me. "Why, Miss Conklin, I think I love the South after all." As I scooped up a forkful of food, I added. "We'll be staying a week longer, if that's alright."

She nodded, then glanced back at the B&B. "I'll even give you a discount if you help me get rid of those awful metal bars."

Littlewing wasn't the only one going to be busy. I focused on the food and the sound of the sprite's laughter from somewhere in the woods. A chance to run naked through the trees as a wolf. Littlewing getting laid. No FBI to drag me into cases. "You got yourself a deal, Ruth."

The End

ABOUT THE AUTHOR

MICHAEL DON ANDERSON was born and raised in Fresno County, California. His first professional publication was in *Marion Zimmer Bradley's Fantasy Magazine* with a short story called '*The Lamp*,' although his writings have appeared in school-related newspapers, journals and competitions since his early teens. His published books include *The Pride of the Pard* (teen fantasy series), *Dragon's Reach* (family focused traditional fantasy), *Murder at the Undead Comedy Club* (fey urban crime fantasy); and *The Dark Elf's Pet* (the first of his popular *Devon Mosteller* gay-themed adult contemporary fantasy series).

His educational background includes two B.A.s (Anthropology and Linguistics) and an M.A. (Linguistics) from the California State University at Fresno, as well as an M.A. and Ph.D. (Linguistics) from the University of Arizona.

To contact Michael Don Anderson, please write him in care of the publisher CRIMSON WEREWOLF LIMITED, at 7260 W. Azure Dr., Ste 140-798, Las Vegas, NV 89130-7999.

For more information about our books, please visit our website at *www.crimsonwerewolf.com*